THE R
B

SEE ME

by Michelle Lee

Blue Forge Press
Port Orchard ✿ Washington

Blue Forge Press is the print division of the volunteer-run, federal 501(c)3 nonprofit company, Blue Forge Group, founded in 1989 and dedicated to bringing light to the shadows and voice to the silence. We strive to empower storytellers across all walks of life with our four divisions: Blue Forge Press, Blue Forge Films, Blue Forge Gaming, and Blue Forge Records. Find out more at www.BlueForgeGroup.com

Blue Forge Press
7419 Ebbert Drive Southeast
Port Orchard, Washington 98367
blueforgepress@gmail.com
360-550-2071 ph.txt

For my Mom
who saved me before I knew
I needed to be saved.

For Jonielle and Loleta
who gave me the needed push
to get past fear.

THE RAVEN'S JOURNEY
BOOK ONE

SEE ME

by Michelle Lee

Chapter One

From my bedroom window I can see a tree, maybe not a large one, but it was a good enough size for what I needed it for. I angled my head back into my pillows a bit, so my face was pointing slightly upwards. I fluffed the blankets in front of me so that they blocked out the houses in the background and golden light of the street lamps. Now I can just see the tree, and the cloudy sky behind it with stars and the half-moon peeking at me as the clouds rolled through.

It was enough for me to pretend I was the only human around and that I was surrounded by peace and Mother Earth and whatever mysteries she wanted to reveal tonight. The air was calm with an occasional breeze, but cool, the fresh rain scent still lingered, and I couldn't breathe it in fast enough. I'm an air sign with an earth affinity, yet I'm also drawn to the water. So, the scent of fresh rain on the earth with a little breeze was like magic to me.

I've been called many things, some not so nice, all because I'm different in ways that aren't obvious to me all the time. Most call me an empath, which I guess I can agree with on a base level though more recently I think there's more to it than just that. Some have called me magic, or an earth angel, some say I'm like a drug, others say I am light. The not so nice ones call me weird, a freak, a loser, a loner and a whole bunch of other words I try not to dwell on.

My differences are also what feed into my suitcase of insecurities which are on constant repeat on a roll of film playing in my brain in the background. Most of the time I can block it out with whatever else is going on in my life, though at times like this when I am just trying to be in the moment and relax, they come to play front and center in my mind. I guess this means not much sleep tonight.

I shift in my bed and change my position to try and get more comfortable and just focus on the tree. The branches now naked of all its leaves, spindly and reaching for the sky with gnarled fingers, swaying gently when a little breeze blows through bringing me the scent that soothes my soul. I do some yoga breathing in hopes that I can arrive at that calm and centered place inside where I need to be, but it feels like it is blocked off right now.

I feel unsettled and a little restless. The scent that usually calms me feels like it's calling me and pulling at me. Kicking off the covers in frustration, I climb out of bed and walk into my closet, blindly reaching into my drawers for clothes to put on. It's dark out, so I don't really care if I match or not. I get dressed in leggings and a t-shirt and grope around for a pair of thick socks. I wander into the bathroom and feel around the counter for the hair tie I threw down there earlier and pull my hair up into a messy pony tail.

I headed downstairs to pull my tennis shoes on and glanced at the clock on the microwave, 11:24 PM. I winced slightly wondering how smart it was to go on a walk at this time of night, even though the area I lived in was relatively safe. Recalling the restless feeling I had I grabbed my hiking backpack and dug around in the bottom of it for my little gun. I don't think I needed it, but I can't shake the feeling that it would be better to have it. So, I clipped it on the waistband of my leggings and hid it with my shirt.

I grabbed my coat and wallet, and then I paused

and grabbed my car keys. Something was telling me walking around my neighborhood wasn't going to be enough. Some part of my brain was thinking so I grabbed my flashlight too. The pull to leave was getting stronger so I just gave into it and headed into the garage to leave.

This feeling doesn't usually hit me this hard at night, so I was struggling a bit with just going on autopilot and letting my brain direct me to where I should be. I pulled out of the garage and turned the heat on and focused inward while waiting for my garage door to close. East, I needed to go east. The tug was insistent, and I wondered if one of my friends was in trouble.

I pulled out of my neighborhood and headed east, letting the tug direct me, and noticed there was some low-lying fog rolling in. I glanced up at the sky when I hit the next stop light, looking for rain clouds, because of course I didn't grab a rain coat. There were clouds, but it didn't look like rain. The moon was bright, but hazy looking with the wispy clouds in front of it, giving an odd glow reflecting off the clouds.

I agreed with being an empath at the base level, but when I started to think that there was something more to it, this was what I was talking about. This compulsion that leads me off in different directions. It's part of being an empath because it is an emotion pulling me, but I think that there is something more to it that just that. It doesn't feel the same. It has this weird sense of just knowing that I am supposed to be there that is separate from the emotion. Like it is two different pieces of thread pulling me in the same direction, and while the threads may cross, the energy of the two have their own distinct feel.

Being an empath is hard, and it's exhausting. Emotions can be heavy, and I can almost always tell when someone is lying to me. An empath is someone that can read the emotions of others, feel what they are feeling, and in my case, take on the emotions of others in order to ease their burden. Empath's are usually healers of some sort, and people are drawn to them. It's even harder when they touch me, and its skin on skin contact.

See Me

When I go into a crowded place, it's sensory overload. My brain tries to shut everything down because I can't process the amount of emotion hitting me from every side, pressing down on me until it feels like I have become gravity itself. It has taken me years to learn how to build walls inside to protect myself from that. When the emotions are that heavy and that many it gets difficult to tell what my emotion is and what belongs to others. If I am not careful, I can suddenly find myself in an all-consuming rage, or deep depression without knowing why. It becomes a never-ending rollercoaster of emotional insanity.

Add that to the chronic pain I seem to suffer from, and life can get pretty intense. The past couple of years I've been able to get a better grip on it all. I attribute that to yoga, it's been a life saver for me, even though I suck at it. I am definitely not one of those graceful people you see on the videos that everyone strives to look like. I look more like a lump of playdoh twisted into weird shapes. At least I am trying, and it's made a huge difference in my everyday life.

Suddenly I snap back into reality and find myself turning down the road I take to go to Mt. Peak, but I pull off on to the shoulder by what looks like a tiny little trail. The only light is the moon and my headlights which will disappear once I get out of the car. Strange. I haven't been here in at least a year. The pull is strong though. I grab my coat and flashlight and get out of the car slowly taking in my surroundings.

My instincts are screaming at me to get back in the car as the darkness starts to swallow me up, but the pull is so intense that it overrules me. Fear has never stopped me from doing something, though it will sometimes slow me down. Nor am I one of those slight in stature, fragile looking females. I've always been thick, and I have curves. I am short, but I am strong. Even still, this was an isolated forest area, in the patchy fog and dark. So yeah, I was going slow.

I refused to allow myself to relax because I didn't know what was pulling me here, and I really couldn't see what I was walking into. The farther in I walked, the thicker the fog became, and the beam of the flashlight was just reflecting off it. It rolled over and around the exposed skin of my face like it had a heavy texture to it, dampening the sounds around me.

I paused to try and get my bearings because it sounded like I was approaching water, and as much as I love the water, I didn't want to fall in it. I didn't bring a change of clothes and it was not warm out. I searched through my memory to try and remember the area around me. I think a river was dead ahead, and that there was a stream offshoot to my left that dumped into the river. The last time I was here it was a bank on either side of the stream, probably at least a five foot drop on either side.

Given how many big storms we had the past year though, I really couldn't say if it was going to be the same. I'd already encountered a bunch of fallen trees. I focused on the pull again and it was leading me to the right, away from the stream, but towards the river. I couldn't remember what that way was, so I just resumed a slow walk. The path started to have a downhill grade to it, and it felt like I was getting closer to the river. The fog thinned a bit in places, and then suddenly, the terrain changed, and I was standing on rocks.

I looked around and saw that I could see the river and my breath caught. All the heavy emotions of others I had collected over the past week evaporated as where I stood filled me with a healing energy and I felt light again. I smiled in the dark and ignored the pull for a moment. I think I forgot to mention that for me to recharge as an empath and let go of whatever I had taken on, I needed nature. I needed the energy of the earth to release all those collected emotions.

It wasn't just any nature area either. I had to go until I felt a spot that filled me with light energy, something to combat all the darkness that I took from others, and there was no other feeling quite like it for me when that baggage was stripped away by the nature around me. Often it brought me to tears feeling the release. It was no different tonight. I let the tears fall and gazed out on the river.

The moon showing enough of itself to spark tiny diamonds of moonlight over the little peaks of the rapids as they flowed around the rocks. The fog thin and hovering about a foot above the water in places, and small tendrils flowing with the river in others with just enough moonlight to reflect off it all to make it mystical and magical feeling. Like I had stepped into another world.

I needed this, I knew it deep in my bones, and let myself stand there and just breathe it all in. Slow, deep breaths that cleansed me inside and out. The moonlight and fog wrapping around me like a blanket of heavenly light, freeing my soul and mind. As the last tears fell, I whispered a thank you to the universe and reached out for the pull again.

It led me parallel to the river and farther to the right. A bridge came into sight, the pull leading me to go under it, and I paused a moment to shine the flashlight around. There was no fog under the bridge, but there wasn't any moonlight either, and it was just a dense darkness that had an otherworldly feel to it. A not natural feel, but it also didn't feel dangerous.

The feeling was intense though, and when I didn't see anything with the flashlight, I let it pull me forward, under the bridge. I swear it felt like I entered a portal to another place. All sound stopped when I was under the bridge, I couldn't even hear the river flowing two feet to my left. Not even the sound of my breathing was heard.

I wasn't scared, though I would be hard pressed to name the feeling that was taking over me. I just knew it wasn't fear. I kept walking. I was about halfway under the bridge when a sound made me stop. It was the first thing I had heard since stepping under the bridge, but I couldn't identify it, or where it came from. My heart didn't race, I didn't speak or cry out, just moved the flashlight around to try and see what it was I heard.

"Are you real?" a voice said somewhere in front of me, though I couldn't see anything.

"Are *you* real?" I replied in a whisper. At this point I wasn't sure my mind wasn't playing tricks on me since I couldn't see anything but rocks in front of me. Hell, I couldn't even tell if the voice was male or female, or young or old.

"Strange, you aren't scared. Define real," the voice said.

"No, not scared. Curious, maybe a little concerned. Why do I need to define real?" I questioned, starting to move forward again. I felt like I needed to be out from under the bridge.

"What is real to some, is not real to others," the voice said, a tinge of sadness coloring the voice making me sense it was female.

"Well, I'm starting to feel like Alice falling down the rabbit hole," I answered, doing my best not to let sarcasm taint my words. "I guess to me real would be something I can see, hear and touch."

"You can't see me?" she asked, definitely female I thought, and certainly sad. I could feel it.

"No, not yet," I replied softly, feeling the sadness and pulling on it with my mind.

"I can feel you doing that," she said. "It feels weird. Are you an angel?"

I laughed quietly, "No, I'm not an angel, but I am real. Just a human. Where are you?" There was an odd energy in the air that felt like little electric tingles on my face.

"I'm not far from you, in front of you," she said and made a sniffing sound.

"Are you smelling me?" I asked wondering if I smelled bad.

"You don't smell like a person, you don't feel like a person, you feel like an angel," she said softly, and I felt a whisper of a touch on my mind and a slight cinnamon scent wafted in front of me.

"What do angels feel like?" I questioned, still walking forward slowly, keeping my voice even and calm, even though strong emotions were hitting me like rocks

13

being thrown.

"Light," she replied.

"Light," I repeated back to her as I finally stepped out from under the bridge and slowly looked around, realizing I could see better on this side of the bridge. There was less fog, and less trees, but the river still looked like magic to me, stealing my attention for a moment.

"It's beautiful," she said.

Taken off guard I wasn't sure what she was talking about. "What's beautiful?"

"The river of course, since that is where you were looking, but also I was describing what an angel feels like," she answered, her voice coming from behind me now.

"I've never met an angel," I told her. "Although I do not believe I am one." I still faced the river, but began to gently tug at the sadness, fear and anger that were rolling around me, trying to collect them and ease her pain.

"You need to stop that," she said in a firm voice, still behind me. "Those are for me to carry, not you." Her anger spiked with that statement, but also the sadness.

I walked towards the river and squatted down in front of it, balancing on a couple of rocks before I let my fingers trail across the icy cold surface of the water. The cold seeping into my fingers and up my arm before I pulled my hand back. I traced my cheeks with my wet fingers, letting the essence of the river soak into my face. I took a deep breath before I spoke to her again.

"Sweet girl, you are allowed to share your loads, you don't have to carry them alone," I said quietly, but in the voice I used only when I needed to convince someone to let me help them. I stood up and carefully turned around to face the direction her voice was coming from.

Then I saw her. I stifled a gasp and just focused on her. She was there, but she wasn't. Ethereal is the word that came to mind. She was completely bathed in moonlight that made her shimmer like the river I was just touching. Though I could see colors, she glowed a blue that made me think of starlight. Her hair was red, long, straight and moved like the wind was teasing it. Her mouth was wide, but her lips were thin, nose slightly off center like it had been broken before. Large almond shaped eyes that glowed with the same blue light making it so I couldn't see what color they were. She appeared waiflike, but not fragile. Maybe in her early twenties.

"Are you real?" I couldn't help but ask her again, as the energy rolling off her was unlike anything I had ever felt before and I was drawn to her. I wanted to wrap her up in a hug.

She smiled sadly, "Again, it depends on your definition. You can hear me, you can even feel me, and now you see me, so, am I real?"

Understanding seemed to sink into me then, and I tilted my head to the side and asked, "Will I be able to touch you?"

"I don't think so," she replied with the sadness I was beginning to associate with her.

"You are a ghost," I told her. "Am I right?"

She nodded, looking down at her folded hands in her lap. I took a little more notice then to try and figure out how long she's been one without having to ask the question. Her clothes could have been from any time period. She was wearing jeans and a V-necked shirt, long sleeved. Her shoes were Chucks, so that didn't give me a whole lot to go on either. She just appeared ageless. Striking, but ageless.

"You are studying me, looking for answers to questions you don't want to ask," she said, still looking at her hands. "It's okay. You can ask them."

She wasn't wrong, I had been studying her, I just wasn't aware she knew I had been doing it since she wasn't looking up. "I can ask those questions later, I think there are more important things I need to know first," I said, deciding to jump feet first into this very weird situation I found myself in. "I've never been able to see a ghost before, I'm not sure why I can now."

"Do you have to see something in order to believe it?" she asked.

"No. For me, that's a hard no. I'm willing to take leaps of faith to believe in things that I can't see. But that doesn't mean I understand it," I carefully answered. It was true though; I was one of the few people that I knew of that would just accept things without having to see it. "Just because I can't see something, doesn't make it not true, and because I can see it, doesn't mean it's real. I tend to go by what I feel."

"What do you feel?" came her anticipated quiet question.

"Well right now, I am feeling everything that you are feeling, and that makes you quite real to me. I've found emotions don't lie, they can be misleading when you don't understand where they are coming from, but they don't lie," I told her. I moved closer to her where she was sitting on a fallen tree. "May I sit?"

She nodded and swept her hand out in a go-ahead gesture. "You glow," she said, looking at me.

Thrown off guard a second, I must have given her a strange look because she chuckled. "I glow?" I asked with a what the fuck tone to my voice.

"That's why I think you are an angel," she answered in a matter of fact voice. "I have seen a few, and you have the same glow as they do. It's light. It's inviting, and warm. It feels safe, like love."

I snorted at that and couldn't stop the words from coming from my mouth even if I had tried. "Love is anything but safe." I looked down at the ground, angry with myself for letting that slip. "So, are we on a time limit?" I asked, changing the subject.

"What do you mean?" she asked, curious.

"Well I assume this takes energy, and I assume that you have limited amounts of that, being a ghost," I said, studying her again.

"I suppose that would be true, but there is an energy here that I can draw from that doesn't feel like it has a limit," she told me.

Thinking back to my cleansing moment on the other side of the bridge I guess I could understand that. I nodded and looked at her again. She was studying me this time, and again, the words just came flying from my mouth, "I'm not an angel."

She looked like she wanted to argue with me but must have picked up a facial cue from me because she gave me a curt nod and dropped it. We sat there in silence for a few minutes. It wasn't uncomfortable, and while we weren't talking, I took the time to see what else I could feel from her.

I pulled up the walls I used to block my emotions from others and dropped all the other ones I put up to keep everything else out. Instantly energy from all around me bombarded me with such force I almost fell off the log. I quickly put walls back up and dropped only one at a time until I was just getting her. It was still strong but filtering out the earth energy which was potent here, helped.

I will still picking up the sadness the strongest, along with lesser feelings of anger and fear. There was a bit of grief, and below it all was a tiny little strand of hope. I grabbed a hold of that hope and fed my own energy into it until it glowed brighter and was more substantial. She gave me a look, and I knew she understood what I was doing, but that little bit was enough to change her appearance.

Her eyes really were blue. With the blue glow she emanated they became mesmerizing pools you could drown in. The little hope I gave her changed her from striking to absolutely beautiful. I gave her a gentle smile, and she sighed. Not a sad sigh, but a sigh that spoke of letting go. "Thank you," she murmured.

"I can take the rest of that away from you and just leave the hope," I prodded, wanting to help.

"No, I just needed the hope to be real," she said wistfully. "Do you believe in destiny?"

I sighed, thinking about it carefully before answering. "Maybe. I believe that some things have been foreseen by those with the sight to be able to see it, but I don't believe that the outcome is set in stone. I believe that people make their own destiny. While it may have been destined for me to be here talking with you in this moment, the outcome is ultimately up to me. I can choose to walk away and not speak to you anymore, or I can choose to hear you out. Both of those will have different outcomes. Also, no matter which I choose, the options of that choice will also vary. Maybe one of those choices will lead me to what someone has predicted will happen, and maybe it won't. In any case, whatever scenario happens is my choice, and yours. You can choose not to tell me why you called me here, and again, the destiny changes."

"You are the first person to be able to see me. I've been searching for twelve years, all over, and you were the only one strong enough," she said with wonder in her voice. "You are quite strong, far stronger than I ever was."

Startled by her declaration a bit, I latched on to the only thing that stood out to me, "Twelve years? Is that how long you have been a ghost?"

She nodded but refused to allow the topic change. "I don't think you understand just what you are capable of. Your strength is what brought me here after years of searching. It drew me in like a siren song. Your strength wrapped around me like a warm jacket on a frigid winter night. I was powerless against it. But, I can't get around your walls to learn you like I want to. There is something unique about you. I need you to understand that, I need you to be open to possibilities that you might not want to accept."

She couldn't read me? It seemed to me like she was doing a damn good job of it. I hesitated, but drew in a breath and asked anyway, "Strength meaning what?"

She looked at me like she was confused, and her voice was heavy with question, but she answered me bluntly, "You."

"I'm not following," I told her, shaking my head.

Her eyes grew wide with understanding. "You as a whole. You literally shine with it. I told you earlier, you glow. I was not kidding. Your strength shines right out of you in so many forms. It's so potent that I don't get why it has taken me this long to find you."

I'm not one for talking about myself, so this was making me uncomfortable, and I was working hard at not letting it show, because I didn't want to give away too many things about myself. Especially to a stranger who also happened to be a ghost, that in my own opinion, saw way more than I wanted her to. I didn't have anything to say to that, so I just shrugged at her.

"I have tried communication with hundreds of empaths. At most, the strongest one felt some of my emotions, but that was it. I had to exert so much energy to even make that happen, I had all but given up. The universe is funny that way. It took me almost giving up in order to see the beacon you put out, figuratively speaking. I was halfway around the world when you hit my radar. Since I had no idea where you actually were, I just had to keep moving in the direction I thought I felt you, and wait for more signals. I don't claim to understand it any more than you do, but it is what it is. I'm here, and now so are you," she said, watching me intently.

I made my face relax, not wanting to give anything away. I still didn't know anything about her, or why she called me here. Or even how. I was so far out of my comfort zone that it felt like I was losing my mind. Not even realizing I was speaking aloud as I thought it, I said, "Is this a dream? Am I dreaming right now?"

I felt a blast of very dense and cold air against my cheek and flinched. When I looked over, I saw her pull her hand away. "Nope, not dreaming," she chuckled.

"Did you just touch me? Is that what I just felt?" I asked, trying not to feel shocked.

"Hi, my name is Gwendolyn, but my friends call me Winnie," she said with a genuine smile and held her glowing blue hand out to me.

I stared at it for a moment, then tried to shake it as I mumbled, "Hi, did you know you are glowing blue?" I widened my eyes with the realization of what I just said. "Shit. Sorry. Hi Winnie, nice to meet you, I'm Airiella, though most of my friends call me Airy." My hand passed right through hers, though I could feel where it was.

She laughed, "Awkward handshake out of the way."

A noise to my left that sounded like someone approaching us made me jolt around as I saw Winnie blink out of existence. I held my breath and waited for more noise. Suddenly a dark shape was coming right at me and I bolted upright fumbling for my flashlight and shone it right into a pair of glowing eyes.

Waiting for my brain to catch up to my vision, what I saw had me bursting out in laughter. A racoon was sitting in front of me on its hind legs with his front legs sticking straight out like he was impersonating a zombie. He made a chittering sound at me, and I quieted down as I watched the sharp claws. I had a moment of panic that I was about to be clawed to death. He didn't move, so I didn't either.

Winnie must have popped back in because I heard her laughing at the same moment that the raccoon tipped his head to the side and looked at her weird. "See? Must be an angel, even raccoons come up to you."

"I'm not an angel," I growled at her, getting annoyed. "I've got plenty of stains on my soul."

Her laughter grew quiet and I could feel her studying me, though I didn't take my eyes off the raccoon eying us. They were cute creatures, but they could be mean and devious little bastards. I did not want to get clawed. "He won't hurt you Airy, it's okay."

"How could you possibly know that?" I asked.

"I can read him. There is no harm in his intent. I think he is just curious about you. I don't blame him, as I am too. If you let down some of your walls, you'll be able to read him too," she explained.

"Dammit, I have no idea if this is a ploy by you to get me to let you in or not," I spat out in frustration, not even realizing that I was starting to show emotion. She was getting to me.

"In life, I was strong. I had a strong talent in clairvoyance, a minor one in empathy, and a few mystic types said I could read destiny, though, I am not sure that I agree with that. Regardless, I had more power than most people and picked up things quite easily. I'm still strong, even in death, but less so than I was. My power level isn't even remotely close to what yours is at. I promise you, I will not attempt to read you, or get in your head without your permission. I can't help what bleeds out of you past your walls though; that is out there for anyone to see. Let down your walls and focus on the raccoon, you'll see he is just very curious about you," she said gently.

"Fuck. Fine. I'm trusting you," I said and slowly sat back down. I dropped a couple more walls and was once again bombarded with several emotions. I started to breathe deep and sort through them, and sure enough, I found a little warm curiosity. I wondered what would happen if I fed that curiosity, and slowly started to pour some of my energy into that strand. I watched as the little guy twitched and lowered his front feet to the ground.

"Careful," Winnie said into my ear. "He's not the only one curious."

I ignored her for a moment and held the strand of curiosity still, waiting. He twitched again and took a step towards me. I focused my energy on a feeling of trust, and fed that into little guy and inwardly smiled as he took another couple of steps towards me until he was right in front of me. "Hi little guy, we won't hurt you," I crooned at him. I dared a glance over at Winnie and saw her watching me with a look of amazement on her face.

The raccoon looked at Winnie, and back at me. He leaned forward and smelled me, his front paws landing on my shoes. Seemingly satisfied at what he found, he turned around and sauntered off, tail twitching. I felt laughter bubble up in me and let it out quietly.

"Put your walls back up, now!" Winnie whispered into my ear in fright.

I slammed my walls back up and looked around frantically, wondering what she saw that made her scared. "What's going on?" I asked quietly.

"Is it only me you see?" Winnie questioned.

"Well you and the raccoon that just left, yes. Why?" I asked, still looking around.

"We aren't alone. You might only be able to see me, but I see seven others. You are drawing them out," she explained.

"People? Or ghosts?" I asked as I touched my

waistband to make sure my gun was still there.

"Ghosts, like me. It's weird you can only see me. But, with your walls down it would be easy for them to latch on to you. I could feel your emotions without having to try," Winnie said. "You are still healing from being hurt badly by someone," she said, her voice kind.

"I am assuming you didn't call me here to talk about me, so let's drop that shitty train of thought please," I retorted defensively. Mentally I was reinforcing those walls as I continued to look around for signs of others. I was acutely aware of being a lone, living female, alone out in the woods at night.

"I'm sorry, I wasn't intruding, that was just what hit me. You're right though, that isn't why you are here. When I was alive, I was in a relationship that I fully believed would last a lifetime. The love I had for him was pure, and strong, until suddenly it wasn't. I was in an accident, and lived long enough for him to get to the hospital where they took me. I don't know if he is aware of what he did, but he bound me to the earth before I died. He promised that he would find my soul, and stay with me forever." She sighed deeply, and I could feel the overwhelming love and sadness she carried in her words.

"I'm stuck here. I can't find peace; I can't move on. I'm stuck watching him spiral out of control. He didn't bind me to himself, but, in whatever he did, I am bound to the earth. And I always feel his emotions. No matter where I go, they go with me. It's tainting the love I have for him, darkening it, twisting it. If I had a body, I would be in physical pain all the time. I called you here for help. Help me figure out how to undo this. I want to move on. Twelve years of this, I'm a slave to his emotions. It's a cage, trapping me and killing my soul. I don't want to be stuck here forever, getting darker and darker, or to have to move on and remember him and his love in this way," she said, her words rushing out in a mad dash for escape. Pain coloring her eyes and changing the blue of her glow.

My heart broke at the weight of her sadness, tears running down my cheeks unchecked. "I'm not a medium, I don't know how to help you or undo this. I'm at a loss here Winnie," I choked out.

"You gave me hope, it's a start. You can see me. You are the only one," she whispered.

"I can help by taking some of the darkness from you," I said. "Share the sadness with me, allow me to carry the burden. I have ways of releasing it," I explained.

"What happens if I let you take it and I can't remember him?" she said, her voice breaking.

"I'm not taking the love, that will always remain. I can't take that. It's not mine," I told her.

"The darkness isn't yours either, it's mine to bear," she whispered forlornly.

"This is just an assumption, but I am guessing that the accident that killed you wasn't your fault. So how is this your burden to bear? You didn't choose to die," I said gently. "Besides, if I am to help you, I would have to meet him, and I would have to pull this sadness from him. Either way you look at it, I am going to have to do it for both of you."

"I get the feeling that it has to be at the same time," she said sadly. "I had a vision of my own death, years before I died. I saw it happen; I didn't do anything to change it."

"That is quite the load to bear. If it was your time, there was nothing you could have done to change it, the path of the accident would have changed and become something else. Sometimes the destiny can't be changed, regardless of the choices you make to try and change it," I argued.

"You are correct, but I also had a vision of you, though I didn't know it was you, or what you were. And because of your belief about Destiny, I am not going to tell you what this vision was, because I do believe that this is a choice," Winnie stated.

The look on her face let me know that this wasn't the time to push for information on that, but at the same time, the sadness of the situation was weighing heavily on her and I could visually see its effect on her. "Trust me," I whispered to her, using the soothing voice that gets me results. I reached out to her energy and pulled some of the darkness I saw tangled up around the sadness and pulled it to me.

She gasped and immediately I felt the oily stain it carried, and how hard it settled on me. I instinctively knew this was something I couldn't hold on to for long without it becoming a danger to me, so I worked fast. I pulled more of the darkness, leaving her with the sadness she clung to. I pulled it and took it on until I saw her color start to get lighter. "He's been playing with things he shouldn't be playing with," she murmured as an excuse for the darkness. "You need to release it as soon as possible."

Standing up, I had every intention of doing that, "I don't like how it feels. If I am going to help you, you must trust me to take what I need to for you to do whatever it is that needs to be done. For now, I have to go. I need to find somewhere safe to let this go," I said looking around.

"I'll call for you again," she said. "Thank you."

I smiled at her gently, "Allow me a couple days to think about this. I'm out of my element in this situation, Winnie."

"I know. I'm sorry for that. He was never mine though, I saw that much, but he won't acknowledge it. The love was there for both of us, but we weren't supposed to be," her voice was getting fainter. "I feel so tired."

"Go, Winnie. I need to get this out of me," I said, an urgent tone creeping into my voice as I started to feel like the darkness was moving around my soul looking for cracks to plant roots inside of me.

"The water, wade into the river, you'll feel it," she said, and disappeared.

"Well fuck, of course it's in the damn freezing cold water in the dead of winter. Where else would it be?" I muttered out loud, looking for the safest route into the river without falling. I pulled my shoes off and stuffed my socks into them to keep them dry and rolled up my leggings. I wasn't sure how far I had to go in, but I knew it was going to be cold.

I braced myself and gingerly stepped into the river and immediately felt that I needed to move to my left, towards the bridge. In a rush of cold water, I felt the slimy darkness seep away, still trying to find cracks to get inside of me. I opened myself further to the release and let the emotions of Winnie and this unnamed guy flow out of me.

Teeth chattering and feet numb I made my way back to my shoes and quickly headed back to my car, checking my watch. It had been three hours! I was hit with a wave of exhaustion as I settled in my car and cranked the heater up. Needing sleep, I hurried home and crawled into bed. Not sure I've ever fallen asleep that fast.

Chapter Two

She didn't lie to Airy, she really was worn out for a ghost. That used up a ton of stored energy, but she at least had the signature of Airy now, so to speak. That meant she could pop in on her by following her unique energy. She wandered around the woods where Airy left and tried to follow the trail she left behind her but found she was too tired.

She sat back down and watched the river that had Airy so transfixed. It was beautiful she had to admit. She vaguely felt the pockets of energy Airy had mentioned, but she didn't think she felt them the same way that Airy did. The one in the water had felt the strongest to her though.

She thought about the way it felt when Airy had pulled the darkness from her that Jax called into creation. It was amazing to feel that removed from her soul, though it had hurt when she did it. She knew it had been feeding on her, and she was pretty sure that there were some parts of her now missing. It was gone though, for now at least.

She also wondered if a piece of her got stuck to Airy, much like it had to Jax. Because she could now feel Airy like she did Jax. Maybe that would help her figure out why

Airy thought she had stains on her soul and couldn't possibly be an angel. She shook her head, she couldn't go diving around in her head, she had made Airy a promise she wouldn't. But it didn't mean she couldn't ask.

She felt compelled to help Airy just as she was asking Airy for help. She knew what she had seen all those years ago, she knew it was Airy, without any doubt in her mind. She felt a pang of sadness strike her at what she had lost, but told herself to let it go. Dwelling on it wouldn't help.

Besides, if she was honest with herself, she knew before she died that her feelings for Jax had changed. She knew his had changed for her as well, though he would never admit it. They still loved each other, she knew that with a deep certainty, but it wasn't the same love as it had been. It had shifted for her.

She walked around a bit more, trailing her ghostly hand over the branches of the trees she could reach, wishing she could feel the scratch of the bark against her skin once more. She dropped her head back and stared up at the hazy moon, her mind racing, and her heart breaking all over again as she got lost in the memories.

"Winnie! Don't you dare die on me, come on!" Jax whispered frantically as he clung to her hand. "Fight! I can't lose you now. I need you so much. You are a part of me, heart and soul. Please God, make her stay! Please!"

She felt his tears rolling over the back of her hand, leaving a warm trace on her skin. She heard the relentless beeping of the machines they had her hooked up to, the sterile and medicinal smell of the hospital around her. The bright lights blinding even through her closed eye lids. She knew, without even opening her eyes what she would see.

"Winnie, baby, I know you can hear me, I feel you in there. Don't go. I'm so sorry," Jax sobbed. "I'm so damned sorry things have changed between us. I don't know why, but we can figure it out. Just don't go. Stay here. I'm being a selfish prick I know, but I need you. I'm so sorry. I still love you." He squeezed her hand, hard.

Guilt was rolling off him in waves of thick need that smothered her and made her feel like she was suffocating in it. She knew though, she had seen it. She wasn't going to live. And she herself felt guilty for leaving him like this. She loved him too, just not the way he needed. She felt her eyes water behind her closed eye lids, and she thought maybe some leaked out, because she felt moisture on her face. She wasn't really feeling any pain; the drugs were making her fuzzy.

"You are going to stay here, even if you die, your spirit stays here so I can find you. I will find you. I will keep looking until I find you. You are staying, do you hear me? You are staying here. That's the price of my love, you have to stay. You don't get to leave me," Jax all but shouted in her ear. She willed her eyes to open then.

She looked up and saw Jax, his tears splashing down over her face, his eyes bloodshot and angry like they were on fire. His hair was sticking up all over everywhere like he had been pulling at it in fistfuls. His skin was pale, and guilt lined his face in every crease she saw, and she broke a little more knowing that he wouldn't ever forgive her for leaving.

"I love you Jax, let me go," she croaked out in pain, her throat burning with the effort it took to get the words out. She felt him let go of her hand and pain engulfed her soul, burning and searing her every fiber. Her mouth opened in a silent scream, her eyes only focusing on the white ceiling tiles above her.

"No Winnie! I am never letting you go! Stay here!" Jax shouted as he stood, his face wild and turning red. Guilt and sorrow flooding her every cell.

She felt her body go rigid, and something inside her felt like it was being ripped apart, and then nothing. She saw herself from above, lying still on the hospital bed, her body bloody and broken as doctors and nurses rushed into the room and silenced the machines that were screaming out their alarms. She watched in despair as they pulled the sheet over her, a universal sign that she was no more.

SEE ME

She watched as a nurse tried to lay a calming hand on Jax and he exploded in anger shoving her away. She watched helpless, as he fell boneless to the floor, his sobs so powerful they were silent, but racking his body. She felt his anguish, outrage, guilt and love wash over her, pulling her down like the gravity that no longer ruled her body. She sank on to the ground next to him, unable to move away. She watched as a nurse led in Ronnie to help him. She cried, knowing nothing she could do would help.

She didn't have the ability to take on his emotions, he had to shoulder this and move on, but she felt from him he wouldn't do that. She saw Ronnie walk over to the hospital bed, kiss his hand and place it on the sheet over her head. She heard him say goodbye, she saw his tears, felt his sadness weigh down on her more, adding to the heavy weight of Jax and if felt like she was pressed even harder down on to the earth below her.

She kept reaching out, trying to console Jax, but she couldn't touch him, he didn't even notice. She didn't think he even noticed Ronnie picking him up off the floor. She owed it to him to stay, he was catatonic in his grief. She watched as Ronnie put him in a wheelchair and talked to a nurse quietly. The nurse nodded and left the room. Ronnie kneeled in front of Jax and tried talking to him, but there was no response. He just shook as the silent sobs tore through his body, his eyes blind to everything but his own pain, his ears deaf except the sound of his heart breaking.

Ronnie dropped his head down between his shoulders and stared at the floor as tears fell from his eyes. She hated every second of watching this, but she was unable to move from here. She crawled over to Ronnie and placed her hand on top of his that was on the floor bracing him. "Ronnie, I'm here, please take care of him," she pleaded with him.

She swore, for just a second that Ronnie looked right at her and whispered, "I promise Winnie." Stunned she sat there, trying to hold his hand, but he picked it up, looked at it and touched it with his other hand and then stood up as the nurse came back in.

"The doctor approved it," she told Ronnie, and then leaned over Jax and gave him an injection in his arm. "Do you want him to stay here where we can watch him?" she asked.

"No, I'll take him home and stay with him, I made a promise," he choked out, looking around the room as if he were looking for her.

"I'm sorry for your loss," she said gently and laid her hand on his arm before she walked back out of the room.

"Me too," he whispered. He sat back down on the floor in front of Jax waiting until whatever was in the shot they gave him started to work and his body went slack. Only then did Ronnie get up and push the wheelchair and Jax out of the room, where he paused and made a call on his cell phone before wheeling Jax out.

She wondered then if it was the guilt that tied her here, and if it would really be as easy as pulling the guilt out of Jax to get this cycle to end. She doubted it, but at least she had a vein of hope now. She had confidence in Airy, she felt that Airy would help her before it was too late for all of them.

Chapter Three

"Fuck Aedan! What the hell do you mean we need to hire someone else?!" Jax shouted across the table at one of his best friends, brother, and co-worker in their cable TV show.

"The producers think they need someone to help calm the situations where you, or any of us, get out of control," Aedan tried to explain. "Look, our hands are tied here. This isn't something we get a say in. It's affecting the show."

"HOW?" Jax yelled. "Ratings are up! I check this shit all the time!"

"The social media platforms have a general negative persuasion about the show, despite people watching," Ronnie stated, his tone flat. "People are starting to watch just to verbally bash you when you fly off the handle and treat the rest of us like shit."

"So, what...you guys called me here for a meeting to tell me I'm an asshole?" Jax asked, incredulous.

"No, bro," Art said, using logic to try and argue the point. "We called the meeting to see if we could put our heads together and come up with a list of attributes we would like the person they are going to hire to have. We don't have a say in who they pick, but if we can provide a list to them of things we think will help us, we may be able to have a little influence, so they don't pick someone we are going to end up hating and making things worse."

"Look, I know I've been a prick, this just seems like an extreme response to that," Jax argued.

"Dude, prick is a bit of an understatement, but we all also know why. We know why we formed this group; we know what we are looking for, but they don't. Do you want to open up to all the brass about why we came to be?" Art asked. Ronnie snorted and Aedan grimaced.

"So the one producer I think that will actually listen to us if we are reasonable, also told me that if we fight them about this, they are going to mandate that you, Jax," Ronnie pointed, "are going to either start getting professional counseling, or regular exorcisms, because they think that this asshole behavior is influenced by a negative entity you pissed off somewhere. Oh, and anger management classes. If you don't agree to that, they have been talking about replacing you."

"Choice is yours," Art replied dejectedly. "I'm not any happier about it than you are. We are a family, and I agree that this is a bit extreme. But shit bro, you damn near knocked me out this last time because I tried to pull you away from whatever was affecting you. We all knew it wasn't Winnie."

"Maybe counseling isn't a bad idea," Aedan said quietly. "If Ronnie hadn't knocked Smitty out of your way, you would have decked him. That's bad." He dropped his head refusing to look at Jax. "It's been twelve years Jax. You can't hold on to this grief forever, it's killing you, it's damaging our relationships with each other."

"Is this coming from Mags?" Jax asked defensively, his jaw clenched and his cheek twitching in anger. Hearing Winnie's name was like a knife in the heart.

"Seriously? You are really asking me that?" Aedan stiffened in anger, his hazel eyes tight and voice tinged with hurt.

"Jax, come on man. This is serious shit. We need to put all our cards out on the table and get through this. This could be the end of our show," Ronnie growled.

Jax dropped his head on to the table with a thud. "Fuck. I need you guys to have my back," he said, his voice muffled.

"When have we not had your back?" Art "Smitty" asked Jax, his tone hardening. "You're being ridiculous."

"Well, it feels like you don't right now," Jax whined childishly. He sighed, knowing that it wasn't true, but he felt like his emotions were careening out of control and he honestly didn't know how he would react. He was secretly afraid he *would* lash out and physically harm one of them. Regardless of how he was acting, he didn't want that, they were his brothers. He heard a chair scrape across the floor and hoped they weren't walking out on him.

Ronnie stood up and walked over next to Jax and sat down, all playfulness gone from his demeanor. He laid his hand on Jax's arm. "Dude, I was there with you. I know what this group is about, I know what is driving you. I get it. We all lost her. We all agreed to join you in your search for her, we all mourned. We *all* miss her. But something has twisted in you, man. Something over this past year has changed. We aren't here to question the reasons we are together doing this; we are here to try and figure out what has changed. There's a darkness about you that concerns us all. Not just for our safety while taping, but our concern for you, as our friend, our brother."

Jax's fist clenched tight at Ronnie's hand on his arm, the muscles in his forearms almost vibrating, but Ronnie didn't move his hand. Jax lifted his head and looked at Ronnie, saw the tears in his eyes, heard the thin thread of control he was using in his voice. Jax saw the haunted memories play across Ronnie's face, and something finally reached him under those layers he was hiding behind, and he deflated. Dropping his head back down on the table, the fight left his body.

Ronnie moved his hand to Jax's back in a show of support. Ronnie never left him alone. Every day for the past twelve years, Ronnie was there. Taking care of Jax, defending him, picking him up and putting him back on his feet. Cleaning up after him after a bender where he just lost his shit. Taking care of the girls he used and dumped the next day. Ronnie was always there.

Hell, Jax knew they all were, but they followed Ronnie's lead when it came to him. Aedan and Smitty weren't at the hospital. They hadn't seen him break, they didn't see Winnie's bloody shattered body, they didn't hear Jax lose his shit the moment her heart stopped, that was all Ronnie. Aedan and Smitty knew, Ronnie had called them. He kept them at bay the next couple of days, but then they were there. Ronnie was right, they were here to help him.

"I'm still broken," Jax whispered, fighting the tears that were threatening to break free. He heard the other two chairs move and knew they all moved closer to him.

"I made Winnie a promise Jax," Ronnie's voice cracked, "in that hospital room where she died. I felt her, I heard her. She told me to take care of you," Ronnie broke down, his chest heaving as he gulped in air. "I was kneeling in front of you, though I don't think you saw me, you didn't see anything. I felt her touch my hand, and I promised her I would take care of you. I can't see you like that again, dude. It haunts me, every day. Every time I see something in you twist, it kills me. You've got to work with us. Let us in, help us help you. Do you know what it would do to her to see you like this?" Ronnie pleaded.

"Jax, we can handle it, whatever it is, just work with us," Aedan choked out quietly, not immune to the emotions cascading over them.

"Please bro, we love you," Smitty added. "I think the work we are doing is important, but you are crossing lines you shouldn't be crossing. Let's figure out how to fix this shit. I want my brother back."

Jax felt all them touch his back, and he resolved to work with them, though there was still a part of him that wouldn't share this darkness with them. They didn't deserve it. He'd just have to work harder to try and get rid of it. But they couldn't ask him to give up or let Winnie go.

The weight of his reaction and words at the hospital were a dark stain on his heart. The guilt that ate at him every day wouldn't let that happen. Maybe if he had loved her more, she wouldn't have died. Maybe if he hadn't been so selfish, things would be different.

"What's it going to be Jax?" Ronnie asked him softly.

"I think we should request an empath," Jax answered.

"Wait, what?" Aedan asked, confused.

"The person they want to hire," Jax replied, "I think it should be an empath. I've heard of a few that can diffuse situations with intense emotions. Might be hard to find one, but it at least buys us a little time."

"Holy shit! Jax is right," Smitty said, getting excited. "I read something in an article about someone like that. Damn it, I can't remember where I read it though."

"Okay, so we have our first quality for our list," Ronnie said happily, whipping out a piece of paper and wrote it down. "What else?"

Chapter Four

It has been five days since I heard from Winnie. If I hadn't felt her energy a couple of times, I would have thought I made the whole thing up. Or dreamed it, or something. I'm not sure my imagination is good enough to have come up with that whole scene that happened. Besides the whole part where I could now feel Winnie's emotions. I'm not sure how that happened, but it's a good argument against having made the whole thing up.

I shook myself and tried to focus back on work. It's been a struggle these past five days. My brain keeps wandering off leash, and I keep trying to put these puzzle pieces together in hopes that an answer will present itself. All I end up with is more questions. I feel like I am missing important information, and if I had it, maybe I could research it and have options. I'd already resolved myself to agreeing to help her, I just didn't know how to do it.

Staring back at my computer screen I noticed I had completely screwed up the report that I was working on. I sighed, tired of looking at spreadsheets with data that didn't match the train of thought in my head. I deleted my work and started over again, deciding to turn on music to try and lull my brain into a cadence.

Music usually centered me and allowed my brain to focus on the beat of the music while some other distant part was able to go on autopilot and work the reports that I needed to do. Sounds like opposite for most people because it appears my attention is divided, but it's not. I sat there for a few moments listening to the song that was on and following the beat of the music.

Then I lost myself in my reports a while, the music playing in the background and my fingers flying over the keyboard, cranking these things out. I had a good pace going until a voice near my ear said, "The music you listen to is telling."

I jumped, swiveling my chair around but didn't see anyone. "Shit! Winnie? Is that you?" I whispered, even though I was alone in the office.

I heard her chuckle. "Yes, it's me. I don't have to appear for you to hear me. It's easier and less of a drain on me if I don't appear. Though if disembodied voices bother you, helping me really won't work out well. But I admit, that was funny."

Willing my heart rate to slow back down I raised an eyebrow assuming she could see me and plastered a not amused look on my face. "I'm happy to be able to make you laugh," I said, sarcasm dripping from my voice. "Is there a reason you are here? You know, this place actually pays me to help them. You, not so much."

I heard her draw in a breath, then softly, "You are going to help me?"

"Yeah," I replied, resigned. "I hate the thought of people suffering unnecessarily. It does something to me, especially if there is something I can do to help it. To be honest, I have no idea what I can do in the situation, but I am willing to try."

"Airy," Winnie said breathlessly, "thank you so much. I can't even tell you how much this means to me."

"Well whatever I pulled from you last time did a number on me. Even thinking about someone else feeling that didn't settle right with me. You say this guy has the same feelings? And you are sure he's alive?" I asked cautiously.

"Yes, he's alive, if you can call it that. He's buried himself under so much guilt and anger, that the sadness can't run its normal course. And everything he feels leeches out into me where it collects and for lack of better words, weighs me down. It's become my burden," she said, her tone melancholy.

"What makes you think he is going to accept help from me?" I asked, curious as to what her ghostly plans contain.

"I don't think he will. But his friends will. They've noticed the darkness that's eating at him, changing him into someone else," she said, her voice warring between utter sadness and anger, and a strong mix of emotions slamming into me as I tried to feel out what she was saying.

"Winnie, I can't..." I started.

"Someone is coming," she said quickly, cutting me off.

I turned back around to face my computer, my brain once again roaming around free range style up in my head. I knew I had no chance of reining it in now, not with Winnie close by and the information she keeps hand feeding me bouncing around up there. I startled as the heavy office door swung open making a lot of noise. I looked over to see a delivery driver dropping off packages before the door slammed behind him on his way out.

Winnie giggled, "Imagine him walking in to see you talking to yourself."

I grimaced, knowing that it was all too possible as my brain tends to focus on the issue on hand when it comes to the "other" stuff. I was going to have to walk around with my ear buds in to make it look like I was talking on the phone if she was going to keep doing this. I smiled at picturing my phone ringing as I was talking to her in a public place with people assuming I was on the phone. Pretty sure that scenario was entirely too plausible.

"Did you know this building has a ghost?" she asked me.

"Not for sure, but I figured something was here. Too many weird things happen for there not to be," I told her.

"That doesn't scare you?" she carefully asked.

"Ghosts? No, not really. I wasn't afraid of you when I saw you, nor when I figured out that you were a ghost," I explained, curious to see where she was going with this.

"Well, that's true, I didn't pick up any fear from you, but I wasn't sure if that was because you had your walls locked down tight. That's good to know," she said with little explanation beyond that.

"Okay Winnie, we are going to have to have some boundaries here. The first is that you can't just pop in anywhere you want to at any time you feel like it. Work should be off limits unless there is something drastic happening that needs my immediate attention, which I can't see happening, since I don't know any of the people involved in this situation. But if you do pop in, please find a way to announce yourself without scaring the hell out of me. I don't know," I thought aloud, "maybe a scent or something that allows me to know you are here."

Winnie was quiet enough that I wasn't sure she was still there until I felt around for her. I felt confusion and frustration, but she still didn't say anything. So, I pulled up the report I was working on and let her think through it. "No one else can see me or hear me though, so I don't understand why I can't be here?" she asked.

"I wasn't necessarily banning you from being here, but you can't scare me, and I can't just be seen talking to no one. Anyone walking in the building can see me, look at the two windows right there. It's like a fishbowl," I replied, vaguely waving my hands toward the windows right as people walked into the building and thought I was waving at them. I smiled, looking foolish. "For example, that."

"Alright," she agreed, giggling. "What else?"

"Full disclosure," I added, muttering, "you can't expect me to help without all of the information. I'm losing sleep over this, trying to puzzle it out."

"Part of that is because I don't know exactly what you are capable of yet. I don't like this, but I am going to have to turn that one around on you. I need the same from you," she hedged, her voice almost timid.

"What? Why do you need to know about me? My life has no bearing on this," I argued, getting hot.

"That's where you are wrong Airy. It does. You might have memories locked up in your head that are directly tied to this, but you aren't aware of it. I need to see. If I find what I am looking for, I can tie this up better for you, get a clearer plan together that we can work on," she pleaded with me, desperation in her tone. "I can do it while you are asleep, and you'd never know I was in there. I promise you I won't dredge things up in conversation if they aren't relevant. It would also give me a better idea of what your powers are like and possibly what you might be capable of that you don't know about."

I felt my face pale at the thought of her in my head. Some things were better left buried. I assumed my back was to her, that was the direction of her voice anyway. I have major trust issues, and rarely let anyone in to those parts of my life. Even the thought of it made me break out in a cold sweat. Logically, I understood where she was coming from, and even agreed with her, but logic wasn't ruling on this, fear was. For just a split second, I felt the taint of that darkness that I pulled from her and shuddered at the thought of that getting in those places.

"Winnie, please let this go for right now. I can't do this here at work. Please," I begged her, straining to keep my emotions in check, but scared I wasn't. I felt my hair ruffle and guessed she was playing with it.

"I will Airy, as long as you promise me, we can talk about it later," she said gently.

"I promise," I said my voice tight with effort and clamping this shit down.

"You are so beautiful Airy. Beautiful and amazing. I think you need to hear that more often, I'll talk with you later," she told me, a wave of comfort washing over me, and then she was gone.

I stood up shaking, feeling weak and unsteady, a weird tremor running through my veins, and I walked out of the office headed to the bathroom as fast as I could. I pulled open a stall and sunk down onto the toilet with my elbows on my shaking knees, dropped my head down and clasped my hands behind my neck.

Breathing slow and deep I tried to calm myself, but it wasn't working. Things were shifting inside me and it didn't feel good. I braced for the defensive pain that my body seemed to use to break me down, but it didn't arrive. I sat there for a few minutes until my knees stopped shaking at least and walked out of the stall to the sink. I leaned over and turned the faucet on cold and dampened some paper towels to rub on my face.

I looked at my reflection, trying to see what Winnie saw. I didn't see anything amazing, and I've never been beautiful. I shook my head, just needing to move on and get through this day so I could go home. Home was safe.

Chapter Five

Ronnie sat back in his room and leaned his head against the back of his chair and kicked his bare feet up on his disorganized desk, knocking a stack of papers to the floor. He didn't care now. He was emotionally wrung out. The meeting with Jax and the guys took everything he had.

He could feel the call in his blood wanting to revert to his old ways and drink to numb the pain or take something that would make him forget. He knew there was some sort of chemical out there to just wash it all away, even if it was temporary. And he felt the pull to give in strong. It always hit him the hardest when he had to talk about Winnie. That shit was in the past though.

When he made that promise to take care of Jax in that hospital room, he also made the choice to be sober. He owed her that much, and it was a debt he intended to repay even if it drove him insane. His skin felt like icicles were crawling all over it the need was so powerful. Growling, he pushed the chair back and stomped his feet on the ground, standing up. He needed to move. To do something.

He paced his room, itching absently at his arms,

desperately seeking something to occupy his attention, without causing a commotion in the house he shared with Jax. He knew he needed some energy, so he headed to the kitchen to grab a protein bar and a Coke to wash it down with. The caffeine and sugar might help.

He headed for the garage they had converted into a gym thinking about using the punching bag. Right now, he wanted to picture his own face on it and beat the hell out of it. He was so pissed at himself for revealing that he believed he saw Winnie in that hospital room. Twelve damn years he kept that a secret, he fumed at himself as he wrapped his hands in tape.

Twelve years! He punched over and over, picturing his face under his fists as each blow landed. He didn't even know if Jax had caught that slip during that meeting, but he kept imagining the pain it would inflict on him if he had. Twelve years Jax has been putting himself through hell looking for Winnie. Punch. Twelve years he had been keeping the secret that he felt her, heard her. Punch, punch, punch.

He felt his skin split over his knuckles with a tear, but he kept going. Hitting, splattering blood all over the bag, his shirt, the coppery scent filling his nose. Tears cascading out of his eyes, his vision blurred, waves of anguish washing through him like a rip tide trying to drown him. Over and over until he collapsed on the floor, giving in to the darkness creeping across his eyes and he let it take him, needing the punishment.

Jax had called him a sensitive, but Ronnie knew it was more than that. He could see and hear things others couldn't. He always could, for as long as he remembered. It was one of the things he shared with Winnie, that drew them closer, secrets shared between them that Jax wouldn't understand. He sat there watching them together and fought back a stab of jealousy. They'd been together since grade school.

It was always Jax and Winnie, with Ronnie tagging along. At least until high school when Smitty

46

moved to town. Aedan was a year and a half younger than Jax, half-brothers by blood, though they didn't know that until high school either. But at least then, Ronnie was no longer the third wheel.

Lately, something had changed with Winnie and Jax though, their bond felt different, but Ronnie hadn't had a chance with Winnie alone to ask her about it. He wasn't even sure he should ask. Another stab of jealousy pricked at him and he did his best to tame it down, knowing Winnie would pick up on it sooner or later. He tried to focus on the TV instead of the developing feelings he was working so hard to ignore.

"Hey Ronnie, can you take Winnie home? Aedan needs me to pick him up," Jax called from across the room.

"Sure," Ronnie grumbled, standing up. He guessed this was his chance to ask Winnie questions.

"I can walk if you have something to do Ronnie, it's not that big of a deal," Winne said.

"Nope, not a problem. You ready?" Ronnie asked, grabbing his keys off the kitchen table.

Winnie nodded, picking up her purse with a little hesitation, which Ronnie noticed right away, but didn't comment on. Jax walked by, gave her a peck on the cheek and kept on going. Ronnie saw her watch him walk away, and he studied her face for any tells on what she was feeling. He'd gotten good at reading her recently. She looked troubled, but he couldn't tell why.

Ronnie held the door open for her as they walked out and her fragrance teased him as it had started doing lately, she smelled like fresh rain. He bit back a groan and followed her feeling like a huge ass for even entertaining these thoughts. God what was he thinking? She was Jax's! Shit, shit, shit! Jax was his best friend!

"You okay Ronnie? I mean, I know you aren't, but do you want to talk about it?" Winnie asked him, grabbing his hand.

He snatched it back from her, feeling guilty at her hurt look. Pretty sure he couldn't make this worse at this point. "Sorry Winnie. Just frustrated I guess."

She let out a huge sigh as she settled in the car and buckled up. "Me too," she said cryptically. She gave him a half smile and asked, "Girl trouble?"

There was no way he could hold back the snort of incredulous laughter that bubbled out of him. Blushing furiously, he started the car, grumbling, "You could say that."

"Tell me about it, please, I could use the distraction," she said, looking out her window, but he didn't think she was seeing anything by her tone.

"Is everything okay with you and Jax?" Ronnie asked, changing the subject.

She flinched, and he knew then that it wasn't. "Just between us, right?" she looked at Ronnie.

"Of course," he answered immediately, guilt swamping him.

"Don't Ronnie, no guilt. You are allowed to have relationships with others. Jax knows we are friends," she said, stuttering on the word friends.

"Yeah, but he doesn't know we have secrets between us, I don't think he would be okay with that," Ronnie said glumly, and turned down Winnie's street.

"Pull over at the park," she demanded.

Too startled to argue with the turn right there, he just pulled into the parking lot. He sat there gaping at her, and she was out of the car in a flash slamming the door behind her. Not quite sure what to do, he slowly got out of the car and followed her as she sat on a swing.

He took a quick look around and noticed that they were alone in the park, but in plain view of anyone walking or driving by. Why that mattered to him, he didn't understand, but it was something he noticed. He kept quiet as she pushed herself back and forth slowly on the swing, and he decided to sit in the swing on her other side. He watched as her red hair floated around her face, then swung out behind her, catching the sunlight so it glowed like a fiery sunset.

Caught up in the mesmerizing spell of color he didn't notice her watching him. "Ronnie, I had some visions that will change everything as we know it," she said softly, paying attention to the expression on his face and the wary confusion emanating from him.

He stilled on the swing, focusing on her blue eyes, "Bad ones?"

"For me, yes," she whispered. Her eyes shining with unshed tears. "Well that was kind of selfish, but bad in more than one way," she tried to explain.

He reached out for her hand, very aware of the public area surrounding them, even though it was still empty. "Want to tell me?" he asked, stroking his thumb along her skin.

"I do, but I'm scared," she admitted in a weak voice that was trembling.

He had never known her to be scared a day in her life. He gulped back fear, his entire body going rigid as thoughts assaulted his mind. Visions of them together shattering, death, a darkness he was too naïve yet to understand. "Who?" he choked out.

"Mine. I saw my death," she gasped out as the dam of tears broke. "Not only that, I saw who Jax is supposed to be with. There are bad times coming Ronnie," she stammered out through her tears.

"Fuck!" Ronnie shouted, dropping to his knees in front of her as he pulled her off the swing and onto his lap, wrapping his arms around her, rocking them both back and forth.

She shifted on his lap, wrapping her legs and arms around him in a death grip as she shook with the force of the cries coming from her. He held her, not knowing what else to do. He fought back his own emotions, knowing it wasn't the time. He just held her sitting on the ground in front of the swings until her cries eased up, his shirt wet.

"I don't think we will have much time to even explore what is growing between us," she whispered sadly in his ear.

Ronnie's eyes snapped open as someone walked into the garage, not bothering to move from where he was laying on the ground. "What the fuck Ronnie?" Jax exclaimed as he took in the blood splatters. "What happened?"

"You've got your secrets, I've got mine," Ronnie snapped out, getting up. He saw the anger flutter across Jax's face, but he was too raw to care. He turned away and headed back to his room, ignoring Jax as he called him back. He couldn't do this right now.

Chapter Six

I pulled out of the parking lot at work while fumbling in my purse with my other hand for my MP3 player for music. I hated driving. I'll be the first to admit I have awful road rage. I finally felt it and pulled it out to plug it in. Within seconds I had blaring music to numb my tired brain. As the traffic came to a grinding halt as it does here, I grabbed the device and scrolled through until I found a song to fit my mood.

I sang along as loudly as I could as we inched forward, letting the lyrics wash over me like a soothing balm, even though the music itself wasn't soothing. I don't care, it worked for me, to hell with what anyone else thought. The song Haunting by Halsey came on next, and it seemed oddly appropriate.

Once again, I was lost in the music when I happened to glance in my rear-view mirror and damn near drove off the road in fright and smacked my head hard against the window. "What the hell Winnie?! You can't do that shit while I'm driving, didn't we talk about this earlier?" I yelled once I realized the blue glowing body in my backseat was hers.

"Sorry," she said with a smirk, not really sounding sorry as I rubbed my head. "This song is good, makes me feel, plus it struck as me as funny for a ghost to talk to you while listening to a song called Haunting."

"Well great, I'm glad popping in and scaring the hell out of me while I'm driving and trying to relax to music works out so good for you. Now that the person behind me thinks I'm drunk and crazy," I muttered sarcastically. "I thought appearing drained you," I said as an afterthought.

"It does, but I'm pulling from your batteries," she said smugly. "That's why your dashboard lights are flickering."

"Fuck. Stop it! The last thing I need is a car to fix," I shouted at her. "Disappear then, I need downtime. Or if you are going to stay here then just disappear and listen to music. Please. No talking."

"Okay Airy, I really am sorry. I just haven't gotten to talk to anyone in twelve years. Been kinda lonely," Winnie said sadly.

Wincing as I understood how harsh my words sounded, I felt like a jerk. "It's not that I don't want to talk to you, I just need to unwind, music helps me do that, especially when I'm driving."

She blinked out of sight, and I heard a quiet, "Okay."

Feeling awful now, I kept flipping through music as I made my way home and smiled a little as I stopped on the song Ghost by Halsey as well.

Jax stared at the door as it slammed shut behind Ronnie, a rage starting to boil up in his chest, one he knew didn't stem from his own emotions. He tried to fight it back but the smell of the blood and sweat in the room was feeding it, feeding the darkness inside him, triggering things that should be left alone. He didn't think he was strong enough to take this on right now.

He was an empath, like he told everyone he was, but he wasn't as strong at it as he let on to be. But he still felt the barely contained anger and aggression that Ronnie left in his wake, and it too, was feeding this thing inside him. He knew even before he took the first step towards the house it wasn't going to let this go. He didn't think anything good was going to come out of this, was his last thought before the rage overtook him.

Jax flung the door open and stepped back into the house, the tension ratcheting up near danger levels. Jax has never really been the brave one out of the group, that was usually Ronnie or Aedan. He knew Ronnie was bigger, but Ronnie was a fighter. He briefly thought back to the blood he saw in the garage and felt the anger take over him again.

God, he felt like he was on a roller coaster from hell. He scanned around for Ronnie and heard him down the hall towards the kitchen. Scratch that, in the kitchen, he decided as he heard cupboard doors slamming. Jax stormed off after him, his feet pounding the floor with heavy thuds. He rounded the corner just in time to see Ronnie pull his hidden bottle of whisky out. Jax froze, his thoughts catching up to his vision as he watched Ronnie start to twist off the cap.

He launched himself at Ronnie, angrily snatching the bottle out of his hands and smashing it against the wall, not caring about the glass shredding his palms. The thing inside him ate it up. It loved the blood and anger. "Fucking shit, Ronnie! What the actual fucking hell are you thinking?!" Jax railed at him.

He watched in fascination as Ronnie's face became stone hard and cold. Shut down. He had a moment of fear as he remembered what this look meant for his friend. Jax didn't have time to move, and he didn't think he would have even if he could. On some level deep inside he knew he had this coming.

Ronnie shoved him, hard. His back slammed into the wall hard enough to break the plasterboard. The darkness inside took back over and he threw a punch that landed on his best friends' jaw. He had never once in his life raised a hand against Ronnie, and he watched in horror as the shock of it settled on Ronnie. Fuck, what had he done?

The anguish Jax saw in his friend's face was enough to snap him back into himself as he sunk down to the floor, repeating, "I'm sorry, I'm so sorry."

Jax couldn't even look at him as Ronnie crouched down. "You know what Jax? I don't care. I don't care anymore. I'm done. That was it, the last straw. I'm fucking done. I'm gone." He stood back up, his voice as cold and hard as Jax had ever heard it. Especially when talking to him.

Ronnie walked away, and Jax pushed himself to his feet to follow, smearing his whisky and blood coated hands over everything, leaving a visible trail behind him on this path to destruction. He couldn't leave this alone though. He couldn't lose Ronnie too. Holy shit this is so fucked up, Jax thought as he followed Ronnie.

Anger blasted him again and he punched the wall next to him, leaving a bloody hole as Ronnie stopped ahead of him and slowly turned around to look at Jax. "You hoping that was my face again?" Ronnie spat out.

"No. Fuck no. That wasn't me Ron, I swear that wasn't me," Jax pleaded, his voice raw with pain.

"You fucking hit me!" Ronnie shouted. "You fucking hit me, knowing my history of abuse, and yet you still fucking hit me," his voice quieted but vibrating with anger and something else Jax couldn't put his finger on.

"It wasn't me," was all Jax could think of to say.

"That's what you have to say, after that? After twelve years of me doing *everything* for you?" Ronnie's voice dropped even lower, sounding guttural and it tore Jax open. "Twelve years. Twelve years and not fucking one goddamned time did you ask me if I was okay. Not once. I lost her too. We all did. We all suffered in silence because of you. To take care of you. And not one goddamned time did you think to check on anyone else. I fucking lost her too."

Jax was floored, he hadn't expected this, and he cracked open even farther watching as this played out in front of him, with the guy who was closer to him than his own brother. Jax watched as Ronnie broke, and couldn't do anything about it. Because it was all true. He was the biggest asshole alive, and he knew it.

"Twelve years I have stuck with you, through absolute hell, chasing your fucking dream of finding her again. Watching as you descend into whatever the hell this is that you've become. Standing by as you have no idea what this is doing to me. Not one clue as to what I'm feeling, for twelve years. Swallowing my own pain so that you can have yours. Never once thinking that it's something we might share. That fucking all of us share!" Ronnie's voice broke and his fists clenched.

Jax refused to step back, if Ronnie was going to hit him, he'd let it happen. "Ronnie..." Jax whispered.

"No! You don't get to talk! Not now. No." Ronnie hung his head, tears falling unabashedly down his face, dripping from his chin, wetting the blood smeared shirt. "I can't do this anymore Jax. I can't. You have no fucking clue what I've given up for you, out of love, out of respect. You just take from me, like there's an endless pit inside I can draw from." He held up his bloodied hands. "Do you know why these are like this?"

Jax shook his head, afraid of where this was going, afraid there was no going back to how they were before. Even as he had the thought, he knew how wrong it was, that it shouldn't go back to how they were.

"Today Jax, that meeting. Having to pull you back from the edge once again, as I fell farther and farther over it." Ronnie started pacing back and forth across the hall. "When we got home, I couldn't sit still, everything I've pushed away for the last twelve years was flooding me, filling my head. I went down there and pictured my own face on that bag, and I beat it until I collapsed because I fucking felt guilty! I felt guilty for mourning! I felt guilty for loving Winnie!"

Jax felt his face crumble and he took a step forward towards Ronnie, his eyes spilling tears that should have been spent by now.

"Do not come closer to me," Ronnie growled out. His face bloody from rubbing his hands across it, a bruise forming where Jax hit him. His eyes bloodshot. "I went down there, to avoid this," Ronnie's hands gestured between them, then dropped listlessly to his side. "I know it wasn't you that did this," he said pointing to his face. "But I also know, you didn't fight it. Jax...I just can't right now." He sagged against the wall.

Jax could see he was barely holding on to his sanity. "Don't leave."

"Fine, whatever. Just leave me alone," Ronnie said flatly. He walked away from Jax and went in his room, shutting the door with a sound Jax would describe as finality.

She felt it. She felt the explosion between Jax and Ronnie, and she knew. She knew things were accelerating and if she didn't want her vision to happen, she had to find a way to change it. She needed to go. It was time. She believed Ronnie would be able to hear her.

She hadn't tried in all these years because she didn't want him to hurt anymore. "Airy," she spoke softly, not wanting to startle her again. She had put so much pressure on her to help already.

"Yeah?" Airy answered, sounding distracted.

Winnie paused a moment to get a read on her, the music she was selecting was a good indicator of how she was feeling as well as the way she felt things. "I need to leave for a little bit, and my energy is low. I hate to ask for another favor, but I need help."

"You can't drain my car battery," she replied.

Winnie laughed quietly. "I'm glad you still have a sense of humor."

"Look, I know something is wrong, your emotions just went off the charts crazy. What do you need?"

"Can we go somewhere really quick where a spot is like we met at? One where I can pull from nature?" Winnie asked timidly.

"Um, sure, but I don't think there is anything around this immediate vicinity." Airy concentrated a moment on something but Winnie couldn't tell what, Airy has her walls firmly in place. "How quickly do you need to get there?"

"Well, as soon as I can, but I think the damage has been done already. I can block myself there, but I need a full tank to try and communicate," Winnie told her.

She saw the understanding light Airy's eyes. "Okay, ETA: fifteen minutes," she said as she turned off the road and headed the opposite direction.

Jax, feeling shell shocked and raw like an exposed nerve walked back to the kitchen. He grabbed his phone and texted Aedan to come over ASAP. His phone rang less than thirty seconds later.

"What did you do now?" Aedan demanded as Jax answered.

"I seriously fucked up with Ronnie," Jax told him, beyond ashamed.

"How did you manage that? He has the patience of a saint with you," Aedan said, incredulous.

"I hit him," Jax said, dropping to the bloody glass covered floor.

"Fuck. I'm on my way," Aedan hung up.

Jax looked around him at the destruction and couldn't find it in himself to care. He deserved this. He'd been a fucking asshole to all of them. He picked up his phone again to text Smitty.

"I need you to come over. I need help. Fucked up majorly with Ron. I hit him."

Five seconds later he had a reply, "On my way, don't do anything else stupid."

Chapter Seven

I was thankful I had my hiking pack in the car with me and an extra pair of shoes. Even though it was a beautiful winter day, work clothes weren't my favorite thing to play around in nature with. As I changed my socks and shoes, I looked around me reveling in the beauty of the earth and the changing seasons.

Tying my shoes, I wondered again not for the first-time what kind of shit storm I was going to be walking into. Some remote part of me knew I was doing the right thing, but another part of me was worried that I was not what was needed to help this situation along. I had a lot of baggage.

Despite Winnie's going on about angels, there was no part of me that believed I was one in any way. I was on an up close and personal basis with my flaws and faults. If the emotions that I picked up from her on the way here were anything to go by, it was a volatile situation, maybe even dangerous. I didn't know if I wanted to be held responsible for the life of someone else, or at the very least the well-being of their soul.

I sucked in a giant breath of fresh air and let it out slowly, soaking in the feeling of the clean air working its way through my body. I quieted my thoughts for a moment and dropped my walls, immediately feeling Winnie close by, but ignoring her, I searched for the feel of the energy. Locking into it, I shifted out of my car locking the doors behind me and headed towards it.

Winnie stayed quiet, which concerned me, but I was also thankful for. I liked being alone in nature with my thoughts; it's where I learned myself the best, although I was quick to acknowledge I still had a long way to go. I left my walls down as I walked; momentarily glad I hadn't brought my music with me. I guess I needed the silence.

It wasn't long before I noticed Winnie feeling the energy. It grew stronger the closer I got to the lake, but this spot wasn't as powerful as the river where I met her. In my experience the flowing water had better energy spots. This would work for what she would need though. The energy pulls me to the left, so I veered off course heading to a spot on the edge of the lake hidden by trees.

The cold winter air was refreshing, and the scenery didn't disappoint. It wasn't a large lake, but it was the closest to where I had been sitting in traffic. The water was clear and smooth, reflecting the sky and the sinking sun. The trees were all pine, tall and full, ripe with the scent of the needles. Due to the winter rains the fields were all green, but the ground too cold for any flowers yet.

I perched on a large semi flat rock near the water and drew one knee up to my chest wrapping my arms around my leg. I dropped my forehead to my knee and concentrated on my breathing. As I already had my walls down, the bad energy I had drawn from people over the past week had slowly leeched out of me as I approached the lake. I let the earth scents cleanse my lungs and mind washing away the worries about everything that I had no control of.

I lifted my head off my knee and looked over to the east as my gaze settled on the majestic mountain looming there. "Thank you," I whispered out to the universe. I never really felt all the way better unless I gave thanks for everything I could, especially when it came to releasing all the negative energy. I felt like it was a gift that the earth and universe was giving me in that release.

"Who are you thanking?" Winnie asked softly from my other side.

"The earth, the universe," I replied, glancing over to see her blue form sitting next to me on the rock.

"Makes sense. You are one of the few I've seen do that," she said. "My tank is full, I need to head out, will you be okay?" Winnie asked me.

Surprised that she thought I wouldn't be, I stuttered out, "Of course. Why wouldn't I be?"

"I realize I've thrown a lot at you this week," she said as I felt her stroking my hair again. "It would be understandable for you to be not as alright as you pretend to be sometimes. Airy, you are truly remarkable."

Surprised again, I wasn't sure how to respond to that. I looked at her questioningly as she studied me. Pushing myself to face fears, I left my walls down and said with hesitation, "You sure have a lot of faith in me."

"I see you in ways you don't see yourself," she answered gently, still playing with my hair, which I had to admit has always been relaxing to me.

"I hope I don't let you down," I told her, my insecurities creeping up again.

"You are so much more than you think. I hope that you will allow me to help you as you help me, so that maybe you can start to see it too. I won't abuse your trust," she promised me and stood up. "I'll be back as soon as I can, and we can talk. I thought about what you said about appearing suddenly, and I think I can do the scent thing. Someone special told me that I smelled like a fresh rainfall, so if you smell that, you will know I am near. Wish me luck, I'm going to need it."

I smiled at her and sent a strand of good energy into the hope she was holding on to and she smiled gratefully at me, then was gone. I stood up and drew some more of that same energy into myself and headed back to my car to go home. Times like this I was grateful for the gift of being able to use energy in this manner.

He heard voices from the other room and knew at once Jax had called in reinforcements. He closed his eyes just wanting it all to go away. He was devastated at what had taken place. They both had snapped, and Ronnie feared it was *his* fault Jax had snapped like that. He absently rubbed at the bruise settling on his cheek and couldn't believe Jax had hit him.

That was the one line he had never crossed. He had fought with Aedan and Smitty before, but never Ronnie. It wasn't even something Ronnie has ever considered a possibility before. He threw his arm over his eyes and started to wonder if they could come back from this. Ronnie knew it wasn't Jax that hit him, he wasn't even present in his eyes when that took place. He had looked possessed.

The guilt he felt over everything told him he deserved it for the secrets he was keeping from Jax, but in his heart he knew it wasn't deserved. Jax was just beyond obsessed with whatever was going on in his mind, he wasn't even sure it was about Winnie anymore. He knew she was still a part of it by the way Jax reacted when anyone said her name, but he didn't believe she was the driving force like she once was.

Ronnie's phone on his nightstand made some weird noise and Ronnie glanced over at it. He didn't see any notifications, but he winced at the blood all over it. He held his hands up and looked at the back of them. Split knuckles, dried blood caked under his nails, pooling in the nail beds, running down the back of his hands. He cursed himself for losing control like that.

He cursed himself for taking that bottle of whisky down too. Fuck, he was glad Jax had knocked it out of his hands, what was he thinking? Was he really going to take a drink? He shuddered at how close he came, and his eyes welled up at the thought of breaking his silent promise to not do that again.

"I wonder what you would think of me right now Winnie," he thought aloud, disgusted with himself and fully immersed in self-loathing. "Pity party of one, now serving Ronnie," he said to the empty room.

He saw his phone screen light up out of the corner of his eye and he looked over again expecting an alert for a message, but there wasn't anything. He stared at it a moment and felt his jaw drop open as it started playing a song. He froze on the bed as some female voice was singing about being haunted.

He slowly sat up and moved closer to the phone but didn't reach for it. He had a wild fleeting hope that Winnie was trying to communicate with him, but just as quickly dismissed it. Why would she have waited this long? Right as that thought crossed his mind, he smelled it. He smelled her. The scent of fresh rain filled his room.

He shot to his feet and frantically scanned every inch of his room looking for her. "Winnie?" He whispered; his voice thick with hope. "Oh God, please don't let this be a joke," he begged out loud.

His phone started replaying the song and he grabbed his iPad and listened to the lyrics and typed in a line on Google. Haunting by Halsey came up. He read through the lyrics and then dropped his iPad, the corner bouncing off his bed and falling to the floor. He stared at his phone as the song played.

The scent of fresh rain washed over him again, teasing his senses. His heartbeat was thundering in his ears and he was afraid to move, afraid he'd lose her again. The song started to replay, and he bent over and grabbed his iPad again to reread the lyrics. He felt like his heart was about to burst between the warring joy held at her being here and the sadness in the message of the song and missed opportunities.

He felt something run over the back of his hands and he lifted them, holding them out, staring, hoping. He felt it again, she was touching his hands, icy cold velvety tingles ran over his split knuckles. "Winnie..." he groaned, his voice cracking as he felt a wave of love wash over him. His knees buckled and he started to drop but was shoved backwards and he fell to the bed.

He rolled on to his side and let the tears fall. After a few minutes the song stopped playing and he sat up fast, worried she was gone, and not knowing. He heard a tap on his window and swiveled around to face it, pulling the curtains to the side and squinting at the light of the setting sun blinding him for a moment. When his eyes adjusted Ronnie saw an outline of a hand pressed to the window. His heart stopped as he leaned forward to place his hand over it, and at contact he sucked air greedily back in his lungs, his heart racing because he knew she was here with.

"Baby, can you hear me? If you can hear me, I'm going to fog up the window, write me a message," Ronnie said quietly. He leaned forward again and used his breath to fog up the window as much as he could and watched.

I am here

"Good job Winnie. I'm so happy right now I want to shout it out loud!" He fogged the window again for her.

can't tell Jax he is not ready
but I found her

"Who, Winnie? Who did you find?" He fogged the window again and waited.

the one who can help fix him

"Fix who? Jax? Give me more." He fogged up a large portion of the window feeling lightheaded he sat back down.

choose Airiella for job
meet me at a river tomorrow with ovilus, alone, I'll find you

"Can I tell any of the guys? What river, what time, are you leaving now?" Ronnie fired off questions as fast as possible. "Do you know I love you?" He fogged up the window again.

any river, at five, no tell others, I love you even in death, remember choose Airiella, hands hurt, why - face bruised, why, who

"You don't sound ready to leave yet, babe. I hurt my hands. Jax hurt my face. Things are complicated right now. Jax is not okay, and as you can see me, I'm clearly not ok." He fogged up the windows again.

bring ovilus and something I can pull energy from I'm low now, need to go, love you miss you

"God, Winnie, I miss you so much. Thank you for this, I'll meet you at the river I threw you in on Halloween. Tomorrow at five. Go rest." He laid back on the bed, his heart lighter than it felt in years and a smile on his face. He closed his eyes and drifted off to sleep, unaware that she was watching him.

Aedan pulled up in Jax's driveway and saw Ronnie's car still there, so all wasn't lost. He looked over at Mags, his wife, and asked her again, "Are you sure you want to be here?"

She nodded, "I might be able to help with something, you never know. Plus, I can check on Ronnie." She swallowed her fear. "I can't believe Jax hit him."

"Yeah, this isn't good," Aedan muttered. He grabbed her hand and kissed the back of it. "I love you, baby."

"Love you too, Aed. Are we waiting for Smitty, or should we just go in?" Mags asked.

"Let's wait, be a unified front at least, or maybe that there is safety in numbers," Aedan said, looking around the yard. "We don't really know what we are dealing with as far as Jax is concerned. He's kept everything inside locked up tight, the only time we see something is when he isn't really him."

"Yet you continue to be around him," Mags said accusingly. "He almost hit Smitty last time. What's going to happen if he hits you? I don't want you getting hurt."

"He's my brother Mags. We will figure it out. I can't walk away from him. And come on, we've fought before, I can hold my own," Aedan rationalized.

"That's beside the point," Mags said, feeling frustrated. She sighed and looked over at Aedan again. "I know you can't walk away, and it's one of the many reasons I love you. I'm just scared."

"I know. We are working on it. The producers of the show want to hire someone to be a kind of mediator or something when he gets out of control. Though the memo they sent us didn't specify Jax, we all know that's who they meant. They worded it so that if on an investigation it looks like something is affecting any one of us, this person would come in and diffuse the situation. That's what the meeting was about today. Ronnie, once again, pulled Jax back from whatever edge he's balancing on and finally got him to agree. Jax said for us to request an empath. So, once things calmed down, we made a list of attributes we think could help any possible situation we run into, and sent it back to the producers. It's just a hurry up and wait game now," Aedan told her as he kept scanning for Smitty.

"I guess it's a start," Mags hemmed, "but you are still adding an unknown person into a volatile situation. Empath? Isn't that what Jax is? How is an empath going to help?"

"Yeah, Jax is an empath, but he isn't as strong as he wants people to think he is. I read an article a while ago where an empath was used by authorities to help in a hostage situation. It was one of the paranormal journals, but I can't remember which one. The reporter interviewed her, and she said she had the ability to pull the emotions from someone and take them on herself, which allowed the negotiator to then diffuse the situation. So that was one of the requests we made. An empath that has that ability," Aedan explained.

"I can see where that would be a handy skill to have. Jax actually agreed to this?" Mags asked, surprised.

"It was his idea," Aedan said. He saw Smitty's car coming down the street. "He's here," Aedan said as he turned to get out of the car.

"How will you know if this person has these abilities or not? People lie all the time," Mags asked as she got out of the car.

"Well, we are going to test them," Aedan replied. He looked over at his wife who was studying the clear sky. "Are you looking for something?" Aedan asked looking up, when suddenly he understood why she was looking it.

"It smells like rain," they both said at the same time. Aedan felt a shiver run down his spine as he tried to shake off the feeling.

"You guys haven't been in yet?" Aedan heard Smitty call out to them as he came up the driveway.

"No, man, we were waiting for you. United front and all that shit. Not sure what we are walking into," Aedan called back.

"Hey Mags, looking good," Smitty said as he walked up and gave her a hug. "Let's do this."

Aedan led them both into the house without knocking, and they could feel the tension in the air. Mags shifted uncomfortably behind him. Absently he reached back for her hand and squeezed. He slowly started towards the kitchen when they all saw a trail of blood leading down the hallway. "Shit," Aedan muttered quietly.

"Wonder which one of them that belongs to," Smitty said, his voice soft.

They followed the trail leading back to the kitchen and they all froze in their tracks. Bloody handprints smeared the walls, leading back, there were shards of broken glass, and the stench of whisky. "Fuck, I hope neither one of them is drinking," Aedan replied looking back at Smitty.

They paused before walking around the wall into the kitchen and saw Jax. Sitting on the floor amidst shattered glass of what looked like a whisky bottle, blood splattered everywhere. Mags stepped around Aedan and called out quietly, "Jax?" While Aedan tried to pull her back behind him.

"She's fine dude, he's not going to hurt Mags," Smitty said. "He doesn't look like he could hurt anyone right now."

"Bro, we're here, man, you okay?" Aedan asked, not using a gentle tone. Based off the cracked plasterboard behind him, the time was way past gentle. This was ugly.

Jax looked up and Mags gasped, rushing over to him. His face was streaked with blood, his eyes puffy and bloodshot, anguish rolling off him. "I fucking hit him," Jax rasped out.

Aedan couldn't move, he stood there staring at the

scene in front of him while Mags grabbed a broom and tried to sweep the glass up. Smitty walked across the room and took it from her, while Aedan stared. "Mags go check on Ronnie," Smitty suggested.

She looked back at Aedan, and he nodded at her, watching her as she followed the trail of blood down the hall. They both heard her mutter, "Shit," as she must have found something else.

"Get up Jax," Aedan demanded, his voice hard. "Get up now."

Aedan didn't make a move towards him and he watched Jax's still bleeding hands fall to the broken glass and try to lift himself off the ground. Smitty gave Aedan a dirty look and went over to help Jax up. Aedan grabbed a chair and pulled it out, "Sit down there," he directed.

"Dude, look at this mess, take it a little easy on him," Smitty whispered to Aedan.

"No, this mess is made by him. I'm not sure why, but if this was the work of Ronnie, it would be worse," Aedan declared. "You've seen Ronnie fight."

"It was me," Jax said sadly. "I followed him into the kitchen in time to see him try to take the top off the whisky bottle and I just reacted badly. I didn't try to talk to him, I was yelling, and I smacked it out of his hand and threw the bottle against the wall. See the wall," Jax said pointing to where it looked like it caved in, "that was Ronnie. He shoved me. But something came over me, I don't know man, I just couldn't leave it alone. I was yelling at him, and then I sucker punched him. Right in the face."

Aedan squatted down in front of Jax and took his hands and held them palm up as he looked them over. "And these? It's from breaking the bottle?"

Jax nodded, his face coloring in shame. "I didn't even really feel it, but it wasn't Ronnie that did this. It was me. I found him lying on the floor in the garage, blood on his shirt, his hands, on the floor, on the bag. Something in me triggered at the scent of the blood and seeing him like that. I fucking flipped out."

Aedan sighed and ran a hand through his hair. This

was bad. Ronnie and Jax never fought. Aedan stood up and grabbed a dish towel and ran it under the faucet to get it wet. He went back over and squeezed the water over Jax's hands to try and see where the cuts were. "Come over to the sink," he told Jax.

It was like Aedan was watching a puppet, Jax just did what he was told. Aedan shook his head again. This was very bad. He looked back to Smitty, "You got the clean up?" Smitty nodded to him, not saying anything out loud, but carefully watching Jax every time he glanced up. "Mags will help when she's done checking on Ronnie," Aedan said softly to Smitty. He just nodded again.

Aedan turned the faucet on, letting the water get warmer and then pulled one of Jax's hands to get it under the stream. He felt Jax flinch, but it was hard to care after seeing the devastation in here. As he rinsed the blood off, he saw several pieces of glass still embedded in his palm. He pulled the other hand under the water too and told Jax to leave them there.

He walked out of the kitchen following the blood down the hall and saw another hole in the wall, blood here too. This hole he knew was Ronnie. He shook his head and walked by Ronnie's room where the door was closed and entered Jax's room to get some tweezers and the first aid kit he kept there. He shook his head again wondering if he should take Jax to the hospital. He figured he would get him cleaned up first and then see. Aedan wasn't sure having Jax around too many people right now would be a good thing.

As he walked back into the kitchen, he noticed that Jax hadn't moved a muscle. He reached over and turned the water off and held one of his hands up to try and see better. "Hey Smitty, can you grab a flashlight and hold it over Jax's hands so I can pick the glass out?" Aedan asked over his shoulder.

"Sure thing," Smitty said, grabbing the emergency flashlight from on top of the fridge.

He held it over Jax's hand while Aedan gingerly picked pieces of broken glass from Jax's palm, wincing every time Jax flinched. A couple of the wounds were still bleeding heavily, and Aedan thought he might need stitches, and he also wasn't sure he got all the glass out. He repeated the process with the other hand and then wrapped them tightly in gauze to staunch the bleeding.

"We'll need to look at these in a few hours, I think a few of these need stitches, and I'm not sure I got all the glass out," Aedan explained to Jax.

Jax woodenly nodded and just stood there, like he was waiting for direction. "I'll do whatever you think is best."

Aedan sighed again, "Just go sit down somewhere while I help Smitty finishing cleaning this mess up." Aedan handed him the first aid kit and pushed him out of the kitchen. This day had gone from bad to worse. He tried to shrug it off and got to work cleaning up.

Aedan paused while pulling the bag out of the garbage can as he felt an icy sensation down his back, wrapping around his chest, like someone was squeezing him from behind. He looked around and felt a tingling sensation at the same time as he smelled rain again. Unnerved he grabbed the garbage bag and stepped away, when he noticed Smitty paused too.

Smitty's eyes were scanning the room around him, but the rest of him wasn't moving. "You okay Smitty?" Aedan asked him.

"Um, yeah. Do you smell rain?" he asked Aedan, confusion coloring his voice. "And did it get cold in here?"

Aedan gaped at him, "Uh...do you think..." Aedan paused, "never mind, it couldn't be." He shrugged.

"It's her, isn't it?" Smitty whispered quietly, hoping Jax couldn't hear them.

"I don't know dude, I don't know," Aedan replied as he walked out.

Winnie was very concerned. Jax wasn't really Jax, Ronnie felt broken, and she could feel the tension radiating from Mags, Aedan and Smitty. The group was falling apart. She stayed in Ronnie's room while Mags checked on him, not because she didn't trust him to not say anything, but she wanted to make sure he was okay.

She wished that had had more time together while she was alive. She felt they both believed it could have been something special, but it just wasn't meant to be. She knew that, felt it down deep within. Knowing it didn't make it any easier though. And he was a hot mess now.

She smiled, thinking about that. He was hot. All those guys were, but Ronnie, he had always made her melt. Even when she believed her and Jax would last through anything and their bond was the tightest, it was always Ronnie she had the strongest attraction to. Over six feet tall, and broad, his body was thick and solid, but very strong. His hair was a rich milk chocolate color, longer on the top than it was underneath, but he rarely styled it, he just let it do whatever it was going to do. Ronnie's eyes always got her, they were the greenest emeralds, it made her think of the wild jungles they showed on Discovery Channel shows. But when his moods changed, his eyes did to, from an iridescent hazel color to a light lime. He had nice full lips and a wide smile, with a very classic roman nose. Put all together he was incredible. Like one of those impossibly perfect underwear models.

She shook her head and returned to Mags and Ronnie. Mags was cleaning his hands and checking out the split knuckles, softly clucking her tongue at him. "What did you do?"

"I snapped, Mags. I just totally lost it. I hated myself, hated the secrets I kept from Jax, my feelings, everything. I have done everything for him since Winnie died, been there for everything, and today it was just all too much, and I hated myself for it. I went to the garage to release some tension, and I pictured my own face on that punching bag, and I lost it. I kept punching, like I was beating myself, until I just collapsed," Ronnie said in shame.

Winnie jolted as if being tased as she heard this. Anger and desperation radiated out of her. She saw both

Ronnie and Mags flinch and look around, before she got emotions under control. For a moment she wanted to go full poltergeist and just scare them all straight. Ronnie should have never been pushed to feel this way.

Winnie knew she didn't have time to go slow and ease Airy into this anymore, things were so out of control. She tuned out Mags as she started to plot out a course in her mind and was distracted by large movement on the bed and glanced over as Ronnie was taking his shirt off. If possible, she would have left puddles of drool on the floor.

He had more ink work done. From his shoulder down around a pec, trailing around his belly button to below the waistband of his pants. Black and red wavy lines twisted and intertwined around each other in a hypnotizing pattern that rippled when he moved. She wished she could trail her fingers down it.

"Well, why not?" she said aloud, "No one can hear me or see me." So, she moved over next to the bed as Ronnie wadded up his shirt and threw it through her to the laundry basket across the room. She even noticed Mags eyeballing him appreciatively. Humming, she leaned over and followed every inch of that beautiful ink down to his pants, not for the first time wishing she could remove them.

She watched as goose-pimples broke out across his skin and he tried to suppress a shiver. Winnie giggled as Ronnie's face flushed, and his nipples got hard. She watched as Mags cleaned the blood off him, wishing it was her hands on him. Damn, she needed to leave the room.

As she turned to go, Mags said, "What happened after that? It's a pretty big mess out there." Winnie paused as she wanted to hear his version of this as well.

"Jax came out into the garage and found me on the floor. Not exactly sure why he lost his shit like he did, it was kinda crazy really. I got angry and walked away. It was like a Mentos dropped in a Diet Coke, you know? Shit just started fizzing up to the top and I exploded. He followed me in, saw me grab his whiskey and got even angrier. It wasn't him, I know that at least. Something had control of him, and I shoved him hard when he knocked the bottle out of my hand, I think the wall broke. Anyway, whatever was in him took over and he punched me."

"Oh Ronnie," Mags sighed, sitting back on her heels.

"That's not all Mags," he said. "I spewed off some shit about being done and said I was leaving. I started walking back here, and I'm pretty sure he was back to himself then, but he followed me again and I lost it. I told him how sick of taking care of him I was, things along those lines, and something about him never taking the time to ask any of the rest of us how we were. Then I said I loved Winnie. It's all a blur. I punched a hole in the wall I think."

Winnie has heard enough. She was afraid of her reactions if she hung around longer. She went to the kitchen and saw Aedan patching up Jax's hands and Smitty cleaning. She took a moment to look hard at Jax, looking for signs of what was happening to him. She felt the darkness in him. It scared her. She saw it scared all of them. She didn't have very much sympathy for Jax now, but like Ronnie, she knew it wasn't all him. She watched him walk out when Aedan was done, and she took in the damage that had been done. Without thinking, she let her love for these guys loose and gave them both hugs, then left. Back to Airy.

I decided to go to bed early, hoping for more sleep, as I gave the cats their bedtime treats, I smelled rain. I didn't see Winnie anywhere, and I glanced outside noticing that a storm was brewing. Could be a coincidence. I shrugged my shoulders and put the cat treats away when I saw both my cats cock theirs heads sideways and stare behind me.

"Winnie?" I said to the empty room. The cats turning their 'what is this weird human doing now' look on me.

"Sorry, I'm here, just trying to collect my thoughts. I can't appear, I've used way too much energy," she said apologetically.

See Me

"It's okay," I replied. "It's only the cats here, and I'm pretty sure they already think I'm crazy, so me talking to nothing shouldn't surprise them. Everything okay?"

"No, not at all. So, I'm sorry in advance for pushing you. But we gotta move fast on this now. Things have escalated so much. So, if you want, I can give you the highlights of me, things you'll need to know and what we need to do if you'd like?" She asked gently but with an urgency in her tone that set me on edge.

"Highlights?" I hedged. "Not details?"

"Well we are short on time for the major story of my little makeshift family, plus, it's also their story and they should tell you themselves," she explained.

"Okay," I said drawing the word out. "Do you think they will?"

"Yep, I do. But my highlights will at least arm you with enough to make an educated guess about most of it. But I need to know you as well. We are essentially working together to save lives here and I need to know all I can because really, at the base level of this, you are walking into a train wreck and I can't help you if I don't know triggers, and what not."

"So, you want me to let you have free range privileges in the dirty pastures of my brain?" I said, my spine stiffening.

"Yeah, I'm sorry Airy. I really am. I won't use anything against you, I won't even bring it up unless I think it's relevant to what is on hand." She chuckled somewhat darkly, "Anyway if it all goes well, I'll be moving on, so I won't be here as a reminder that I know things you don't want me to know."

"That's a fucked-up way of looking at it," I snapped at her. "But fine. You'll do it when I'm asleep?"

"Sorry, yes I will. You won't even notice," she said.

"Oh, I'll notice," I mumbled. I walked away heading upstairs, wanting to be at least comfortable for her story.

74

Smitty walked down the hallway after cleaning up the mess Jax made, something close to anger boiling under his skin. Ronnie's door was shut, and Aedan was finishing patching up the hole in the wall. He nodded his head toward Jax's room and Aedan gave him a brief nod as a go ahead.

Smitty didn't knock, just opened the door and walked in. Jax looked like he had taken a shower, his hair wet and he sat shirtless on the edge of his bed with his head ducked down like he had fallen asleep, medical gloves taped around both hands to keep water out. He shut the door behind him and leaned against the wall.

"You've gotta find a way to fix this," Smitty warned. "We can't keep rescuing you, it won't work out in the end."

"I know," Jax replied, his voice rough. "I get that I've been just about the shittiest friend I could have been. To all of you."

"Look dude, people grieve in their own way and in their own time. We all know that. It just seems like you haven't even tried to move on. You just diverted attention away from the problem and now it's so big it seems insurmountable. I understand. Twelve years is a long time to hold on to that grief. You crossed a big line tonight and I've got to be straight with you, I have no idea if Ronnie will even want to try and fix this."

Jax gripped the blankets so tight in his hands that blood started seeping through the gauze making it look like the gloves were filling with blood. He didn't even seem aware of. "Something has a hold of me," Jax admitted.

Smitty let out a bark of laughter, "No shit! So, what are you going to do about it? It appears to us like you are just rolling over and letting it happen."

Jax stiffened, "Fuck you, you don't know what this is like."

Smitty pushed off the wall and stalked over to Jax, getting right up in his face. "I don't know, huh? Because I haven't been here the past twelve years watching it? I haven't been on the receiving end of the abuse you dole out in the name of grief? I haven't been driven mad with nightmares over the shit you've put us through? I haven't suffered sleepless nights wondering if one of my best friends was going to let whatever this is kill him? What have I missed? I don't live here like Ronnie does, that's true, so I'm not here twenty-four seven. I'm not related by blood like Aedan is, so I can't claim you are family like he can. But I have never turned my back on you or what you need. I've let you drive long enough. You fucking find a way to fix this, or you stand to lose a lot. This must stop. You've become the biggest narcissistic asshole I've ever met!"

Jax wilted in front of him. "I'm starting to see that."

"Tough love time, bro. Nothing else is working. I better start to see an effort out of you or I'm gonna walk. Watching a friend self-destruct isn't high on my list and it gets old. Twelve years of this Jax. I don't know what Ronnie said, and I don't need to know. But I know if he blew up like this, you pushed way too far."

"I did. I own that. It's just...it feels like I black out, but I'm still aware of my reactions. Like I'm watching a movie. Seeing him lying there, blood all over, triggered something. Memories, something, I don't know. The smell of the blood hit me hard and it was over. Like I craved it. I felt powerless," Jax struggled to explain, his voice cracking and breaking.

"Here's my suggestion. The producers sent a job listing to the agency today for our team and listed the qualifications they wanted. Whoever they hire, if they find that empath, let them help. I don't think an exorcism will help you. Your belief in God has twisted into something ugly. Do more meditation too, man, I'm sick of the selfish streak," Smitty retorted.

"I can't do this alone," Jax begged.

"You might not have a choice if something doesn't change really quick," Smitty warned, turning around. Jax nodded even though Smitty couldn't see him.

"Tell Aedan no hospital tonight please. He can take me in the morning," Jax called after Smitty's retreating back.

Chapter Eight

Hey! Where are you going?" Winnie called out to Airy. "To take a shower, you aren't invited," Airy called down the stairs.

Smiling Winnie followed Airy to her room, "Okay, I won't join you in the bathroom," she chuckled. "Do you mind if I pop over to that spot in the river for a moment? I am nintey percent sure I can get there. I need to recharge for this, but only a little since I don't need to appear."

"Of course, I don't mind. Are you sure you can get there, or do you want me to drive there for you?" Airy asked.

"Let me check," Winnie said, and she pictured the spot that she met Airy, and imagined herself there. When she opened her eyes, she was there, but the energy didn't feel right. With a flash of understanding she blinked out of there and back to Airy's bedroom.

"Well I can get there, but your spot is now tainted," Winnie told her glumly.

"Tainted? How?" Airy asked, her face crinkled up in confusion.

"I think when you pulled from me and released it, it

might have stuck to the area," she told Airy. "It is just a guess, but the energy didn't feel right."

"Well shit, that's not good. I wonder if I can pull it from the earth and release it somewhere else?" Airy mused as she started her routine.

"No, you'll have a chance to figure that out later, for now take your shower. I am going to pop back over there and wander around looking to see if it feels like that everywhere or just there. I'll probably be back before you are done," Winnie said distractedly, and then popped out.

She went back to the river and opened herself up fully with her eyes closed and focused her attention on the feel of the energy. She learned that trick from watching Airy and feeling her out while she did it. Winnie felt a slight tug pulling here and she let it guide her to a different area. She opened her eyes and looked around, not worried about other people, just to see where she was.

She could feel Airy's energy signature here, so it must be one of the spots she used. She sat on the ground like Airy does sometimes and let the earth energy fill her up again. It felt amazing to have this pure energy sink into her being, she almost felt alive again. Not wanting the feeling to end she just sat there for a bit and soaked it up like she was trying to get an energy tan. Giggling, she started to feel a little drunk.

"Time to go," she said giggling again. It was a heady feeling and as she stood up a raccoon appeared. Wondering if it was the same one from when Airy met her here. "Hey little buddy, do you remember me?" Winnie made herself appear and the raccoon approached her with no fear. "It *is* you!" she sighed.

She reached her senses out and felt the taint of the darkness that Airy pulled from her and she winced. "This isn't good now is it?" she told the raccoon. "I'll have her come back tomorrow and take it from you. I don't imagine that feels very good." The raccoon looked at Winnie and nodded his head and walked away. "Huh," she said, "interesting."

As she stood up to leave, she started putting a few

things together in her mind, it seemed like Airy was a grounding force for her, she felt drunk coming here on her own, but with Airy, it was just soothing. She knew Airy was an angel, it just felt right to her. She smiled, and still feeling drunk she popped back over to Airy.

As she popped over, before appearing she focused and sharing her scent as a warning and waited until Airy said, "Hi Winnie."

She appeared so Airy could see her. "A couple of things first, you might want to get dressed again sorry, I know you just showered. But first, I need you to send a text to one of the guys, you don't have to say who you are, just please text this message: A message from Winnie, can't meet tomorrow, something has come up. Will be in contact."

Airy was giving her a crazy look. "You know that this person will then have my phone number?"

"Yes," Winnie sighed, "but he's one of the good guys. Ready? I'll tell you the number."

As Airy sent the text, Winnie thought about how to word the energy tainting part. Based off what she knew about Airy, it wouldn't go over well that the raccoon was suffering. It didn't sit well with Winnie either. She looked up and saw Airy watching her expectantly. "Oh sorry, Airy. Get dressed, I'll meet you downstairs," she said distractedly. She heard Airy's phone beep. "Don't answer him. He can wait."

Winnie went downstairs and tried to work it out before Airy got there. If she was an angel, she was one of the touched, so it meant she had more abilities than she was using, and she didn't know it. What would a work around solution be to rid an area of evil? Religion was the obvious answer, but she didn't think the raccoon, or the earth followed any particular denomination. Actually, she didn't even know if Airy did. But maybe hallowed grounds would work. It wasn't earth energy there, it was spirit energy though.

If Airy released tainted energy in an area where spirits rested, would it make those spirits evil? Winnie shuddered, that wouldn't do. A church itself was hallowed ground though, wasn't it? Not just a cemetery. If she released the energy into a holy place, she didn't think it would spread. She hoped it wouldn't.

Airy came back downstairs and started to put her shoes on as she asked Winnie, "So where are we going?"

Winnie thought for a moment, "Is there a Catholic church around here that is still open? And first we are going back to the river."

Surprised at Winnie's answer, Airy silently grabbed her iPad and searched for a church. Sending the address to her phone, she grabbed her coat and the flashlight and nodded to Winnie to follow her.

Jax didn't think it was possible for him to feel any worse than he had before Smitty walked in, but he was sadly mistaken. Nothing that was told to him came as a shock, it was just hard to hear. Smitty basically said the same things Ronnie did, and that Aedan alluded to. He had to admit to himself that he's always been a bit selfish, that was part of the reason Winnie balanced him so well.

He needed to talk things out with Ronnie if he would give him a chance. Jax knew it would be a messy and painful talk, but it was a necessary one. He pulled off the gloves he had on and unwrapped his hands, they were still bleeding. He rinsed them off and pulled out fresh gauze and a roll of paper tape and started to wrap them back up and then covering the gauze with the tape to seal them up. Infection is the last thing he needed.

His hands properly mummified, he grabbed a pillow and a few blankets off his bed and went and laid in front of Ronnie's closed bedroom door. Jax didn't want him to leave without him knowing it, and it struck him that *that* was a selfish thought as well, but at least he had good intentions behind it. That's what he told himself anyway.

He was as quiet as he could be as he tried to find the most comfortable way to lay with his body feeling battered, not to mention his shredded ego and heart. Sleep would come he knew; he was just praying to whatever God would

listen to him that he would have a night without the
nightmares.

"Aedan, do you honestly think that Jax will be okay?"
Mags asked her husband.

"I don't know, my love," he answered
truthfully. "I want to answer yes, but from what I saw today
and heard from him, he's at the point of no return. Even if
he comes back from this, I don't think it will be the same
Jax we knew."

"That's what I am afraid of," she admitted as she
slipped into a slinky nightgown, hoping for a fun sort of
distraction from all this. She turned as Aedan hummed
deep in his throat as he saw what she was wearing. She
smiled and bent over on purpose so he could see her
breasts as her nipples rubbed against the rough lace,
getting hard.

"You planning something tonight babe?" Aedan
asked huskily.

She smiled at the tone in his voice and knew she
was going to get exactly what she wanted. "I think Ronnie is
borderline suicidal," she mentioned.

"Wait, what?" Aedan demanded, shocked.

"He imagined his face on that punching bag, and he
kept hitting until he passed out," she told him, walking to
the bathroom swaying her hips seductively. She glanced
back to see if he was watching her, and she was happy to
see his eyes were glued to her ass.

"Ronnie will be okay," Aedan said distractedly, and
started pulling off his clothes as fast as he could.

Mags loved watching him undress, his body was like
priceless art. Sculpted muscles, narrow hips, tanned skin,
selective inkwork, and just a light brown smattering of hair
for his happy trail. One she would happily follow with her
mouth in a few minutes. She looked back at her reflection
in the mirror and brushed her teeth, and then her hair.

Mags was blonde and fair skinned to Aedan's tan
skin tone, and light brown hair. Her eyes a royal blue color
and Aedan's a mesmerizing hazel. She was lean, where he

was a muscled Adonis. His voice had a gentle timber to it, and her voice was a more high-pitched tone. He was calm, but had an edge, while she was higher strung, but soft.

She smoothed the scented lotion he liked over her arms and legs and watched as he slowly stroked himself as he watched her. No more waiting, she needed him, needed the release, needed the distraction. She knew he needed it too, probably more than she did.

She sashayed back over to him, the silky gown hugging her body in a way she knew drove him crazy. "Nothing but us for the rest of the night, okay babe?" she told him, her voice thick with need. All he could do was nod his acceptance as he watched her trail her tongue down his body, his hands fisted in the sheets next to his hips and she took him in her mouth. Yep, they both needed this. Mags sighed around him as he trembled below her.

Care to fill me in on why we are headed to the river you just came from and why I looked up a Catholic church?" I questioned Winnie.

"Um, well, I told you about the area feeling like it was tainted, so you know that. But as I was getting ready to leave, our buddy the raccoon came back. He had the same taint," Winnie explained softly.

Tears immediately sprung to my eyes at the thought of the poor animal feeling that disgusting energy. I had poisoned the area with that release. The pieces started falling together. "We are going back so I can pull the energy out of the earth and the animals, and the church is where you want me to release it?"

"It was the best idea I could come up with," Winnie admitted.

"I've only ever released in nature, I'm not sure I can in a church," I muttered. "You can bet your ass that I will try though. No way am I letting innocent creatures or that beautiful land be host to that shit," I said angrily. "I can't believe I didn't think of that."

"I honestly thought that releasing in the water would take care of it," Winnie defended, "but maybe the raccoon was in the water when you did it? I don't know. I just know whatever this is, it's very invasive."

"I remember," I replied, shuddering. "I can't hold it too long or I think it will try to take root in me. This is new for me, so I can't be sure of anything. By the way, whoever you had me text wrote back with a name of some talent agency."

"Can you take the rest of the week off work?" Winnie asked.

"I'd rather not, but I have some sick leave I could use I guess," I hated calling in. I'd have to remember to try and text one of my co-workers to see if they could cover the office for me. "I'm the only one that works in that office, so it's not as easy as just calling in. I need to try to find someone to be there. You will probably have to remind me, because once that energy is in me, I need to stay super focused on it."

"Okay, I'm sorry," Winnie said weakly. "I've turned your whole life upside down and I feel awful about it."

"Don't dwell on it, I'm good with change," I muttered. I pulled off the road and slammed my car door and damn near ran until I felt the energy of that darkness. Stopping, I opened all my senses, dropped all my walls and invited the energy into me. I felt for that dark strand with my mind, and I pulled as hard as I could. I felt sick as tendrils of darkness wove in me, over me, through me.

"The land is clear Airy, pull back," Winnie warned. "We aren't alone."

I snapped my walls back in place but left my senses open, searching for the little raccoon, or any creatures that got tainted by this oily evil shit. Feeling a pull, I let it lead me for a ways and then I stopped. I figured I was close enough to grab the tendrils and pull them in. "Can I drop my walls Winnie?"

"Do it fast," she told me.

I dropped and pulled hard, not being gentle and sent a little message of sorry out to the universe. I felt it wrap around me deeper, and then I felt more, and pulled as many of the strands that were appearing as I could. I was starting to feel heavy and overwhelmed.

"Airy, pull some of the pure energy too, and do it fast, your glow is changing colors," Winnie said frantically.

I didn't know how much more capacity I had, but I mentally searched for the good energy and pulled it into me until I felt like my soul was battling with itself. The raccoon appeared in front of me, and I cried because of the hurt I caused the poor little guy. He came right up to me and put his cute little face up close to mine and then licked my nose. I smiled through my tears at his little thank you and waited until he moved before I got up.

"Walls Airy," Winnie warned again.

Feeling restless I snapped them back into place. "Is the area clear? Did I get it all?" I asked weakly.

"Yes, you have it," Winnie said sadly. "It's affecting you."

"Then let's not waste any time," I snapped, grabbing my cell phone and pulling up the address for the church and ran back to my car, my chest heaving at the unexpected exercise. I wasn't a runner; my boobs were too big for that. Hell, I was too big for that.

Back in the car I followed the GPS to the church and hoped like hell someone was in there. "I don't know what to do Winnie, I've never done this before."

"Can you open up and see if you feel anything? My thought was it should be hallowed ground, but when I thought of a cemetery, I didn't want zombie spirits created by that evil energy invading their resting place," Winnie said hurriedly.

"Nope, don't want that. Horrifying thought. I don't even want to know if zombies are real, so let's move on, shall we?" I opened my senses and searched for energy. I didn't feel any of the earth energy here, but I felt a sense of peace and worried about what a release here would do to that.

"Probably a little late to ask this, but what are your religious beliefs?" Winnie asked.

"I was baptized roman catholic, so they can't turn me away, but I don't practice or conform to any religion. I just consider myself spiritual, I guess. I believe in God, but don't believe he needs a church or rules to be praised," I clarified.

"Maybe a priest will be in there that can help us," Winnie suggested.

"You want me to tell a priest I am full up of evil energy that I pulled from a ghost and released into the earth, which then tainted the land and the poor little animals, so I had to go pull it back again and now I'm here to release it?" I asked dumbfounded as I got out of the car.

Winnie let out a belly laugh. "Maybe not all that much. *I'm* the ghost and hearing that sounds crazy to me!" She kept laughing.

I chuckled darkly, "I'd probably find that funny too if I wasn't harboring this shit in me."

Winnie stopped laughing and we headed inside the church as she said deadpanned, "I hope lightning doesn't strike you as you walk in."

"Not funny Winnie," I told her with a glare. Though at this point, it wouldn't surprise me if I did get struck by lightning. I pushed the doors open, and only paused for a moment before continuing as I heard Winnie laughing quietly next to me. "Ass," I whispered to her.

As we entered though I felt the darkness inside me start swirling around like it was frantic and it was making me sick to my stomach. I stumbled and heard Winnie cry out, "Airy!" I caught myself on a pedestal and in the back of my mind I realized it was holy water. In desperation I plunged my hand in it and immediately recoiled at the pain that tore through my body, bile rising in my throat.

"Over here!" Winnie shouted and l looked around and saw a garbage can and stumbled over to it, barely in time to empty the entire contents of my stomach and pain slammed through every nerve in my body. I could feel a cold sweat dripping down my face. Not good.

"My senses are open; how do I get rid of this shit before it kills me?" I whispered to Winne, mentally cringing at the cuss word in a church, I should know better than that.

"I don't know, what did the holy water do?" She asked me gently. I could feel her cool hand on my head and noted the relief it brought at her touch.

"It hurt, like, everything, my whole body," I told her. "It's tearing me up inside."

I heard footsteps approaching me, then a soft voice, "Are you okay, my child?" I looked up to see a man in black with a priest's collar. No clerical robes, but it had been so long since I had been to a service I didn't know if they wore those all the time or not.

"Not feeling my best at the moment, father," I told him. My stomach turning again as he placed his hand on my arm. He pulled it back fast and gave me a quizzical look.

"You've been touched," he said in amazement.

I wasn't sure how to take that. Even Winnie was silent, which I didn't know if that was a good thing or not, but I was here, so I was going to just go with it. "I need help father," I beseeched him.

"I see," he said, standing up, "are you well enough to walk?" he asked indicating the garbage can. I nodded weakly though I still felt unsettled. I grabbed the can and stood with it in hand. With a nod of his head he said, "Follow me."

Like an obedient puppy I followed along and heard Winnie whisper next to me, "Walls." I didn't even know I had dropped them. I snapped them back in place with a slight nod of my head and saw her relax. Guess we weren't alone here either. What was happening?

The priest went through some doors on the side of the altar and I followed meekly, feeling revulsion when I looked at the religious items around me. I knew immediately that was the energy in me reacting and I fought to control it, my head beading up with sweat again. We were in some sort of office and the priest reached into the desk in the room and handed me a handkerchief. Grateful for the consideration, I smiled and thanked him.

"Airy, your glow is getting dark, something needs to happen soon," she said with fear.

"Father, in your experience what is the best way to

get rid of evil energy that is attacking you?" I asked him bluntly.

"In your case, I am not sure. You are different because you've been touched. I don't think it can take over you," he said watching me closely. "Would you like to try drinking holy water?"

Winnie gasped next to me. "It might hurt you Airy."

"Will it hurt me?" I asked the priest.

"It's just water that has been blessed in the church," he said, his eyebrows furrowing together. "Physically, I do not know how it will react with the energy."

"Well, it's worth a shot, I feel like it's killing me, so might as well," I said resigned. Pain was nothing new to me.

The priest held out his hand for me to take, reminding myself to just go along with this, I gave him my hand and the energy in me jolted violently making me shake. I grasped on to the garbage can with my other hand in case of an emergency projectile situation. "It can't beat you, child," he said softly, his eyes slightly out of focus.

"I'm thirty-four, hardly a child," I told him, my patience wearing thin. "What do you mean it can't beat me?"

"We are all God's children, but you are young enough to be my child, though if it bothers you, kindly tell me your name and that is what I shall call you," the priest said sternly, but not unkindly.

"I apologize father, I don't take offense. Just feeling a little on edge, and maybe names aren't a good thing in this situation," I hemmed.

Ignoring my statement, he continued, "It can't hurt you because of the blessing you have on your soul. Put plainly, you are stronger than what is trying to kill you."

"How do I beat it?" I asked, my curiosity now peaked despite the painfully violent tremors running through me.

"Well, let's start with the holy water for the moment, it would be the quickest way I believe. Beyond that, I am not sure. I'm not well versed in things like this, but I do have the sight," he said, standing up and reaching for a jug behind him.

"The sight?" I repeated, sounding dumb.

"I can see the blessings bestowed by angels," he said matter of fact.

Biting back a curse, I shot a warning look at Winnie silently telling her to keep her mouth shut about the angel shit. "So when you said I was touched, you were referring to an angel? I was touched by an angel? Isn't that a TV show?" I said, unable to hold back the sarcasm.

The priest chuckled, at least he had a sense of humor. "It was a TV show," he said as he poured some water into a cup and then performed the holy rites to bless it. The words he was mumbling over the water making my insides quake and I leaned over and hurled again into the garbage can. I didn't see how anything else could be inside me and this was embarrassing.

"You have been touched by God himself," the priest said. Several inappropriate comments sprung into my head and I had to literally bite my tongue to keep the verbal diarrhea from flying out. "As for what gifts you have, they will reveal themselves when it's time. I think it's just important for you to remember that you are stronger than this evil is. Hold on to that thought and it will help see you through your journey."

Oh yay, more cryptic messages delivered by an elderly priest this time. He handed me the cup of water and I lifted it up in a salute and said, "Bottom's up." I drank it down like I was dying of thirst and gripped the rapidly filling garbage can in case it came back up. Throwing it up would have been easier.

Pain slammed through every fiber of my being as the energy fought back. I fell out of the chair, the garbage can falling from my grip, thankfully upright, because, well, eeeww. I think it was me that cried out as it felt like something was trying to physically rip my nerves from my body, and all the hair on my body stood on end. I felt the priest lay his hand on my forehead, the contact burning my skin like I was on fire. The lightning strike comment came to mind and I could only hope my skin wouldn't burn the holy man trying to help me.

I heard Winnie somewhere in the background of the screaming that was filling my ears say, "Hold on Airy!" I felt her cool touch on my leg. The screaming in my ears got so loud that it drowned out all rational thought from my head until all I heard was "You are stronger than this." Then I blacked out.

Not sure how long I was out, but there was now a pillow under my head and a blanket over me and I felt soaked. I cracked open one eye to see the lights had been dimmed, and I was grateful for that. I opened both eyes and saw Winnie hovering over me, fear etched into her face. "Oh my God, I thought you died," she cried out. "You were here on my side of things."

"Nope, not dead," I replied, my voice scratchy and rough.

I heard the priest chuckle, "No child, you are certainly not dead at the moment. Are you okay?"

Shit, I forgot where I was for a moment. I shot a glare at Winnie and she got the hint and went silent. "Define okay," I said. "If by okay you mean did I survive some evil energy trying to kill me after I found out God touched me," I couldn't help the snicker that escaped there, "and an old priest made me drink holy water that scorched my insides, then yeah, I'm okay."

"Well child, I can say you certainly made this old priest's heart race. That has to have been the scariest thing I have ever witnessed in my life. I'm eternally grateful for my position in this holy war against evil in this quiet church. Well, quiet before tonight that is," the priest said, chuckling. "You've got quite a set of lungs on you."

Surprised, I sat up, then grimaced as my body revolted against the movement. "The screams I heard were mine?"

Winnie was nodding her head frantically, her eyes wide. "Most certainly were," the priest told me. "Might I suggest carrying around a blessed object with you?"

"Why not? I just drank holy water, something I

didn't think was ever going to happen," I said dryly.

"While you were, um, out, I ran out to lock the church doors, well I didn't run, but I walked as briskly as I could. I dropped an old rosary I had in here in the holy water out front. If you will excuse me for a moment, I would like to go get it and bless it at the altar. Just sit here and rest. There is water in the jug on my desk if you need it."

I looked at him sideways before eyeballing the jug of water, remembering what happened last time I drank water that came from the jug. The priest suddenly burst out laughing. "You, my child, are precious. The look on your face was one that will carry me through any dark times I have headed my way. The water in the jug is not blessed, it's just plain water," he said still laughing as he stood up. "I'll be back in a moment."

I glanced over at Winnie who was also trying to hide the fact that she was laughing. Jerks. They wouldn't be laughing if they had gone through that shit! I thought about it for a moment, and then laughter overtook me as well. This was just north of crazy, past the border of insanity and around the corner from what the fuck just happened.

My throat was painfully raw, so I stood up and poured myself a fresh cup of water in a cup that didn't have holy water previously in it, and greedily drank it down, the coolness soothing my throat. "What the hell happened Winnie?"

"I don't know, but you were screaming so loud that the priest was worried someone passing by would hear it, but he was afraid to leave you alone. He had his hand on your head, and like someone flipped a switch, you just stopped and were gone. I seriously thought you had died; your glow went away and everything. Your spirit was on my plane with me. You were like that, completely still. I couldn't tell if you were breathing or not. The priest put a pillow under your head and covered you with a blanket and went out of the room. I'm guessing it was about twenty minutes before you opened your eyes," Winnie said in a rush.

"Why am I wet?" I asked, pulling my sticky clothes away from my body.

"Sweat," she said. "It was rolling off you like it was being burned out of you."

"That's about what it felt like," I said recalling the pain.

"That's what what felt like?" the priest asked as he came back in.

I spun around, sloshing water over his desk as he walked towards me. "Um, that's what the pain felt like," I stammered stupidly, trying to gather my thoughts. "Am I clean?"

Winnie nodded at me, while making a zipping her lips motion, and then it clicked. He had walked in on me talking to Winnie. Damn it, I needed to be more aware of my surroundings.

"Do you mean is the energy gone?" the priest asked me for clarification.

"Um yeah," I mumbled, looking down at my drenched in sweat self. "Clearly I need to go take another shower."

"I am not able to see energy like you can, but my assumption is that it is gone. Can you not feel it?" the priest asked, confused.

I paused, trying to gather my thoughts. I couldn't feel anything at all. It was like I was numb. I shot a look of fright at Winnie, then quickly looked back to the priest, "I can't feel anything right now."

"Ah," he said as he wrapped up the rosary in a clean handkerchief, then handed it to me. "I guess that would make sense given what you just went through. From what I saw with my own eyes, which I would have struggled to believe had I not seen it, it felt as though something was expelled from you. There was a violent breeze that bounced around in here until I opened the window."

I looked at him blankly, my mind still muddled. "So, it's just back out there now? I need to go find it and clean up again?"

"No child, I think it's gone back to wherever it came

from," the priest explained. "Holy water would have banished it from here."

"You mean like an exorcism?" I asked, feeling stupid.

"In a way. I think a better description would be that you killed the darkness in it, and it just dissipated," he tried.

Great, I'm a darkness murderer. "Well thank you for your help. Jeez, that feels like a major understatement. Thank you for keeping me alive," I tried again, but it still didn't feel adequate. "Um, just, thank you. For everything. I am eternally grateful," I said, humbled beyond belief.

He smiled at me gently, "Child, the pleasure was mine. It was a first for me to witness one of God's warriors at work. It is I who should be thanking you."

I shook my head, "No. That's not me. Please accept my gratitude," I said, holding out my hand to him.

He took it and shook it gently, then shrugged and pulled me into him and gave me a soft hug that warmed my insides. "Go in peace, child."

"And also with you," I responded automatically, surprising myself yet again. He traced the sign of the cross on my forehead with his thumb and then steered me to the door.

"Not to be rude, but you wore this old man out," he said lightly and escorted me out of the church, Winnie following behind me in silence.

"Thank you again, father," I said gratefully. "Have a good night."

He nodded at me once, and then shut and locked the church doors. I headed to my car, eager to get home and shower and climb into bed until I remembered my night wasn't over and I still needed to find someone to cover for me at work. I got in the car and dug around for my phone and pulled it out, sending a text to my co-workers to see if any of them could cover the office for me, then started the car and headed back home.

Winnie still hadn't said anything, and I didn't know if that was good or bad. I was still shaken up by the whole thing, so I plugged in music for a distraction. I didn't blast it as loud as I normally do, my ears were still ringing from the noise I had apparently been responsible for. I pulled up at a red light as my phone dinged at me with a text message, saw that one of my co-workers was free to cover the office, and quickly shot off a text to my boss telling him that I had a family emergency I needed to tend to and would be out the rest of the week.

His acknowledgement and well wishes came through as I was pulling into my garage. I got out of the car and told Winnie, "Okay, I'm off the rest of the week."

"This was the most eventful day I've had since I've been dead," she said with a straight face. I raised my eyebrow at her and walked into the house.

"I'm going to go shower again," I told her as I pulled an electrolyte drink out of the fridge. "You can do your part after I'm done." She nodded at me and I went to go shower, downing half the drink before I got to my bedroom.

Well, that was one interesting night,' Winnie thought to herself. She heard the shower turn on upstairs and made her way up there and laid on Airy's bed, her eyes closed. Winnie wasn't sure she could process all that just happened, and she had no idea how Airy was. Plus, she felt bad because she was about to dump more stuff on her, and then invade her head, which she had made clear she didn't like. Winnie sighed a sigh of defeat.

She didn't like to be the one pushing the limits of someone else, even if that someone was an angel, and remarkable even without having that quality. Airy had a pure soul. In a nutshell, she was love and she was life. Trying to shake it all off, she gathered her thoughts about what she was going to tell Airy about this mess Winnie had dragged her into. She had to reveal who the guys were.

Winnie felt that not telling her who they were was setting her up for failure. She'd be walking blind into something that could get her injured, and that wasn't fair to her, or the guys. Winnie heard the shower shut off and called out, "Airy I'm on your bed, so unless you want me to see your goodies get dressed before you come out here."

Winnie heard Airy laugh, then, "Got it. Thanks."

It was amazing Airy could even laugh right now. Winnie was pretty sure for a moment, Airy had died. Winnie sat up and rubbed her eyes, hating herself for a minute for doing this to her. She rationalized it by telling herself Airy would be saving lives, instead of dwelling on the thought that Winnie was being selfish and using Airy to ease her own conscience about moving on.

Airy came out of the bathroom in a pink tank top style nightgown with cherries on it, and she smothered a laugh, because the style wasn't Airy at all. Winnie noticed she had her arms crossed over her chest and realized Airy was embarrassed. Winnie kept quiet as Airy plugged her phone in to the charger she had on her nightstand and watched as she pulled out stones from the drawer and placed them near the bed on the nightstand. Curious, she asked, "What's with the stones?"

"They radiate an energy to me, like a vibration that I find when my mind is a mess, they soothe it," Airy explained sheepishly. "I know, cheesy, at least that is what my friends tell me."

"I don't think it's cheesy," Winnie said, "whatever helps is worth it."

"Thanks," Airy said as she stacked her pillows, pulled back the blankets and crawled in. "Okay, let me have it, hit me with both barrels."

"First, I need you to look up the number for the agency my friend texted you and call it and tell them that you are responding to a posting for an empath," Winnie said, her face carefully blank. "Obviously, leave your contact info."

Airy narrowed her eyes at Winnie, "I already have a job," I said, my voice hard.

Winnie sighed dramatically, "Just do it, Airy."

Professional voice on, Winnie listened, "Hello, my name is Airiella Raven, and I'm calling about a job you have available for an empath. Please give me a call," she said as she recited her phone number and hung up. "Happy?" she said to Winnie.

"Oh, you know it," Winnie replied. "So, you know my name, and that I'm dead, and that I had some abilities in life," Winnie started. Airy nodded. "Well, my abilities were a bit more than I let on, but until you had agreed to help me, I wasn't sure how much to share with you. The clairvoyance I had was a little different, some specialists called me a seer. I would get visions of things that were destined," she made air quotes with her fingers, "to happen in the future. Along with that, I could sometimes look at a person and see what their destiny had in store for them. The destiny thing always appeared to be more set-in stone than the visions, but not always. I also had the ability to see aura's, and read people a little deeper than most, which I think is the minor talent as an empath. But when you combined them all together, I knew things that I shouldn't really know."

"Okay," Airy drawled out. "Must have made for an interesting childhood."

Winnie smiled. "My parents took me at face value, so it wasn't too bad. I had known two of my friends since I was a young kid. We went to the same schools, and just melded together well. Do you ever watch any of those ghost hunting shows on TV?" she asked Airy, kind of in a side note type of way.

"Um, yeah. That was an odd question," Airy replied scrunching her face up.

"Sorry. Jumping ahead of myself there. One of those friends became my boyfriend, the one I told you about, since about fifth grade on, until about a month before I died. The other one was our best friend. We were always together, throughout everything. Because of my abilities, they knew about so called paranormal things as they related to me. My boyfriend had an interest in the field, and my friend, he had abilities as well, though he kept them well and truly hidden, but I knew. I think because of that, there was a bond between us that always felt strong and unbreakable to me. In a very different way than I had with my boyfriend," Winnie paused and looked at Airy who was watching her with rapt attention. "Following?"

"Of course, but do these people have names?" Airy asked.

"Yes, I was getting there. Jax was my boyfriend, Ronnie, my best friend, well our best friend really," Winnie paused again to gage Airy's reaction. She hadn't made the connection to the show yet. Internally, Winnie sighed in happiness. "During high school—well, ninth grade—we met two others that we had an instant connection with as well, Aedan and Art. Art we all called Smitty, because his last name was Smith," she explained and watched as Airy had a glimmer or recognition flit across her face, but it passed just as fast.

"All throughout high school we were together, we all got good grades, we all were good kids for the most part. Ronnie had a pretty rough go of it though, out of all of us. Purely by chance we stumbled on the fact that Aedan was Jax's half-brother. Their father had an affair no one knew about, and during a science class our instructor was talking about DNA, turns out after a test we submitted came back, they were related. Small world. But that revelation caused some tension between them, and some hard feelings between them and their dad," Winnie went on.

"I can only imagine," Airy said, riveted by the not so exciting story yet. But Winnie enjoyed the attention that was focused on her, it made her feel warm.

"Ronnie was getting into a lot of fights around that time, but we never really figured out with who, he would just show up battered. He also started drinking heavily, and at the minimum was smoking weed. Smitty was the one who put it together finally, that it was at home that it was happening. I'm just giving you the basics here because it's not my story to tell. Bottom line, his dad was abusing his mom, cheating, drunk all the time and heavily involved in drugs, which is where we think Ronnie got them from. Being Ronnie, he kept trying to protect his mom and took the brunt of things for a while."

"Oh my God," Airy breathed out, her eyes shining with tears. "Awful for a kid to see happen to a parent."

"It was bad," Winnie agreed. "Smitty mentioned something to us, but Jax took it, and went to a school counselor, who went to the police, who then put together a sting operation to bust the drugs he was peddling. But it lasted for a couple of years. Though not blood, Ronnie was Jax's brother, and seeing him show up at school beat up and broken inside tore Jax up. Ronnie had started taking martial arts classes and boxing after school, determined to not be a victim," Winnie continued, staring out into space, remembering.

"I can understand," Airy said cryptically, which snapped Winnie back into the now and she squinted at Airy, studying her.

She kept going, she'd get her answers later. "The rest of our high school years were spent putting Ronnie back together and watching as he became a pretty tough opponent in any ring he chose. But he was still drinking and using. We graduated, and I went to school and became a mental health counselor," Winnie said wistfully. "I loved it."

"Ronnie's situation influenced that decision?" Airy asked quietly.

Winnie nodded. "I was good at it too. That was when I started getting the visions that changed everything though. I also noticed that the relationship between me and Jax was strained, and the feelings we once had, weren't there. If I'm honest with myself he had been pulling away for a while, but I was so occupied with work that I just ignored it. The same way I ignored the feelings that popped up every time I was around Ronnie. Classic love triangle. But wait, dun, dun DUN," Winnie sang. "There's a twist. The visions."

Airy shifted a bit and rolled on her side while she propped her head up with her arm and watched Winnie. "You had a vision about you and Ronnie?" she asked.

"Kind of," Winnie hedged. "I had visions about all of us. I saw the way each of us died, but only mine was one that was imminent. Theirs, I saw they were all older, the age they are now," she said remorsefully. "Those visions, something about them told me those could be changed, it wasn't set it in stone, but they all revolved around Jax. Even mine. I kept them a secret from everyone because really, who wants to hear that someone saw their death? I was only twenty-two, but I knew that mine was set in stone. I had a few others as well that seem to be playing out as we speak, but they are becoming a reality much faster than I anticipated," she exhaled.

"That's where I come in," Airy guessed.

"Yep, sorry," Winnie said, her eyes filled with regret. "But I'm jumping ahead again. I kept them secret as long as I could, but with the developing relationship I had with Ronnie, it got harder and harder, because he saw more than I thought he did. He could feel my emotions, he felt the others too, but he always felt mine the strongest. It's only now I realized that is because he was in love with me," Winnie's voice cracked with that statement. She cleared her throat and continued. "Jax was becoming more and more selfish and demanding of everyone. He'd been researching starting up his own investigation company and he just automatically assumed that the rest would join him. Smitty had gone to a tech school and gotten an IT degree, electronics and coding were his thing. Aedan had gone to school and gotten a business degree. Ronnie, well, he was extremely intelligent, but he was still drinking, smoking and fighting in a club to earn money. Granted, he earned a lot, but it didn't help his disposition."

"He's moody?" Airy asked.

"No, but he hadn't really dealt with the fallout from the stuff with his dad, so fighting was his way of letting go of things. He also had a habit of rescuing people he thought needed rescuing," she smiled wistfully. "He's got such a good heart." She closed her eyes and paused again.

"Winnie," Airy started, but Winnie cut her off.

"I'm fine. The weight of the visions started to affect me at work, and even Jax was picking up on it. It finally came to a head with him and he called me out, telling me I was pulling away from him and he thought we needed some space. The truth was we were both pulling away, but it was always easier for him to put the responsibility off on others. Aedan had met Mags, his wife now, and they were getting serious. I'm not sure why that set Jax off so much, but it did. Neither of us told any of the others that him and I were slowly ending things. We still loved each other, but it was in a different way now. I would have spent the rest of my life with him if he had asked before that, but somewhere, even before the visions, I knew he wasn't the one for me," she scoffed, "well, I didn't know that I didn't have anyone because I wasn't going to live, but that's the way things work out sometimes."

Airy stood up, her eyes watery, "Excuse me a moment, I need to pee." She walked into the bathroom and Winnie heard her blow her nose and flush the toilet before she came back out.

"I've come to terms with it Airy, it's okay," Winnie said softly. Airy nodded at her, so she went on. "So, no one knew about Jax and I, but Ronnie felt it, because one day when he took me home, he asked me. It was all just too much for me then, and I told him to pull over at a park, and I got out and was swinging. He looked so beautiful sitting there next to me, watching me, that it all just bubbled out. Everything came out in a mad rush, all the visions, I told him everything. Even about you, Airy," she whispered that last part.

Airy startled, "What?"

"I saw you in one of my visions, though I had no idea who you were. I didn't even know how to start looking for you. Anyway, Ronnie and I got so close that day. I knew I was in love with him, and I knew then he was in love with me. I also knew my time was short. We made the most of it we could, but I couldn't be sneaking around with Ronnie, so I had to tell Jax. I didn't tell him about the visions, other than I told him I saw my death. He didn't ask, so I didn't tell him. It was a thing we had. Some things were just too much for him to handle. But I also told him about how I was developing feelings for Ronnie, and Jax admitted that he saw it, even understood it. He didn't like it though. He wanted Ronnie to be the one to tell him, and I couldn't ever see Ronnie doing that. He'd have felt like he was betraying Jax. We had a good talk that day though, and we left each other on good terms, I am almost a hundred certain we were broken up, but Jax hadn't really said those exact words," Winnie's voice cracked a little then.

"It's like a soap opera," Airy quipped with a little smile, trying to lighten the mood.

Winnie laughed, "It is. In my heart I felt like Jax and I were over, and I wanted Ronnie. I wanted to be with him before I died. I went to his house after I left Jax's and found him outside leaning against his car talking on the phone. Of course, he was talking to Jax and I was somewhat hopeful Jax and told he we were over and that he was okay with us, but I knew Jax wouldn't do that. I told Ronnie about my conversation with Jax and how I felt like we were over, but for some reason I never told him that Jax knew I had feelings Ronnie. It was a distinct line in the sand that Ronnie would never cross without expressed consent from Jax. I was so angry with the situation that I cried, a big, fat, ugly cry, all over Ronnie. He held me, just like he did before, and even dropped kisses on my head," Winnie's voice got quiet then. "I still remember the feel of his arms around me, tight like a vise grip, but so gentle. So warm, so safe. He felt like home to me."

Airy sniffled next to Winnie, and quickly wiped her eyes, pretending she hadn't just cried for Winnie.

Winnie reached her hand out and cupped Airy's cheek. "You feel like home to me too, Airy." Winnie took in another deep breath, closed her eyes like she was in pain, and continued. "While he was holding me and I was dripping snot and tears all over him, my anger just grew. I eventually pulled away from him, and tried to kiss him, but he wouldn't let me. I snapped, and stormed off, getting in my car and peeling off out of there, the sight of Ronnie standing there alone in his driveway getting smaller in my rearview mirror. That was my last sight of him while I was alive. When he was out of sight, I grabbed my cell phone, which, I knew better, but my anger had a hold of me. I called Jax and went off on him like I never had before. I'm pretty sure I said some hateful things, which I do regret, because I didn't mean them. I had told him he was ruining what was left of my life and depriving his best friend of an opportunity for love, a bunch of stuff along those lines. Then it happened, it wasn't even my fault, though I was the one the phone. A pickup truck ran a red light, slamming into me on the driver's side, crushing my car door in on me and flipped my car over several times. On the other side of me was an embankment, maybe a ten foot drop down the city made for overflow when it rained and flooded. My car flipped over the guard rail and rolled to land upside down in the little creek. Jax heard everything. My phone had bounced around the inside of the car, but it never lost signal."

Airy gasped next to me, tears falling and soaking her pink nightgown and she stared at Winnie in horror. "He heard you die?" she choked out.

"No," Winnie said carefully trying to keep her emotions in check, but she knew she couldn't. This was the first time she had gotten to share her story. "He had grabbed the landline in his house and called 911 to report I had been hit and that the signal was open on his cell phone. He knew the route I was on because he knew I had left Ronnie's. The ambulance found me quick, but my car was so damaged and twisted they couldn't get me out very fast. Plus, the pickup was half hanging over the embankment and they were trying to keep that from falling over too. I had seen it all already, I knew what this meant. I just hadn't known it would be that day, or I would have worked harder to have a memory of Ronnie to last me. I would have not said the hateful things I had said to Jax," Winnie whispered. "Anyway, they got me out eventually and I was rushed to the hospital, where Jax was already waiting. He lied and told them he was my fiancée, so they let him in while they checked me over. They were going to prep for surgery because they saw the signs of internal bleeding, and they knew my time was limited. I remember shaking my head at the doctors telling them that it was too late, to not bother, but Jax was yelling then, telling me not to leave him, that I couldn't go. He was yelling that he would search for me forever until he found me again. Something in the words he was yelling bound me here, I don't know what it was. Maybe it's the guilt we both felt, well, still feel," Winnie admitted, ghostly blue glowing tears rolling down her cheeks. "But I told him I loved him, and I died. Not only did he have to hear the accident happen, which I hadn't seen in my vision, he had to be there when I died. The pain I felt was horrific, watching you after you drank that holy water today brought back those memories fast. They had given me a shot of something to numb the pain while they prepped me, but I still felt everything. Curse of having empath abilities."

"A few seconds after I died, I don't remember anything but feeling numb, and I was able to watch my soul pull out of my body. I was hovering there, above myself, watching the aftermath unfold around me with Jax, and then Ronnie was there too," Winnie choked then. "I saw him kiss his fingers and place it over the sheet they covered me with. Even though I was stuck, I couldn't move on, it was too painful for me to stay around them. So, for twelve years, I've been wandering. From people to people who had some sort of ability I could try to use to get them to see me or communicate with me. The closest I got was one weird machine where my words came out in a weird jumbled mess and the ghost hunters completely got the message wrong." Winnie shrugged. "What's a girl to do?"

"Oh my God, Winnie, that's awful," Airy rasped out through her sobs.

"I popped in on Aedan a couple of times," Winnie went on, "I saw that they themselves had formed a paranormal investigative team. Jax was holding on to his promise to seek me out, which is also what I think is keeping me here. It's also why I tried to keep getting through to someone in hopes that he would let me go. It never worked, until you."

Airy stilled, her eyes filled with understanding. "Are you telling me these guys are a part of a ghost show?" Her eyes got wide as she whispered, "Shit. Jax, Aedan, Ronnie and Smitty... oh my God!" Airy had put the pieces together. She jumped out of bed, "No!"

"Airy, calm down," Winnie tried to console her.

"You are asking me to join them as an empath so you can talk to them?" the words tore out of her mouth in a tragically funny way to Winnie. She nodded at Airy.

"But...wait. Jax has been an asshole lately," she said aloud as she paced along her bed. She looked up at Winnie, "Is he possessed?"

"I don't know, I think it's a good possibility," Winnie quietly admitted.

"That dark energy I pulled from you comes from him? You want me to pull that from him? And do what? Drink more holy water?" Airy was shouting now, her eyes wide in fright.

"I don't have all the answers yet Airy, the first step is to get you hired, and get you introduced to them. Ronnie will help you," Winnie pleaded.

Airy sunk down on the bed and buried her face in her hands, the nightmare of the situation growing by the second. "I'm going to need more than holy water for this," she muttered darkly. "And a life insurance policy."

Winnie smiled remorsefully knowing it was true. She purposefully left out the vision of her being the one for Jax, she felt that was something that would send her straight over the edge. For now, she needed Airy to sleep so she could learn about Airy. "You need to sleep, so I can do my part that you don't want me to do."

Airy laughed harshly, "You think I'm going to sleep after that bombshell? This day went from a shit hole to a full-blown fucking hurricane of shit."

All Winnie could do was nod, she wasn't wrong. Airy leaned back into bed, straightened out her pillows and closed her eyes. "If you've still got magic, you better use it to put me to sleep," Airy told her dryly.

"Just relax, it will happen," Winnie said softly, stroking Airy's hair slowly. She felt the tension start to bleed out of her. Winnie kept stroking until Airy fell asleep, then braced herself and dove into Airy's head.

Chapter Nine

Ronnie woke up feeling disappointed and sore as hell. Every move he made his body ached. He didn't even want to think about how much of a nightmare yesterday was, and how down he felt after getting that strange text of a message relayed from Winnie. He needed a shower and then caffeine.

After showering and getting dressed, he grabbed his phone and opened his door to head to the kitchen and almost tripped over Jax, who asleep on the floor outside his door. Ronnie rolled his eyes and shook his head, fighting the urge to kick him, as he was still pissed at him. Then he had a better idea. He turned back into his room quietly and grabbed his water bottle off the nightstand. Walked back over to where Jax was asleep and upended the bottle on him, watching in satisfaction and glee as Jax bolted awake and in an impressive move was on his feet in the blink of an eye.

Not wanting Jax to see him laugh, he pushed past him and made his way to the kitchen, snickering under his breath as Jax spluttered behind him. It didn't take long for him to hear Jax thudding down the hall after him. Ronnie sighed, it was going to be a hard morning, he could just feel it. He opened the cupboard, grabbed a bottle ibuprofen, dumped out four and swallowed them dry as he looked around the kitchen.

The guys had done a good job of cleanup, but he would need to figure out how to fix the Jax sized hole in the wall. He shook his head wondering again how things had gotten this bad. He heard Jax clear his throat, and oh yeah, that's how they got that bad, he thought as he swallowed the rising anger he felt, and gently rubbed his face.

"God, I'm so sorry Ronnie," Jax choked out as he saw him rub his face.

Ronnie shook his head, "I don't really want to do this now, Jax."

"We have to talk, man," Jax pleaded. "I promised."

Ronnie didn't answer as he pulled open the fridge and grabbed an energy drink and bottle of water, then rooted around in the cupboard until he found a protein bar. He peeled the wrapper off and bit into it as we walked over to the table and sat down. "Go ahead then. I want this over with."

Ronnie saw something flicker behind Jax's eyes and it looked like he was struggling for a second. Ronnie braced himself, not knowing what to expect after yesterday's performance, but it looked like Jax had regained control. Jax grabbed a bottle of water out of the fridge and sat down on the opposite side of the table from Ronnie, which was probably a calculated move on Jax's part, but a smart one considering Ronnie's mood.

"There aren't enough ways for me to say I'm sorry for what I did," Jax started, "and I know it feels and sounds like an excuse, but it wasn't me. I wasn't in control. It's happening more and more often, and I don't even feel like I know who I am anymore. Based off what Aedan and Smitty told me, you all think the same thing. Is that true for you too?"

"Yeah. You aren't the same at all. It started with Winnie's death, but in the past five or so years, you are becoming someone else," Ronnie said, his voice hard.

"Change is good, but not this change. In twenty-eight years, you never once raised a hand to me. Now in the past month, you've gone after Smitty, and hit me. You tell me, is that good?"

Jax choked on the shame flooding him. "Help me. I need to find me again. I'm so lost Ronnie. When this shit takes over, I feel like I'm having an out of body experience, like my life is on a movie reel playing and I can't do anything. I'm starting to think it's killing me. Last night, when I saw you on the floor and bloody, the first thing that happened was memories were triggered, of you know, back then. Then the scent of the blood hit me, and I became someone else. I wanted more blood, it was like it was feeding me or some shit. I swear I felt like a vampire, but I didn't want to drink it." Jax shook his head.

"What do you mean?" Ronnie asked him, watching his face carefully.

"The blood?" Ronnie nodded in answer to Jax's question. "It was like I needed to see more of it spilled. The blood is what triggered whatever happened last night. The memories hit me, and I felt like I was battling over my own body. Part of me wanted to give in to the rage to try and forget the memories, and the other part of me felt like I needed to hold on to the memories to stay human. It's dark shit, man. I don't know how to explain it. It just fucking festers inside me like an infection. An infection that has emotions of its own."

"Somewhere along the line in one of our investigations, you brought something home with you. It's happened before, you've had exorcisms within the past five years. Don't you think that would have taken care of it?" Ronnie prodded, his curiosity winning out over the anger. Also, he was more than a little concerned by what Jax had admitted.

"I talked with the exorcist about it, and he thinks maybe it's not a demon, maybe it's something else. I don't know. I've seen doctors, had more scans done that I care to admit, I even talked with a shrink, which, I am not doing that again." Jax's face was filled with anguish, his voice desperate. "I'm scared. I'm scared to even talk about it, like if I acknowledge it, it will take over more, or it gives it power or something." He pulled at his hair, making it stand up in weird tufts.

"Maybe the producers are right to bring in someone that can calm situations down then. Maybe even you are right to suggest it be an empath. Have you done research on any of this?" Ronnie queried, drinking half the energy drink in one swallow.

"Too scared. It's in my mind, man. I don't want to give power to the thoughts," Jax argued.

"Well you can't keep on the path you are on!" Ronnie shouted in frustration. "Look where that has gotten you." He stood up and paced behind his chair, his mind racing. "I'll do some research, but I need a list of things you think and feel, symptoms, anything to go off of."

"I'll get it to you," Jax said forlornly. "But that's not all I want to talk to you about. Sit back down please."

Ronnie gazed across the table, trying to get a read on what was coming, but Jax had a poker face on, his eyes guarded. His phone chirped in his pocket, and he was tempted to look at it, but kept still. "What?"

"Please. Sit. I know you don't owe me any favors, I'm just asking you to hear me out," Jax replied, his voice even, but quiet.

Ronnie had a bad feeling about it, but he sat, crossed his arms over his chest and slouched down in the chair. He wasn't as good with his poker face as Jax was, but he tried. He also opened his senses to try and get an emotional read, but there was nothing. He was walled off. Not good. "Should the guys be here for this?"

"No, this is between us," Jax said as he shifted uncomfortably. "Really, it's on me. All of it. Everything. The past twelve years, hell, even longer. It's me. You were right last night," Jax admitted.

Ronnie was the one uncomfortable now with where he was heading. "Jax, no amount of guilt over anything, will change the past. Nothing will. It's in the past. No amount of fear, or panic, or anxiety, whatever you want to call it, will alter the future. All it does is ruin the present. Let go of this shit," Ronnie said, exasperated.

"Talking to you is a start, if you'll let me," Jax responded. Ronnie rolled his eyes but nodded for him to go on. "Out of everyone, I've been the biggest dick to you. I own that. I've been petty, childish, and held a grudge you didn't even know I had. I carried it with me and stroked it in any way I could. By letting you bear the brunt of everything. I let you take care of me, I didn't put any effort into anything because somewhere I felt like you owed me for what happened."

Ronnie flinched, an idea of what was coming hitting him and sucking the oxygen out of his lungs. He couldn't do this. He needed to take his own advice about the guilt. Hell, he needed to fess up to his part in this, but the train wreck he was on was barreling too fast down the track.

"It wasn't you, man. None of this was your fault," Jax shook under the weight of his words. "I was too much of a coward and told myself whatever I could to just not face that fact." He looked Ronnie straight in the eye, "I knew."

Everything in Ronnie froze in place, his heart racing, his breathing ragged. "Knew what?" he asked even though he didn't want the answer.

"I knew about you and Winnie," he said, his voice tight. "It's hard for me to even say her name," he confessed. "She told me. She told me everything. She told me before the accident." Ronnie started shaking just as much as Jax was. "I don't know, I guess I was waiting to hear it from you, but you never said anything. I saw signs, but you didn't cross that line. If I were to put myself under a microscope, I'd probably see that you didn't because of me, our relationship, and you wouldn't do anything without my consent," Jax laughed darkly. "But it was so much easier than examining myself to just blame you."

Ronnie felt like there was ice running through his veins, and he briefly wondered if Winnie was here listening, but he didn't smell anything, so he dismissed that thought. Jax was right, this was between the two of them right now.

Ronnie was too tense to say anything, unsure of what would come out of his mouth, so he remained silent, instead watching Jax struggle with himself to get this out.

"After our first time, we decided to cool things off with each other, it was a mutual decision because both of us felt the distance between us had grown too big to really fix. I still loved her, she still loved me, that was never the issue. I think we had fallen out of love with each other though. It wasn't the same as it used to be. We were okay with that too, because we both knew people grew apart and changed," Jax shifted and leaned over the table putting his hands in front of him and stared down at them.

"She told me that she had some bad visions, told me she had seen her death, but she refused to tell me too many details. I don't think she liked talking about it. That confession from her shook me bad. It bothered me every day and weighed on me. Anyway, after that bombshell, she told me she had feelings for you, that she thought were important enough for her to see it through. I'd never denied her anything before, and I didn't even then. I think that moment is when I started to change though. Even though I didn't tell her to not follow through, I think I knew you would never allow it, so it's probably why I never talked to you. Total dick move on my part. But if I think hard enough about that time, I can see patterns emerge that lead me to believe that's when this shit hole I find myself in started," Jax said, still looking down.

Ronnie felt something in him, but he couldn't name the emotion, and he also felt himself trying to tamp down the anger in himself that was threatening to boil over too. Jax dropped his head down onto his arms and looked out into the backyard. "I knew she had considered our relationship over, and that she had free reign to explore other avenues, and I agreed with that, but never voiced it. With the threat of her death looming on my mind I tried to hold on to her in any way that I could," Jax's voice broke. "Because of my selfishness, neither of the people that mattered most to me in my life got to see or feel the beauty of that kind of love, that connection. That shit eats at me. I fucking took something from you, that could have given you the happiness you deserved. I'm not asking for forgiveness from you, that's not what this is," Jax said, stumbling over the grief in his words.

Ronnie felt like the life was being squeezed out of his lungs as the pressure in his chest built. Logically, he knew that all this was in the past, but he also heard the truth of the words Jax was spilling, and they cut him deep. Even still, he understood the reason behind the actions, while they weren't the choices Ronnie would have made, he understood it. It felt like he was losing Winnie all over again.

"I wanted what the two of you had growing between you. In my selfishness, my asshole ways, I thought if I held on long enough, I'd find it. I've never regretted anything before the way I regret that. Even though it hurt me to think I wasn't enough for her, I knew she wasn't enough for me. It kills me that I knew that and still did what I did," Jax took a deep shuddering breath in, and exhaled a sob.

"The day of the accident, she was at my house, talking to me, making it understood and clear that she was going to move forward with you. She left here on good terms with me, I knew she was headed to your house. I had actually called you after she left, my intention was to tell you, to give you my blessing so to speak, but I didn't. I don't know why I didn't. I hate myself for it. I heard her pull up and talk to you and after we hung up, I almost called back three different times, but something held me back. Jealousy? Anger? Hurt? Fear? I don't know. Maybe all of them. It wasn't too long after that, I got a phone call from her. She was going home, and she was pissed. She went off on me like I'd never heard before. She said some hateful things, and while they are true, it's a side of her I'd never seen or experienced. Regardless, while I didn't know of the details of her vision, it unfolded while I was on the phone with her. I heard the accident. Every fucking thing I heard, I kept the line open, using the house phone to call it in, because if she was going to die in that car, then I was going to be there with her. Even as I drove to the hospital, and called you from there, I had that line open. I left it open until the battery in my phone died. After she had already gone. I lied to the people at the hospital to let me back where they had her, told them we were engaged," a ragged cry tore from him.

Ronnie didn't know Jax had heard it all happen and a well of grief opened in him so wide that he felt like there was no coming back. He didn't try to hold back the tears, but he was gripping his own arms so hard that he knew there were going to be bruises. This was turning out to be just as bad as yesterday was. Some wounds just don't heal, and Jax had just ripped this one wide open.

"I know you were at the hospital with me, maybe if you had been in the room with me things would have been different. They'd given her a shot of morphine as she was wheeled in, and they were prepping her for surgery. I was just on repeat, telling her not to leave me, she couldn't go, shit like that. I don't even think I was aware of what was coming out of my mouth. She was so broken, I knew she wasn't coming back from that, anyone could see it, but the doctors were going to try. Until she opened her eyes and told them no. I fucking lost it. She told me she loved me and died. You know the rest. But what I told none of you, well aside from the whole story, was as she died, I felt something grab a hold of my soul and plant itself in me. I don't know what it was, I still don't, and it's still there, but it feeds this evil dark thing in me. Somehow, all this is related. It all ties together," Jax said, his heart and soul laid out on the table.

Ronnie stood up fast, shoving the chair behind him. "What do you want me to do with all this?" he shouted angrily.

"I just wanted you to know the truth," Jax said brokenly.

"Twenty-eight years we have been inseparable," Ronnie spat, "and this is what I get for that?! Do you have any idea how destroyed I feel right now? And yet still, I feel like I should be consoling you, taking care of you!"

Jax nodded. "I'll take care of myself, but I get the

rest. You have every right to hate me. Not only for back then, but for last night. Fuck, I hate myself enough for both of us. Rip open any of my scars and you and Winnie bleed out of them."

Ronnie deflated and sagged back down to the chair, beyond broken, but he didn't hate Jax. He couldn't ever hate him. He was hurt and angry for sure, and he didn't know how to go about healing that, or how to help Jax. This was something that would always be between them now. He knew the relationship would heal in time, Jax was too much a part of his life for it not to, it was just too raw right now.

"I don't hate you Jax. You can bet your ass I'm pissed and hurt. Fucking shattered. No hate though. I'll get over it, we both know it because that is who I am, but you have to give me time," Ronnie ground out. "I'll never turn my back on you," he thumped his chest, "you are a part of me. It might be broken right now, but it's still there. I just need time to process this, give me that much."

"I won't let you walk away from me bro, I love you," Jax cried. "I'll give you time, I'll give you anything you want. I know how much I owe you. I'll even stand here and let you hit me like you hit that bag, I deserve it."

Ronnie barked out a laugh, "The bag barely survived that. You wouldn't. I'm not going to hit you. Go shower or something, you look like hell and I want to be alone." Ronnie felt the turmoil rolling off Jax and was a little worried that suicide would pop in his head with that darkness in him.

Jax nodded resolutely and left back down the hallway without another word, looking like his entire world had collapsed. Ronnie guessed in a way it had. But in that process, he had taken down a good portion of Ronnie's world too. The triangle with Winnie and Jax was just as much his fault. He could have stepped up and talked to Jax about it but chose not to out of his own insecurities that he had battled with every day back then.

Fuck, he didn't know how Jax made it through listening to that phone call. Ronnie thought that part of the story explained so much about Jax's behavior, and it hit him so hard he bowed under the weight of the thought. Ronnie was pretty sure he would have snapped after that, and he gave props to Jax for shouldering that all these years. He shook his head again.

The house was silent and still as Ronnie sat there trying to organize his thoughts which were anything but silent or still. He itched to go at the bag again but knew his knuckles couldn't take another beating like that. His phone chirped again from his pocket and he dug it out to see a couple of texts from Aedan.

They had a lead on an empath, and Aedan wanted to know if they were up, he wanted to take Jax to get his hands looked at. Ronnie responded and waited for Aedan to show up and called the agency. He wanted to be present for the interview and he wanted the council to meet with the empath too. Aedan could stay with Jax and watch him. He texted Smitty his thoughts and got a response of agreement right away. Things were in motion now.

I woke up with a mild headache, and way too many body aches to count, although I felt oddly rested. Given the shit storm I found myself in that was amazing in itself. It felt like I was alone, and not having to work today is a blessing in disguise given how I felt. I rolled out of bed gingerly.

The urge to pee was bigger than the body aches and I made a mad dash for the bathroom. I finished my business and looked in the mirror, expecting to see a haggard old witch, and instead I looked normal. I didn't understand how that could be possible with the way my life had flipped a switch on me, but I'll take it.

I got dressed in yoga pants and a sports bra sans shirt as I figured I'd do a yoga session this morning to try and stretch out the body aches. I grabbed my phone and headed downstairs to get the cats fed so they'd stop howling like I was murdering them, since their breakfast was a little later than normal for a workday. Damn cats.

Cats fed, yoga music on, I set out to unkink my body

after the terrifying experience with holy water. I put myself through the poses paying extra attention to my hips and back which seemed the tightest. My soul loves yoga, but meditation was still the hardest part for me. I lay on the floor and closed my eyes, trying to find that spot in my mind where I could make everything disappear for a few minutes.

It was a struggle keeping my mind clear, and as the sweat from the poses cooled and dried on my skin, I felt like a salt lick. I gave up after about five minutes, though I felt better than I had before. I shut off the music and plugged my iPad into charge and went to go take another shower. I hated feeling like a salt lick, but I never regretted whatever I had done to get me to that point.

Freshly showered I studied my reflection in the mirror carefully, the words of the priest rolling through my head. I didn't look like an angel, that was for sure. Definitely no wings or halo here. I snorted, not much vanity either as my critical eyes took me apart. I didn't see the glow the priest referenced, or that Winnie said she saw. I couldn't even see my own aura.

What I saw was a completely average human, with an above average skill to find herself in odd situations. My hair grew super-fast, I acknowledged, running my fingers through the thick wet locks. It had turned curly about nine years ago. Sometimes it curled up in ringlets, and other times it was just wavy, normally it was a mix between the two. It frizzed out when I was in humidity or causing humidity. It was a medium brown color, but I was often asked if I colored my hair. While someone would look at me and say my hair was brown, it was a variety of shades of brown. In the sunlight, my hair had a red undertone to it that made it look a totally different color.

My eyes were round shaped and a milk chocolate color of brown, until you looked really close at them and saw specks of a gold and copper spattered around the pupil. When I got downright angry, they looked almost black, and when I was really happy, they were a light shade of brown and had an odd sparkle to them. Okay, so I guess maybe that wasn't quite normal, though it didn't scream angel.

My face was what I would call oval, I thought studying it. My cheek bones were visible but not prominent and my cheeks typically had a natural pink tint to them. My nose had a slight crook to it from breaking it when I was little. My bottom lip was fuller than my top lip, and they weren't wide, and I tended to chew on them when I was stressed out. My ears were average size, down to just one piercing now. Eyelashes were a dark brown and very long, but stick straight, eyebrows were the same dark brown and shaped well enough that I didn't need to pluck them or any of the other stuff people did.

My skin had always been good. Rich olive tone and clear. I tanned fast in the summer time, always getting dark much to the annoyance of my friends who laid out for hours and got nothing. I credit that with my Italian heritage. I always looked healthy. Well almost always, there was a period where you could tell I wasn't well.

My body was nothing to write home about. Thick and overweight. Soft belly, dimples where there shouldn't be, stretch marks, and so many scars I looked like a road map. The flip side of that is that I am incredibly strong from the activities I do to maintain sanity. The hiking, walking, yoga, swimming, white water rafting. I was too top heavy to do too many impact sports, bouncing boobs just hurt after a while. In the water, they just floated.

I sighed, nothing special. I had at least made enough progress on myself to admit that I wasn't ugly, but I also didn't think I was beautiful. I was just me. I didn't wear makeup, I didn't fix my hair, I just was. It was enough for me. I put on some deodorant and grabbed a hair tie and mentally started calculating how long I had to go before I cut it again.

At least six months, I thought. I grew my hair out for the sole purpose of donating it for charity. Maybe I guess I did have some vanity; my hair was good, and I liked sharing it. Especially with my history of cancer. I quickly swept it up and out of my way and tried to figure out what to wear. I still hadn't heard from Winnie, so I wasn't sure what my day was going to hold.

I pulled a pair of jeans off a hanger and dug through my shirt drawer for an old worn-out shirt. I felt like comfort today, so I grabbed a pair of my thick fuzzy socks and put them on after I smeared some lotion on my feet. I grabbed my phone and saw I had missed a phone call.

I headed back downstairs trying to Google the phone number as it wasn't one I had recognized, but nothing came up. It wasn't an area code from this state, so I shrugged and put it out of my mind. Back downstairs I rummaged around through the fridge and due to lack of variety, I grabbed an orange and started peeling it.

I was halfway through the tender, juicy fruit when my phone rang again. Of course, while I had sticky fingers, I glanced at the phone and saw the same unknown phone number and debated not answering it, but curiosity won out. "Hello?"

"May I speak to Airiella Raven please?" a bored sounding man asked.

"Speaking," I replied, imitating his tone for my own amusement.

"This is Tony from Spectre Talent Agency, you left us a voice mail last night in regard to an opening we had for an empath," he stated. In my mind I was laughing at the name of the agency.

Faking interest I responded, "Oh yes, nice to speak with you Tony."

"Would you be able to meet with us today if we purchased you an airline ticket?" he asked in the same bored tone. How lucky was I to be able to speak with Mr. Personality?

"Sure, of course," I said. At least I got an airplane ride out of it. I loved flying. "Where will I be travelling to?" I asked, interested in this response.

"We have a building in Colorado that is central to all parties involved in the hiring process that we would use for this. Is this acceptable to you?" he droned one.

"That is fine with me, will someone be contacting

me with flight information?" I questioned.

"Yes. We will also confirm via e-mail if you would be kind enough to give us an e-mail address," Tony continued. I rattled off the e-mail address I rarely used, and thought I heard a slight chuckle at the end of the phone. I had to be mistaken though, robots don't laugh. "See you later today Ms. Raven," Tony ended the phone call.

Well that answered what my plans would be then. I finished up my orange and went back upstairs to look for an appropriate interview outfit. What does one wear to an interview with unnamed people for a position as an empath? And where the hell was Winnie? Ah hell, I flipped through my closet and settled on a pair of black slacks, and my bright red colored tunic. I set the clothes on my bed, grabbed a pair of shoes and socks and went to take stock of my makeup drawer.

Rolling my eyes, I realized I needed to run to a drug store, everything I had makeup wise was seriously old. I grabbed my phone as it dinged with an e-mail and opened it as I went back downstairs to grab my keys and purse. Flight info. Looks like I was leaving in three hours. Didn't leave me a whole lot of time.

I popped my earbuds in my ears and called my brother to see if he could give me a ride to the airport as I drove to the closest drug store. I'm not a shopper either, I don't wander up and down aisles. He agreed to pick me up in fourty-five minutes as I flew down the makeup aisle snatching up mascara, a light brown eye liner, and a brown colored eyeshadow palette. Good enough for my needs.

I drove home and flew up the stairs as fast as I could calling out "Winnie!" as I went, hoping wherever she was she would hear me. I got dressed, leaving off my shirt so I didn't get makeup on it, changed my earrings to pink colored pearls and got down to business with makeup. Not something I am skilled at on the best of days, certainly not when I'm in a hurry and a blue glowing ghost appears out of nowhere.

Needless to say, I looked like the raccoon that had visited us. Winnie looked haggard and it hit me as I was cleaning the smeared eyeliner off my face that she had been in my head last night. Suddenly I wasn't sure what to say anymore to her, she now knew all my secrets, and she looked bad too. "Um, any particular reason you look like death?" I carefully asked.

"No energy," was her weak response.

"Okay, I won't waste time then, the agency called, and they are flying me out to meet with some people in Colorado. My brother is picking me up in a bit," I glanced at my watch. Shit. "Well in fifteen minutes. Anything I need to know?"

"I'll try and find out, just be you. I am sure they will test you in some way, so be prepared," she warned, flickering.

"Okay, and um, about last night," I hemmed.

"I promised you I wouldn't bring it up unless something was relevant, at this moment, nothing is. Focus on this interview. I'll find you in a bit. I need to rest," she said, and then was gone. A little shocked, I was still a moment and then went back to putting on makeup.

Finished, I studied myself and was satisfied overall. I tended to use a natural look when I did wear makeup, and this had covered the vestiges of the dark circles under my eyes. I put my shirt on and decided to add my wrist cuff to my other arm that I had a charm engraved with "Unbreakable" on it. I used it as a reminder to myself that I was a survivor.

I went back downstairs, filled the cats' water and food dishes, locked up, grabbed my purse, phone and iPad and walked out the door as my brother was pulling up. "You got this," I told myself.

Winnie was in no shape to try and communicate with Ronnie, she had barely enough energy to appear for Airy. She just needed not exist for a bit to recharge. She thought about going back to the river, but she didn't even think she had enough energy to pop in there. Last night zapped her more than she had thought it would. Airy would be fine. How hard was it really to interview for an empath position?

Though she might pop in during the interview, but she didn't know what time it was. Focusing the last of her energy she popped in on Airy and smothered a laugh as she jumped when Winnie asked, "What time is the interview?" Airy held up three fingers, mentally calculated the time difference and popped back out, not failing to notice how cute Airy's brother was, and to drain some energy off the car battery before she left.

The energy she took gave her enough to get to the river and she laid there, soaking up the energy. It was alarming how drained she was. She decided to not move until she had to for the interview. She went over the information she learned about Airy and was overwhelmed. She was definitely strong.

Winnie ticked off, emotional abuse, mental abuse, physical abuse, rape, marriage, addiction (not Airy's), cancer, divorce, infidelity, betrayal, loss, abilities, selflessness, humble, strength, and so much love. Her capacity to love was incredible. Beyond her wildest imagination. There was no one shred of doubt in her mind that Airy was an angel, she just didn't know how to convince Airy of that. That girl was humble to a fault.

She sighed as she closed her eyes. There was a storm moving in, but she didn't care. It wasn't like she could get wet. Besides, storms produced a lot of energy that she could draw from. She had seen a memory of a dream that Airy had, Jax was front and center of that dream, and she didn't think Airy remembered it. The evidence was there though, she was destined to be with him. Winnie just needed to work out the details.

Still tired, she drifted off as the glowing dark gray bottomed clouds let loose and rain came down in violence, soaking the ground within moments. Thunder boomed and crackled in the distance, echoing in Winnie's ears like an unrealized premonition of the heavens declaring their intent to the dark forces that they are prepared to fight for their warrior here on earth.

Smitty pulled up outside Ronnie and Jax's place and grabbed his overnight bag. As he was heading to the house Ronnie came out and shook his head, "Let's just go now," he said. "I want to be gone before Jax gets back."

Smitty narrowed his eyes at Ronnie, "You two haven't talked yet?"

"Oh no, we did, and that's why I want to be gone before he gets back. Otherwise he'd argue for coming with us. I need space," Ronnie said, climbing in and buckling up. "You're driving."

"I gathered that," he said wryly, getting back in the car. "You booked flights?"

"Yep, we don't have much time to get there either, sorry. I didn't book return flights though, it didn't feel right," he said confused. "I'm just going with it."

"Alright. I trust you. Can I ask how the talk went?"

"Sure, ask. Doesn't mean I'll respond," he grunted.

Smitty reached out and backhanded Ronnie in the chest. "Cut the shit, man. I'm on your side here."

"Yeah, I know. Just having trouble processing everything," he replied, his voice losing the edge it had.

"So...?" Smitty pushed.

"It's between Jax and I. At least for now. He owned up to shit, gave me more details on what I can only describe as some sort of possession with him. Told him I'd research it," Ronnie said, distracted.

"That hardly seems worthy of this attitude you're sporting," Smitty said caustically. "I'm not saying it's not deserved, just don't take it out on me."

"You're right. I'm just... You know..." he kept starting and stopping his train of thought. "Winnie came to me yesterday," Ronnie blurted out.

"You serious right now?" Smitty sputtered, stunned.

"Yep. As a heart attack, which I almost had because my phone started playing music when I wasn't near it. Happened after out little show down yesterday. Before you ask, no, I haven't said anything to Jax," Ronnie started glumly.

"How do you know it was her? We've had attachments before," Smitty asked very carefully, remembering the moment in the kitchen the night before. He felt like he was on eggshells between Jax and Ronnie.

"I smelled rain," he replied softly. "I'm not crazy."

Momentarily floored, Smitty waited to see if he'd say more. When he didn't, he chose his words with care, knowing this was a sensitive topic. "When Aedan and I were cleaning up in the kitchen, we both smelled rain. I don't know about him, but it felt like something wrapped around me from behind. Cold, but familiar."

"It was her," Ronnie said, sounding totally sure of himself. "I smelled rain first, and then my phone started playing some song I didn't know. I thought I'd lost my damn mind, and then it would repeat. I listened to the lyrics then searched on them. A song called Haunting by Halsey. I read the lyrics and got chills. She was talking to me. I told her to write on the window and I fogged it up. It was the only thing I could think of."

"Pretty ingenious if you ask me, that's quick thinking," Smitty told him, impressed. At that moment, Smitty smelled rain, and just like Ronnie said, the radio blared to life, a driving beat blasting through the car. Smitty was barely able to keep the car on the road it scared him so bad. Thank God for stop lights.

He looked over and saw Ronnie fogging up the car window and sure enough, he watched a message being written on the window. The light changed so he had to drive, but he was stunned. "What's it say?" He asked Ronnie over the music, afraid to touch the radio.

"Song for Jax," Ronnie said tightly. "Gotta be another message. She's trying to tell us something."

Smitty's skin broke out in goosebumps and he shivered. "Hey sweet thing, we've been looking for you," he whispered out loud.

"Came Back Haunted is the song. Nine Inch Nails. Reading the lyrics now," Ronnie said scrolling across his phone.

"I know the song," Smitty said, turning the radio

down. "I think she's telling us something is attached to him."

"We knew that though," Ronnie sounded frustrated. "I think she's referencing a line in the song about it being black, maybe? Or that he's unable to stop? I don't know."

"Just keep it on the back burner, dude. It will make sense when it's supposed to," Smitty suggested.

The radio blared to life again, this time with what sounded like a love song. Out of the corner of his eye, he saw Ronnie typing madly into his phone again. "I Don't Want to Live Forever," he said.

"Maybe just listen to the lyrics," Smitty told him, still dumbfounded by what was taking place in his car. The song started over, so he took his own advice and just listened. He felt like he understood that one when the song was done, and the radio fell silent.

He heard Ronnie breathing raggedly and glanced at him. His face was pale, and eyes were haunted. He reached over and put his hand on Ronnie's shoulder. "I think that message was for both of us," he told him. "We were looking for her, but we never called her out by name, and she just wanted to come home to us."

Ronnie nodded numbly, knowing he got a different message than that, but at a loss on how to put it into words. Instead he kept his mouth shut. His emotions had taken one hell of a beating the past couple of days.

"Did you find anything out about the person they are interviewing?" Smitty decided to change the subject.

"No. We will find out soon enough I suppose," he said tightly.

"Keep it together man," Smitty cautioned. "I can tell we will have some rough road ahead." All Ronnie could do was nod his agreement.

Winnie smiled. Her message got across to both in the way she intended with the last song. She knew they'd figure out the first one. She watched the storm play out around her back at the river, trying to understand the message to her she felt was hidden in it.

Chapter Ten

I flew first class, which was a nice treat. My e-mail said I would have a car waiting to pick me up, so I followed the signs to the pick-up area and looked around. I smelled rain and smiled in relief; Winnie was finally here. I spotted a sign that said Raven and headed over to the guy holding it. "I'm Airiella Raven," I told him.

"Right this way ma'am," he said motioning ahead of him. I winced at the ma'am part, and hoped Winnie was following. I got in the car and pulled my earbuds out of my pocket so if I was seen talking it would look like I was on the phone. As I waited for the driver to leave, I sent a text to my brother letting him know I arrived, and all was okay as he instructed.

"Walls up and locked tight Airy," Winnie said from next to me. "They are going to be trying to get in your head, try reading you, and seeking your power and energy signatures. Give nothing away until the actual tests begin. You won't be able to hide your glow though. A couple of my contacts on this side of the veil gave me some info on this Spectre group. They test all applicants for their clients via their leaders of the company, which they call a Council. The

Council consists of various Shamans, or Medicine Man from tribes that represent different regions. They have a Hoodoo priestess, a Santeria priestess as well, a parapsychologist, a psychiatrist, a Vatican-trained special unit priest for exorcisms, a medium, and there might be a few others, I had mixed messages on that."

"Isn't Santeria another name for voodoo?" I whispered.

"Yes. But first, the production company will interview you to get a feel for your personality. Just play that like a normal interview, but keep your walls up, don't let anything in. If you put out feelers, keep them weak. Play everything close to the chest on this but get hired. I keep getting pieces of a premonition having to do with you, but it doesn't make sense to me yet. The overall message is to be on guard."

"Nothing frightening in that statement at all, is there?" Sarcasm just came rolling out.

"I'm going to try to get as close as I can without anyone sensing me. There are a lot of very powerful people that will be there," Winnie warned.

"I'm good. I've got it under control," I promised her. "Well except the glow part I guess."

"I think Ronnie and Smitty will be somewhere close by, but I'm not entirely sure," Winnie added.

"But not the other two?" I wondered why not all of them, that was curious.

"I pulled you in this mess, I just want you as prepared as possible," she explained.

"Look at me Winnie," I said quietly, "I'm calm, not really nervous or scared. I'm good. Don't worry."

"I'm not worried about you," she clarified, "I just don't want them to know much about you. Your powers far overshadow anyone they have."

"You're worried someone will pick up on my strength and try to use me," I said, understanding now.

"Yes. Stay locked down at all times except during the tests and only then allow your powers to be used but keep them out of your head."

"No worries," I agreed.

"They will try to trip you up too," she said.

"I already expected that," I replied.

"If you need me, don't call me out loud, you know the feel of me, right?" I nodded at her, "Send out a strand looking for me only, and I'll know to come."

"Got it."

"Knock their socks off, babe," Winnie said with a smile.

Head held high, I pulled my earbuds out, silenced my phone and walked in the building.

They had gotten there about an hour early and were waiting in the observation room that was adjacent to the conference room. The walls of the conference room were all mirrored glass inside the room, and floor to ceiling. One wall had a seam running down that was the door to the observation room, just made to look like it was two large pieces of glass. There was a microphone in both rooms, but the observation room had a mute button for the microphone so that they could speak freely.

Ronnie couldn't sit still, kept pacing, then when Smitty got annoyed, he'd sit down, but was restless and fidgety. "What is wrong with me?" He asked rhetorically.

"That list is too long to start now," Smitty retorted.

"Aren't you just the funny one today," Ronnie ground out. "Seriously, why can't I just chill?"

"It's just excess nervous energy man, nothing's wrong with you," Smitty said, checking his watch. "It won't be long now."

Ronnie sat down for about the hundredth time and tipped his head back over the chair. He snapped forward as he heard someone talking out in the hall and watched the room. Sure enough, the door opened, and the receptionist walked in explaining that the interviewers would be there in about ten minutes. As the person, a female, walked in the room, he had an intense visceral reaction to her.

His body went completely rigid as it felt like someone pulled all the air out of his lungs. Desire, lust, need, fear and love tore through him like a storm. He hadn't even been aware he was moving until Smitty yanked him back by the shoulder and stuffed him into the chair.

"What the hell are you doing?" He whispered furiously, "You can't go in there!"

Ronnie visibly shook himself and tried to clear his mind. "I don't know if I am in love with her, or if I am terrified of her or what, but the reaction I had was fucking intense," Ronnie tried to explain, not understanding it himself. "I felt her at a base level inside."

Smitty watched him warily. "She's hot, I'll give you that, but what were you thinking? That you were just going to walk out and introduce yourself?"

"I don't know! I didn't even know that I had moved!" Her hair was brown at first glance, but when the sunlight from the windows hit it, there was a coppery red glow to it, the curls catching the light in an odd way making him think of a sunset. Her body was full of curves, and she was on the short side, but she moved with a natural grace. He wanted to sink his teeth into her lips, that bottom one just begging for attention.

Smitty turned to study her, and Ronnie got irately jealous that he was even looking her way. "Ronnie, chill the fuck out. I'm not going to eat her," he told him.

"I feel insanely protective of her, and I don't even know her. This is so not normal. I'm also absolutely terrified right now, for no reason," Ronnie said, dazed.

Smitty gave him a look and put a hand back on his shoulder, holding him in place. "You are acting fucking crazy right now."

They snapped their gazes back to the female as her voice came through the speakers, "What storm? What premonition?"

Ronnie had a visible reaction again and Smitty tightened his hold on Ronnie's shoulder. "Holy shit! That voice, it felt like it punched a hole in my soul," Ronnie said with amazement. He couldn't even describe the timber of it, there were so many layers to it.

"Okay, I'll give you that one too," Smitty agreed, "it

did something to me too." They looked at each other in wonder for a second and as one they turned back to watch her. "Who is she talking to?" Smitty thought to ask.

"No clue, dude," Ronnie stared in fascination. "Why am I scared?"

"No clue, dude," Smitty mimicked him. "She's not even your type." Both were whispering like they were afraid she would hear them. Exaggerated teenage type whispers.

She looked directly at them, or at least appeared to and said, "Winnie said to tell Jax to listen to the song she sent you earlier. Now." Their jaws dropped. She had been talking to Winnie. "She also said to tell him to listen to Let Me Go," she said, looking at the chair next to her in confusion.

Smitty leaned forward and tapped the mute button to turn the microphone back on, "By who? There are several songs with that title." Ronnie stared at him, unable to speak.

She cocked her head to the side and replied, "Nice to meet you Smitty, my name is Airiella. She said some group that's named after states. I'm not even sure where she heard it. Sorry."

Ronnie reacted like he'd been slapped. "Choose Airiella," he whispered, shaking his head. His eyes seeking hers out, even though she couldn't see him. Winnie's message on the window suddenly making sense to him. He motioned to hit the mute button but Smitty didn't see him as he was doing something on his phone.

"Florida Georgia Line?" Smitty asked looking up.

Ronnie watched as she looked next to her again, and then looked back towards them nodding. "She said to tell him they were from her."

"Shit," Ronnie said. Those eyes were doing something to his heart.

"Um, hello? Is that Ronnie? Nice to meet you too," she said, sounding like sex.

"Hello," he stuttered lamely. Smitty smirked at him and hit the mute button.

"You sound like a teenager that just saw boobs for

the first time," he said laughing. "Do I really say that Winnie wanted us to communicate with him to listen to those songs?"

"Well, I think if we don't, she's going to do to his phone what she did to mine," Ronnie stated. Trying to regain control of his own body and thoughts.

"It might push him over the edge, but I'll send the links," Smitty said, typing on his phone again. He sent the message, and they sat there quietly for about five minutes before Smitty's phone beeped. "Interesting," was his response as he leaned forward to un-mute the microphone again. "He replied with Something I Can Never Have."

Ronnie pulled out his phone frantically looking up the song as he heard a gasp from Airiella, then, "That's just mean." He looked up at that and saw her shaking her head no, looking somewhat pale. Both him and Smitty were looking up the song as Airiella said, "Not now." Pause. "Why? Because it will just hurt you." She paused again then they heard her faintly say, "Yes I know the song, it's one of my favorites." Clearly, she was talking to Winnie. Ronnie read the lyrics and hit the mute button himself and swore.

"Now that we are fully back in high school and doing song dedications via text message, what the fuck?" Ronnie jumped up and started pacing.

"He's on his way here," Smitty said quietly.

"Shit, he's going to eat this poor girl alive," Ronnie said, worried now.

"He won't be able to get to her," Smitty replied as the conference room doors opened. "She will be tied up for a while."

Ronnie smelled rain again, then Smitty's phone started playing the song from Jax. The haunting lyrics sending a wave of pain through the room as the message sunk in. All he could say was, "Shit."

Three men walked into the room, each as nondescript as the next in their same hairstyles, same colored boring suits and plain ties. None of them pulling off the look they were going for, and I struggled not to laugh at their attempt. They didn't need to try so hard, but I was kind of glad they were as nervous as I was.

"My name is Airiella Raven," I stood up and held out my hand at the flustered men. Maybe this wouldn't be as hard as I thought, as I shook their hands, immediately forgetting their names. Then again, maybe it would be if I couldn't even remember their names.

"So why don't we tell you about the job?" Suit guy number one said. "We are producers for the hit TV show Shadow Seekers, and we are looking for a strong empath that has the ability to diffuse situations. Preferably before they get out of hand," he added as an afterthought.

I nodded and suit guy number two piped in. "We are looking for not only strong empath abilities, but strong character as well since these will be intense and possibly emotional situations." I nodded again, content to let them explain what I already knew.

Suit guy number three spoke up then. "All we really had time to do was run a background check on you, which is of course clean." Of course it was. I nodded once more. "Why don't you tell us about yourself?" He stammered out. Why were they so nervous?

"Sure, what areas would you like to touch on?" I asked in my professional voice. They all blushed and shifted around. I had no idea what was going on and was feeling awkward by this point.

"Um, how about your empath skills?" Suit guy number two suggested.

"Of course," I replied, resisting the urge to roll my eyes. "For as long as I can remember I've had the ability to know what people are feeling and through the years have honed my skills to where not only can I feel their emotions, I can read the signs and energy of areas, objects and even animals. When things are bad for some people and I feel they need help, I pull the troubling emotions from them, allowing them clearer perspective to help them get through it," I explained.

"Can you clarify that?" Number three asked.

"Which part?" I responded.

"Uh, well, I'm not sure," he said getting more flustered. I did the only thing I could think of. I opened my senses, and felt around his emotions, grabbing the nervous energy, and embarrassment. I pulled them from him and fed calm energy back into its place. His face changed in amazement and he exclaimed, "Wow! That was incredible." The other two looking at him in utter confusion.

"Better?" I asked kindly. Quickly I started putting my walls back up as I felt curiosity pushing at me from different angles.

"I'm sold," was all he could say. The other two just staring at him, not understanding. "She took away the nervousness I had," he said weakly, failing to mention I took his embarrassment too. Though I still didn't get why he was feeling embarrassed. Number one and two turned their surprised gazes on me.

"Honestly, I have no idea what to ask right now," number one admitted. Winnie started howling with laughter.

Holding back a smile I suggested, "How about I ask you some questions?" They all nodded in relief and pulled out pens to write down my questions. This was the weirdest interview I'd ever had.

"Salary, schedule, location, benefits are the basics," I started.

"Wait, before we get to that I have a few more questions," number three said, getting brave. "How do we know you aren't using some form of mental manipulation?"

Damn, that was a reasonable question, and now it was starting to feel more like an interview. "Well, I guess that would have to be a leap of faith, or belief using logical reasoning and deductions. Aside from the fact that I can't read minds, and don't know your thoughts. In order to manipulate you to get my desired effect I'd need to know that. I simply took your energy that was causing you trouble, and fed you back my own calm. You were aware I was doing it, and you remember everything, and none of your own personal beliefs were changed I am assuming. I have learned valuable people skills over the years, but simply put, I didn't need to use any empath abilities to know what you were feeling. Anyone paying attention could have figured it out."

"How so?" Number one asked, curious.

"First when you three walked in, there was an air of confidence about you. As I stood up, you all became noticeably stiffer in posture, had facial expression changes and you appeared flustered and suddenly unsure. As we sat down you all exuded copious amounts of nervous energy, your voices had intonation changes, and your body language changed frequently. Deductive reason told me, something caught you off guard and made you uneasy. Two of you started to get beads of sweat on your upper lip, and the other started flushing. I have no idea as to the reason for any of those emotions or changes. I do know that when vocal tones match facial expressions and body language, they often mirror emotions. Using more deductive reasoning I can make educated guesses to your thoughts, but that's all it is, just a guess. I'm not a fan of mind games and have zero desire to play them. Does that answer your question?" I tried explaining.

"Does taking emotions from others have an effect on you?" Number two questioned.

"Yes. The stronger the emotion, the more it will affect me. I am essentially taking that emotion into myself and giving you my good ones in return," I responded carefully.

"What do you do after that?" Number one asked.

"It depends on the strength of the emotions. Sometimes I don't need to do anything for a week, other times it could be a matter of hours. For me personally, I need to be in nature, or an area that has a natural earth energy, like a ley line, or a vortex, and I release what's in me, and recharge with the pure energy of the earth so to speak."

"How are you under pressure?" Number three broke in.

Smiling, I said, "You tell me." Which got a chuckle out of them. I knew where they were headed with this, so I continued. "I've been through a lot in my life, just like everyone else has. Imagine growing up knowing what everyone around you feels all the time. Now imagine going to school and knowing things others didn't know, like when someone is depressed, or having violent thoughts. Being honest and wanting to help, I always asked if they needed anything. Kids can be cruel when they see something different and don't understand. Imagine knowing your boss doesn't like you, or knowing you are getting fired. Social outcast became the norm and my circle of friends stayed tight. I play my cards close to my chest and don't offer up a lot of personal information unless I feel it will help the situation, or someone in a similar situation that I faced along the way. Pressure for me is not a big deal."

Number two jumped in again, "You say you've been through a lot. Often times on an investigation you will run into things that can trigger strong emotions, or you learn the history of a person or location that may be a trigger for you. So what kind of things have you gone through in life?"

"You are borderline getting too personal there," I responded gently. "I understand why you are asking, but please know, I don't share very much with others. I will give you a broad answer without details, but I can safely say that in tense situations, or volatile ones, I remain calm. The freak-out happens after everything is done and I'm alone. I've personally dealt with violence, abuse, rape, relationships with people who have addictions, cancer, divorce, betrayal, infidelities, abandonment and mental illness. Most of those situations have touched many people I know, it doesn't single me out. Everyone is, or has been broken in some way, that's how I get through to them."

Flustered, Number three asked, "How did you get through?"

"Well, I overthought every little detail, researched, tore apart the situation until I drove myself crazy looking for where I went wrong and how I could fix it until somewhere along the way I figured out the lesson I was supposed to learn and learned it. I would take the lesson and apply it to the situation and understand where I could improve so as not to repeat it. I wasn't always successful, but I've learned many valuable lessons and am constantly working to improve myself. Yes, life leaves permanent scars, but it's still beautiful. I am my own worst enemy and am harder on myself than anyone else could possibly be. Work in progress," I said pointing to myself.

"You are quite remarkable," Number two said, impressed.

"I disagree, I believe everyone is remarkable, people just tend to not look for it in others," I argued.

"We have a council of people with abilities that we have applicants test with to learn their ability range before we offer any jobs and have you meet the team," Number one stated.

I interrupted, "I know two of them are behind that glass door," I pointed. "I felt them the moment I walked in the room as they had no mental barriers in place to lock away emotions."

"How did you learn about this position?" Number three asked. "It hadn't even been posted yet when we received your voicemail.

"This might require a leap of faith on your part. A ghost told me. Before you ask, I'm not a medium, she is the first and only ghost I've ever seen or talked to, and me applying for this job was helping her, so I did."

"I see," three said, his eyes searching my face. I shrugged. At that moment, three's phone started blaring the Ghostbusters theme song. They all three looked at me in amazement.

"That wasn't me, I'm guessing she was saying hello or something, she is not currently visible," I said, choking on a laugh that was threatening to explode.

"Ah, yes, well...as I was saying," Number one continued, slightly rattled, "You will need to meet with the council over the next two days and test with them and after that we talk offers."

"Okay, sounds good. Thank you for your time. Can you recommend a hotel for me?"

"Oh, we made arrangements for you already. The

council will meet you back here at 8:00 AM tomorrow morning. Some are still in route, I apologize. We have a driver at your disposal," one slid a card across the table to me. "Call that number to arrange a ride in the morning or to take you where you need to go this evening if you need to get out. He's currently waiting in the garage for you and will take you to the hotel."

"We will speak to you soon Ms. Raven, it was a pleasure to meet you," two said. The others nodding. "I'll escort you to the garage, if you'll follow me," he motioned towards the door. I stood, waved at the wall where Smitty and Ronnie hid and left. Winnie trailing after me.

"Thank you again," I told one and three as we parted ways.

As I got into the waiting car and left, I asked the driver if there was some where close to the hotel I could pick up some extra clothes at, not realizing this was going to be a multi-day interview, I only had what I was wearing.

Winnie rode next to Airiella quietly, going over everything in her mind. Jax was on his way, and he knew she was in communication with members of his team now. Airiella blew the producers out of the water and dropped some info bombshells for them all to ponder. It wasn't anything Winnie didn't already know from her trip in Airy's head. But to hear her say some of the things in her own guarded words was different. Winnie felt for her. Though she was also laughing hysterically about the way the producers reacted to her. They felt the angel presence as soon as they walked in the room and when Airy started talking the one guy got a boner.

Winnie couldn't help it, she thought it was hilarious. She wasn't sure how she felt about Ronnie being attracted to her. She wasn't against it, but it made her sad because she never got her chance with him. Then she started thinking about the song Jax replied with and that hole inside her opened a bit more. Winnie completely understood why Airiella said it was one of her favorite songs, but when she applied it to her and her relationship with Jax, it hurt.

She needed to focus now, wrap her mind around how to help Airy with the council tomorrow, because for sure they would feel her, and she wasn't sure that was a good idea yet. Maybe it was, she didn't know. She was also trying to figure out the premonition she had during that storm, it was such a jumble in her head right now that it just wasn't making sense. Almost like it was spoken in a different language. All in due time, she figured.

Chapter Eleven

Smitty sat there a few minutes after everyone left the conference room trying to absorb everything that was just said. "Thoughts?" he asked Ronnie.

"Too many to sort through, and so many more questions," he replied, still awestruck. "We going to leave her alone tonight, or are we going to try to talk to her on our own?"

"My gut says we talk to her, but I'm not sure where they booked her at," Smitty said.

"My guess is the same place they always put us, they don't vary much." Ronnie paused. "She's been through a lot."

"You think?" Smitty said, his eyes wide. "She's got a lot of strength to her though, I could feel it through the wall. This might sound crazy, but I think I could feel her."

"Not crazy, I know I could feel her." Ronnie turned to look at Smitty. "She didn't exhibit any of the nerves that typically happen during an interview, she remained calm, but the producers sure didn't. Wonder what that was about?"

Smitty smiled smugly, "Well Dave had a boner."

Ronnie laughed, "Guess her voice affected more than just us."

"Yeah, we weren't even in the room with her or my guess is we would have been the same way they were," Smitty admitted. "She has a draw to her."

"Yep, makes you want to be close," Ronnie said thickly.

"Easy cowboy," Smitty joked. "Let's find out if she's checked in yet," he suggested, grabbing his phone and calling the hotel. "Yes, hi, has Airiella Raven checked in yet?" Smitty snuck a glance over at Ronnie. "No? Okay, thanks. When she does can you please tell her to keep her dinner schedule open? Thank you."

"Should we bring something to her hotel room then?" Ronnie wondered. "Or should we take her out?"

"I'd say public place would be safer, but we'd be able to ask more questions in a private setting," Smitty argued with himself. "If we bring her food, we could inadvertently pick something she doesn't like. What about the restaurant in the hotel? We are staying there too, right? Dinner and then we could go back and talk."

"Perfect. Hopefully before Jax gets here," Ronnie worried.

"Aedan texted and said they fly out tomorrow morning. She should be with the council then." Smitty's eyes went out of focus for a moment, "Hey did you feel what she did to Dave by any chance?"

"Yeah, she did exactly what she said she did, I could feel the nervousness just disappear, and she didn't even change expressions," Ronnie marveled. "Useful skill to have."

"You heard her describer her life, I don't think she found it useful," Smitty recalled her words.

"I'm like ninety-five percent sure I'm in love with her," Ronnie said, smitten.

"Okay lover boy lets head out," Smitty said, offering a hand up. As Ronnie stood, Smitty had to fight himself not to respond that he felt the same way about the mysterious Airiella, which confused the hell out of him.

Jax paced his room at Aedan's house in a mad fury, his feet falling heavy on the floor. Winnie. A message from Winnie to let her go. Well, and the other one that told him he was haunted, which he already figured out. Everyone knew that by now. After all these years he finally gets a message from her and it's two songs.

He'd been stuck on the letting her go one, that one threw him off. He kept trying to pick apart the other one looking for her message in there, but it wasn't jumping out at him. He was a little ashamed at himself for responding with the song he did, but it was a knee jerk reaction, and spot on as well. He wanted to be in Denver now, not leaving in the morning.

Frustration was close to boiling over. He kept getting this feeling like things were out of his control now and nothing was going to change that. Like he just had to sit there and watch his life play out in front of him. He couldn't even get a hold of his reactions, most of which were being driven by whatever was inside him.

He completely understood why Ronnie had left without telling him, and he harbored no ill will against him for it. Jax had become unpredictable and somewhat unstable. Not a good way to meet someone that was supposed to help you. The feeling in him wouldn't stop pulling at him though that he needed to be there now. He was half tempted to get in the car and drive there, but he knew that would be the wrong decision. Instead he paced.

He could smell something cooking from downstairs and his stomach grumbled in response. He checked himself to make sure he was not too unbalanced to be around Mags and headed towards the kitchen. No one was in there, but whatever she was making smelled fantastic. He grabbed a soda from the fridge and sat at the table and looked at his stitched hands.

Waves of guilt washed over him and settled heavy into his heart. All the lives he was ruining flashing through his mind. Sometimes he wondered why this thing just didn't kill him and be done with it. He hated how his life

141

had become and he was tired of trying to fight this thing. This oily black stain he felt growing in him.

"Whatever you are thinking sweets, stop," Mags said, walking behind him and dropping a kiss on the top of his head.

"Mags..." Jax started.

"No Jax. Stop." She left him no room for argument and pulled out a roast chicken from the oven. Jax's stomach grumbled loudly and she laughed. "That problem I can fix, so that is the only thing we are going to focus on, got it?"

"Yes Mags," Jax smiled wanly.

Mags set dishes out in front of him, "Set the table please."

Like a robot, Jax went through the motions, but still didn't feel like he was present. He'd eat, then hopefully sleep. Get to Denver tomorrow, and try to figure out a way out of this mess before he lost anyone else. Before he lost the rest of himself.

I looked at the name of the driver on the card, Mark, and thanked him for stopping at a store. I jumped out of the car and ran in to the discount store headed straight for the clothing department. I wasn't too concerned about style right now, I was more focused on comfort and versatility since I had no idea what the testing tomorrow was going to consist of.

I spotted jeans, grabbed my size, grabbed a few colorful shirts that caught my eye, and went in search of leggings. Found a couple pair of those and headed to the socks. I could make do with one bra, but I needed more underwear and something to sleep in. I just grabbed the first thing I saw and added it to my growing stack.

I went looking for shoes, needing some tennis shoes, and then went to grab a toothbrush, toothpaste, deodorant, hairbrush and some hair ties. My arms now full I went straight to the register and dumped it all on the counter. I winced at the total, my credit card was near maxed out, and I was thankful that I hadn't had to pay for the hotel room or the flight.

I paid and snatched up the bags and ran back to the car, huffing and puffing at the flurry of sudden activity. "Thank you for waiting!" I told the driver with a smile. "We can go to the hotel now."

I settled the bags next to me on the back seat and wondered where Winnie had gone. She'd show up eventually, so I wasn't too worried. We pulled up to the hotel and Mark went to grab my bags for me, but I waved him off. I was perfectly capable of carrying my own crap. He gave me a kind smile and told me he'd be back tomorrow morning by 7:00.

I noticed the hotel had a restaurant and I was thankful for that, I was starving. I made my way to the front desk and checked in. The gentleman smiled at me and told me everything was already taken care of, handed me my key card and relayed a message to me to keep my dinner plans open. I thanked him and headed up to my room which was on the top floor.

Wall to ceiling windows greeted me as I took in the large suite, a little awestruck at the view of the Rockies and city sprawled out below me. Those mountains called to me on a deep primal level and I longed to just go explore them and the secrets they held.

I dropped my bags on the bed and pulled out the clothes to hang them up. As I pulled out the shirts, I howled in laughter. I should have looked at them instead of just grabbing and running. One had "Gorgeous!" scrawled across the front in neon pink. The other had "Sexy Woman" written on it in a weird violet color. My own fault, but it was funny. Those were two shirts I would have never picked out for myself in any other situation.

I pulled the tags off everything and put it all in the closet and sat down on the couch to just take in the view and be in the moment until whatever dinner plans were being made for me materialized. I must have dozed off for a bit because I suddenly awoke at the sound of knocking on the door. I scrambled off the couch and saw I looked a little rumpled, but really didn't care all that much.

I looked out the peep hole and froze. Ronnie and

Smitty stood out there. Well, I guess we had to meet at some point. I unlocked the door and pulled it open smiling brightly, "Hello! Come on in," I invited with a false sense of bravado. They were mouthwatering hot, and I wiped my hand across my mouth in hopes I wasn't drooling.

"Hi there," Smitty said, somewhat shyly as he walked past me. Then turned around noticing Ronnie wasn't behind him. He was still standing in the hallway staring. Smitty gave me an apologetic look and pulled Ronnie in, closing the door behind them.

"I am going to assume my dinner plans were with you then?" I stammered out. Jeez, I needed to get a grip. I wanted to lick Ronnie. He reminded me of a white Jason Momoa, except that bruise on his jaw. Smitty could have been on a calendar with half-dressed sexy firemen on it. He had that look. Maybe I needed to get laid if my quivering belly was any indication.

"Yes, we were hoping you would join us at the restaurant downstairs," Smitty explained. "We wanted a chance to get to know you without the audience of the producers or the council, or well, to be honest, Jax."

"I'm starving!" I exclaimed. "Let's go." I felt like if I didn't get out of that room, I was going to strip them both and climb them like trees. Damn! I hadn't reacted like this to men in a long time.

Ronnie still hadn't said anything, and I saw Smitty smack him on the back of the head and grinned, herding them towards the door. "Lead on, little lady," Smitty smiled. I liked him. Winnie was in trouble for not telling me how sexy they were in person.

As they got in the elevator Ronnie seemed to stand very close to me, and Smitty stood closer than normal social convention would dictate, even though they were alone on the elevator and had plenty of room to spread out. I didn't really care, I let my eyes rake them up and down, and was only a tiny bit embarrassed when they both caught me doing it.

I looked at Ronnie, "So do you talk only on the show?"

Smitty broke out in laughter, "He's just a smitten kitten. Soon you'll wish he would shut up."

Yep, I liked him. Well, I liked both really. I felt like I had known them for years. I wound my arms between theirs on either side of me and we headed into the restaurant. The hostess's eyes popped out when she saw them, and I felt a little smug. "Can you get a table for me and my dates please?" I asked sweetly. Not having any idea where this personality in me came from. Maybe an alien had taken me over.

"Baby girl, you just crushed that poor girls' dreams," Smitty breathed in my ear. My belly got tingles when he called me baby girl, combined with the warm breath in my ear, I think my underwear were soaked. This was sad.

"I'm living mine," I shot back at him, using my phone sex voice. That got a reaction out of Ronnie and he stepped closer, sliding his arm around my back pulling me to him. "He's alive!" I teased him.

"Oh, I'm definitely alive," he murmured, my insides went to mush and my knees quaked. He was sex on a stick.

"Food," I said fast. "I need food," I quipped, needing to put something in my mouth that wasn't attached to either of these men. They brought us to a table and I moved from between them to sit across from them. I didn't think I would survive dinner sandwiched between them.

Ronnie looked at me, his eyes intense, and I felt something inside me shift. Some weird feeling in me that felt connected to him. "I think I just need you," he said, his voice throaty and deep.

Smitty cleared his throat, "Ease up dude." He looked at me apologetically again. "I think what he means to say is we feel a draw to you," he tried to explain.

I shifted my gaze over to Smitty and felt the same connection. "I don't feel the draw," I said carefully, "but I do feel a sort of connection that I can't explain."

Smitty reached his hand out to me, and I took it as he shook my hand. "Officially now, I'm Smitty and it's a definite pleasure meeting you," he purred at me. My eyes widened at the contact and it felt like an electric current sizzled between our hands. One that was familiar. I pulled my hand back and looked at it, like there was a mark there or something. "Yeah, I felt that too," he said quietly in awe.

Not wanting to be left out, Ronnie clumsily stuck his hand out to me, and I was slower to take it this time. The moment our skin touch it felt like it glowed, but it too was familiar to me. "I'm Ronnie," he said roughly, clearly being affected the same way I was.

I dropped his hand, too startled to say anything, and was saved by the waiter. "Can I get you guys a beer, anything to drink?" he asked.

"Water for me please," I said automatically.

"Iced tea," Ronnie forced out.

"Water for me too please," Smitty said. "Can we get the appetizer platter to start?"

"Sure thing," the waiter smiled, walking away.

"What was that?" Ronnie asked.

I shook my head in confusion, I had no idea. That had never happened to me before. Smitty looked between us, "What are you talking about?"

"When we touched, I saw a glowing line between us," Ronnie said, his voice shaking.

"Did you see anything when I was touching her?" Smitty asked, curious.

"No, I just felt jealous," Ronnie said with honesty. I didn't know what to say. I hadn't seen it, but I certainly felt it. "Did you feel anything Smitty?"

"Yeah, but I don't know that I would describe it as a line. It felt like electricity sparking along a live wire, but not painful, like a tingle," Smitty tried finding words to describe it. I nodded, agreeing with him, that was what it felt like.

"And familiar," I added. "I feel like I know your touch."

Ronnie raised one of his eyebrows at that. "You felt that with Smitty?"

"I felt that with both of you," I clarified. "Can I try something?" I asked slowly, questioning my own sanity at this point. I held out both hands, one to each of them. They caught on and each took a hand, and the connection between us snapped in place, this time I saw it. It startled me so badly I let go of both in the next instant.

We all gasped, and I went silent. "You guys have a bond," Winnie whispered in my ear.

I let out a yelp and jumped. "We talked about that!" I snapped at her. Then my eyes went wide with the realization of what I just done.

I had two sets of eyes glued on me, Winnie laughing next to me, and my thoughts were scattered every direction possible. "It's the angel in you, it calls to them," she explained to me. "It's like a soul mate thing."

Doing my best to ignore her so I didn't look crazy any more than I already did, "Sorry," I said sheepishly.

Smitty to the rescue, "Well, we know you talk to Winnie, I'm guessing that means she just joined us?" I nodded mutely. "Can I ask what she said?" I shook my head no. I wasn't about to repeat the angel nonsense to them. "Fair enough," he conceded.

A plate full of appetizers appeared in front of me suddenly and I was ecstatic for the distraction. I was in way over my head here, and Winnie seemed to know it by her snickering. I grabbed a cheese stick and stuffed it in my mouth, not trusting myself with words.

Ronnie was watching my every move and it unnerved me because I felt like he was seeing things I didn't want him to see, nor knew how to hide. "I can see I have some research to do," he said cryptically. Smitty just nodded, eating like I was. "You'll need to power load on food tonight for the testing tomorrow," he advised.

"What will it be like?" I finally found my voice.

"It's not physically hard, but it takes a lot of energy," Ronnie explained. "It will drain you fast. Well at least it did to me."

Recalling the past few weeks I'd had, I would guarantee that statement. The waiter came back, and we ordered entrée's and he left us alone. "What should I expect?"

"Well the council meets with everyone that has abilities to determine what they are and the strength to see if the job will be a good fit or not. In this case, we requested someone fairly strong because of what has been happening with Jax," Ronnie told me.

"I am guessing then that the testing is different for different people," I surmised.

They both nodded at me. "The council can be a bit difficult sometimes, just please remember, it's not personal. They are testing you, your reactions and your solution to the problem, so to speak. They believed me to be an empath, and while I do have a little of that, they aren't really sure what to classify me as," Ronnie said in a rush. "I have a sensitivity to other energies, but sometimes I can't really read the emotions. I can see manifestations of certain types of energies, but not necessarily ghosts. Other times, I can see and feel things easily. Jax has told everyone he is an empath, and he is, but it's a minor talent, where my talent is significantly stronger than his. I'd place a bet on yours being stronger than all you will meet combined," Ronnie said humbly.

"I'm an empath," I told them both.

"I think it's more than that," Smitty said.

At the same time, Ronnie said, "There's more to you than that."

Winnie chose that moment to burst out laughing again. "Why won't you just believe me? Even they can sense it!"

Aggravated, I exploded with, "I'm not an angel, Winnie!"

And silence reigned across our table with that little outburst. "Research," both men said at the same time.

"I've got a few books I can look in," Ronnie said. "The council would know for sure though."

I sighed, my nerves fraying a bit now. "I'm not an angel," I argued quietly.

"It would make sense if you were," Smitty pushed gently. "Given the way people react to you."

"Can we talk about anything else? Please?" I begged.

"Jax is flying in tomorrow," Ronnie said. "But don't worry, we'll keep him away, and plus, you'll be offsite somewhere testing.

"Offsite? They don't do it at that building?" I asked, startled.

"A couple of them will," Smitty answered.

"The ones that will test your abilities will do so closer to the mountain range to alleviate any danger to the area, and people," Ronnie followed. "The whole process takes a couple of days depending on the abilities. That's why there is no return ticket scheduled yet."

I sighed. "Well I guess I get to see the mountains then, there's my silver lining."

"You like nature?" Smitty asked.

"I'd die without it," I admitted. "Being in nature is how I release the stuff I take from people."

"I remember you saying that," he said as our dinners were put down in front of us. "What do you do for fun?"

"In general? Or in nature?" I asked, inhaling the aromatic scent of my food. I don't usually eat a lot of pasta, but blackened chicken alfredo sounded so good to me. I dug in.

"In general," Ronnie responded, taking a bite of the steak he ordered.

"I read a lot, I white water raft during the spring and summer," I said around my food. "I like movies. I breathe music. I write a lot. I hike, spend copious amounts of time in nature. I walk when I need to burn off restless energy. I do yoga when I need to center myself. I go to the beach and walk for hours on end. I'm not really that exciting," I said. "It's not like I hunt ghosts," I quipped.

Smitty chuckled, "Well if you have been talking to Winnie then you know why we are doing that."

Ronnie's face darkened. "She told you, right?"

I nodded slowly, remembering her feelings for him. I had to tread carefully here, I didn't want to step on her toes and hurt her feelings by diving head first into this man that suddenly had a line connected to me. I reached out across the table and laid my hand on his, "I'm sorry the way things worked out. She loves you."

His face lit up in rapture at the contact and I went to pull my hand away, but he held it tight. "I think I'm in love with you."

Smitty choked on his chicken, and I laughed at that thought. They both looked at me strange. "Smitty is choking on his chicken. Choking the chicken," I said giggling hysterically. Oh yeah, I'd lost my damn mind.

They both cracked up laughing. "Oh, baby girl, I like you. We are going to get along great."

We finished our dinner, talking about nothing important, just getting to know each other, and I felt a warm glow of happiness taking root inside me, getting bigger the longer I spent with them. Most definitely there was a connection between us. I didn't know what that meant, but I couldn't argue it away either. Winnie disappeared before our food was finished, and as they paid the bill I glanced around looking to see if she was near.

Not seeing her anywhere, I went with the guys back up to the top floor. They told me their rooms were up there too, but they came with me into mine. Happy that I wasn't alone, I excused myself to take a shower, and got ready for bed. They looked a little startled when I came back out, but I just climbed in bed, feeling at peace.

I patted the bed next to me on either side. "Can you stay with me until I fall asleep?" Both men settled on either side of me, I held their hands, letting that connection wash through me and lull me off to sleep, wondering who this person was I was becoming around them.

Ronnie watched her sleep, the feelings rolling through him in pleasant soft waves. Winnie had been the only person he had ever fallen in love with, but he knew without a doubt in his mind that love was what he was feeling for the angel laying here. He said it out loud, "Angel."

He saw Smitty nod in agreement. It fit her. That inviting warm pull she emitted was like she was wrapping you up in love. He hadn't felt this kind of peace ever before. It was better than any drug he had ever tried while seeking this feeling. They'd never encountered an angel before, and he had no idea what they were capable of. He knew that this situation had taken an interesting turn, and he worried about what the testing would reveal tomorrow.

"I don't know if I'm comfortable with the council knowing she is an angel," Ronnie whispered across Airiella to Smitty.

"Me neither, but maybe they won't know?" he hoped.

"Maybe," Ronnie muttered. "We should go."

"Yeah, we should, but I don't want to leave," Smitty softly smiled down at her sleeping form. "I feel amazing right now. She's incredible."

Ronnie wholeheartedly agreed. "Think she would be okay if he just stayed like this?"

"Yes, she would be okay with it, but you need to stop talking and go to sleep," she said her voice thick with sleep as she shifted and then drifted back off.

Smitty laughed quietly repositioned himself to get more comfortable but made sure he still had skin on skin contact with her. Ronnie got up and turned the lights out, then pulled off his shirt and climbed in on the other side. He needed that connection to. He could feel Smitty in that connection, making it more solid, but it was her essence that coated him in a cocoon of safety and love. He wouldn't ever be able to get enough of this.

Not even thinking twice about how weird it was to be cuddled up in bed with Smitty and a stranger between them. It just felt natural, he turned on his side to face her and molded as much of her to him as he possibly could. Smitty spooning her from behind. Life as he knew it had just changed forever.

Winnie watched them all sleep, happily humming to herself. Things were starting to fall in place. She felt a pang of longing when she looked at Ronnie, but she didn't hold it against Airy at all. This was how it was supposed to be. And the little piece of her soul that Airy pulled when she took that darkness from her was firmly embedded into her, so she could feel the tingle of the connection Ronnie had with her. And it felt like home.

Winnie blinked out and popped back in on Jax, who was finally sleeping, but in the throes of another nightmare so strong she could feel the darkness in him welcome it. She admitted her feelings about him had changed so drastically since Airy had come into the picture. She still loved him, she always would, he just wasn't the same person as he had been. He'd need to change to make that connection strong with Airy.

She faded into the veil to rest. She wanted to be there for Airy tomorrow, even if they knew she was there. She knew Airy was strong enough to handle it, there wasn't much that girl couldn't handle. Didn't mean she had to face it all alone though.

Chapter Twelve

Aedan texted Smitty in the morning as Mags was packing their bags. "How's it looking?"

"She's fucking amazing," Smitty texted back.

"Female? Think she can handle Jax?" he wrote back.

"I think you should be more worried that Jax can't handle her. She's crazy strong. Testing today."

"Council?" Aedan typed and hit send.

"Yep."

"Will she pass?" Aedan worried, Jax's condition seemed to be getting worse.

"I have zero doubt about that. You'll see when you meet her."

"You've seen her this morning?" Aedan texted.

"I'm lying in bed next to her," was the response. Followed by, "Ronnie is on the other side."

"You both slept with her??" Aedan fired back.

"Not how you think. She asked us to stay, so we did." Attached came a picture of Smitty and Ronnie lying on either side a woman.

Her hair was fanned out on the pillow behind her, and Aedan thought she was glowing, but could just be the picture. Smitty was grinning in the picture, Ronnie was still asleep.

"Behave," Aedan cautioned.

Smitty didn't respond to that, and Aedan went to make sure Jax was ready to go. He knocked on the door, "Fifteen minutes Jax, better be ready."

The door opened and Jax was there, looking tense and strung out. "I'm ready," he replied, pushing past Aedan and out the door.

Aedan shook his head and went to grab the bags from Mags, and they headed out.

W aking up between two sexy men was a new thing for me. And I liked it. A lot. I pried open my eye lids to see Smitty grinning down at me, that meant it was Ronnie wrapped around me from behind. Delicious. I wiggled my butt a little bit realizing that he was hard beneath those jeans of his he kept on.

Smitty laughed, seeing what I was doing. I shrugged innocently, then smirked. Not sorry at all, I did it again and felt his arm tighten around me as he growled low in my ear, "Stop that, angel."

Smitty got up, "I gotta go get cleaned up and changed, baby girl. I'll drag this ape with me, so you can get ready. Make sure you eat breakfast before going. Remember, you'll need the energy. We'll meet you downstairs in thirty minutes."

I nodded as I felt cold with the absence of them around me, and got up, stretching slowly. I heard Ronnie groan from behind me and I turned around and damn near drooled again. I reached out to trace my fingers down the ink on his chest and he stepped closer to me. "If you keep touching me, you are going to be late for your testing," he warned, his voice rough.

I looked up into his eyes and was lost. I didn't care if I ever made it to the damn testing. This was one tasty man in front of me. I felt Smitty come up behind me, his arm wrapped around me under my now very sensitive boobs, and he pulled me away. "Testing," he reminded me.

I decided to test him and leaned back into him as I looked at Ronnie. Needless to say, I was pretty damn distracted and didn't care about much else except the man behind me and the one in front of me. I groaned aloud as Ronnie put his shirt back on as he grinned at me.

Of course, Winnie decided to pop in at that moment, once again making me shriek and jump. "Dammit Winnie!" I grumbled. Stalking off to the bathroom. She followed me as the guys left the room.

"How did you sleep?" she asked sweetly smiling.

"Actually, pretty good," I admitted.

"I bet," she smirked.

I felt guilty then and sat down heavily on the edge of the tub. "I'm sorry Winnie, I'll stop flirting with Ronnie."

"What?! Don't you dare! How else can I live vicariously through you?" she practically shouted at me. "This is supposed to be like this!"

I threw my hands up in front of me in supplication. "Fine, whatever. You should have told me he was built like Jason Momoa."

"If I knew who that was, I would have," she said confused. "Is that a bad thing?"

I laughed, "Oh no, it's pretty damn wonderful."

"Wear jeans," she told me. "You'll need to be comfortable today."

Nodding, I got dressed and headed downstairs for breakfast. "How heavy of a breakfast should I eat?"

"Go heavier on the protein than the carbs, maybe grab a few of the fruit to take with you," Winnie suggested.

I saw the guys in the omelet line, so I decided to go with a three-egg cheese omelet. I placed my order and waited while the chef made it and grabbed a plate and loaded it up with fruit and some extra that I could take with me. I took some toast and grabbed a bottle of water and went and sat down with the guys.

They nodded approvingly at my plate and we all tucked in and just ate. Just as I finished, my phone went off with a text telling me the driver was here. I dropped off my empty plate and grabbed another couple bottles of water and went back to the guys.

"Cars here, I gotta go." I leaned over and gave them both hugs. "Wish me luck," I said.

"You'll blow them out of the water," Ronnie said, sounding totally sure. "Nice shirt," he added smiling. Smitty nodded. I looked down realizing I had on the sexy woman one. And off I went. Winnie trailing after me, her soothing cool touch calming me.

I got in the car and smiled bravely at the driver as he carted me off to meet these mysterious people that were going to push my limits. I didn't know how I felt about that, but I wasn't nervous in a scared type of way. I was more nervous that I wasn't enough and would have to leave and never see those guys again. I already missed them. I shook my head to clear it, what was wrong with me? They were just two guys.

I got out as the driver pulled up, and noticed Winnie following me. I looked at her with a question in my eyes and she nodded, "I'm coming with you. I don't care if they know I'm there, I don't want you to face this alone. Unless they banish me from wherever you are, I'll be there," she told me. Grateful for the support, I smiled at her.

"Thanks," I whispered. Following the receptionist's directions, I got on an elevator and went up to the top floor. It was a different room this time, no windows, and solid walls, not glass. I made sure my walls were firmly in place and walked in.

Ten people were sitting around a large wood conference room table, all along one side, the other side barren, which was apparently where I was supposed to sit. I smiled at each person as I walked around and sat, calmly folding my arms in front of me on the table.

"You are a raven," an elderly man said, possibly a native American.

"That is my name, yes," I said. "Airiella Raven."

"Not your name, you," he said cryptically.

I had no idea what he was talking about, but I didn't ask any questions. I just looked around. Two women were looking at the man, one of them quietly asking, "Are you sure?" and he nodded in answer.

"Interesting," the woman who had asked looked back at me, looking with a critical eye this time.

I didn't know what to do, so I just sat there quietly as they all stared at me, and I focused on the calm feeling inside me that was residual from my night with the guys. I refused to let this group ruffle my feathers, which were apparently raven feathers, whatever that meant. I wasn't knowledgeable about native American legends.

After a few minutes of silence, a silver fox gentleman cleared his throat. Seriously? Did all the men I encountered have to be good looking? "Hello Airiella, my name is Dr. Trevor Stone, and I am the psychiatrist for the council here today, and I will be evaluating your mental state, before and after the testing by the individuals you see in front of you."

I smiled and nodded my understanding, waiting for him to continue. I knew how to get around the test's psychiatrists used to evaluate people. Though I did wonder if being a part of this group his tests were different than others. I wasn't worried. Dr. Stone isn't the one who continued though. A voice from the end of the table spoke up.

"My name is Degataga, welcome Airiella," he bowed his head in respect. "I am a medicine man from the Cherokee tribe." I was fascinated already.

Next, the elderly man who called me a raven spoke. "My name is Taklishim," he said to me. "I am part of the Zuni nation, an Apache warrior." He tipped his head to me as well, and I returned the gesture.

A woman next to him came next, "Hi Airiella, my name is Dr. Sarah Fields, I'm the resident parapsychologist." She smiled at me gently. "I notice you have a guest with you," she said referring to Winnie. I simply nodded in return, not acknowledging the statement. I wasn't going to give anything away.

Next came two identical women, obviously twins, one of which had asked Taklishim if he was sure. "My name is Onida," the sister to the one who asked about me said. "My sister is Tama, we are from the Chinook tribe," she said as they both bowed their heads to me. I bowed back.

A handsome man came next, looking British in his proper attire. "My name is Asher Vance," he spoke, like I was supposed to know who that was. I was right on the British point though. "I'm a medium," he explained when it was clear I didn't know his name, looking a bit put out. I immediately wondered if he felt Winnie too.

Next, we came to a woman with dark ebony skin, and a face so beautiful I wanted to cry. When she spoke, her voice had a musical lilt to it due to an accent I couldn't place. "Airiella," she started, "my name is Kalisha. I am a priestess of hoodoo." Well I can't say I was expecting that. I was intrigued though.

"Hello," said the man next to the priestess, and he had an Irish accent. It was one of my favorites, and I didn't care what he said as long as he kept talking. "My name is Father Patrick Roarke. I am a Catholic priest, specializing in demonology and exorcism, trained by the Vatican." Man, they were covering a lot of bases here in this council.

The last lady spoke. Her skin a mocha color, and her eyes were a soft gray color, absolutely mesmerizing. "My name is Aminda," she said in another musical accent. "I am a priestess of Santeria." I struggled to place that one, when she said with a smile, "Voodoo." Got it.

Dr. Stone spoke back up. "For the next couple of days, you will be spending time with each person, learning about what they represent and being tested by them in whichever way they deem necessary to help us learn about you. Most all these tests will be at an offsite location away from the city," he explained. "A couple will be here, but outside of the building. Do you have any questions?"

I shook my head. "No. I'm eager to proceed," I answered calmly.

"I myself will be observing you before the ones that will take place here in the city, and afterwards. I will also have you wear this fitness watch that is linked to my phone so I can record heartrate and stress levels," he handed me a watch like the one I wore. I put it on my other wrist, so now I was the weirdo with two watches on.

Dr. Fields spoke, "My test will be here in the city, and I will go first with you. When we are done, I'll bring you back here. We are going to go for a little walk," she said standing up. Dr. Stone and she fielded me to the door, nodding at the rest.

Dr. Stone asked me a few generic questions about how I slept last night, my general mood right now, my overall happiness. Trite questions, but he studied me intently as I answered. I fought my impulse to roll my eyes, he struck me as pompous, even though for an older man he was pretty good looking. Silvery hair, of course styled with not a hair out of place. Silver stubble over his chin, and his eyes a sky-blue color. Narrow face, he was tall, and of slight build. Not bad. He wore the suit he had on well, which was a gray that complimented his hair.

I switched my gaze over to Dr. Fields. I guessed her to be somewhere in her forties, her hair was pulled back into a tight bun that sat low on the back of her head. She had a few streaks of gray in the mix of the light brown color. She was fair skinned, hazel eyes. Sharp cheek bones and full lips, she was striking. Maybe only an inch taller than me, but very slender. Her hair contrasted with her clothes which were bright colors and fabric that flowed with her movements. A simple skirt and blouse, but she pulled off the look.

"Airiella, I have skills in precognition, clairvoyance, telepathy and I can see apparitions," Dr. Fields told me. "Are you familiar with all those?"

"To a degree of knowing what they are yes, I am. I don't have any of those skills myself," I replied, my voice controlled.

"You can't see apparitions?" she asked me, surprised. "You have one with you."

I nodded carefully. "The one that is with me is the only one I've ever seen. While I can sometimes pick up the energy of a spirit near me, I am not always sure that it's the energy of a spirit, it could be residual energy left behind from someone experiencing strong emotions," I explained.

We had walked into a cemetery not far from the building we had just left. "Can you feel anything here?" she asked, watching me.

Out of the corner of my eye I saw Winnie move in front of me into my line of vision and she made a motion of zipping her lips. She didn't want me to say anything. Even though I didn't feel anything or see anything. I looked at Dr. Fields and just shrugged. "It's a cemetery, so I just feel sadness," I said vaguely.

Dr. Fields narrowed her eyes at me, "You are hiding something."

Shocked, I looked at her. "Excuse me?"

"What are you hiding?" she demanded, getting in my face, hers all red and blotchy now.

"Sarah," Dr. Stone warned. This wasn't part of the test? What was happening?

"I'm fine Trevor," she replied, instantly back to normal. "I have a feeling Airiella's little ghost friend is giving her tips."

Dr. Stone looked at me. "She hasn't said anything to me at all," I said honestly. She hadn't, she just made motions, but he didn't need to know that.

"Why is she here?" Dr. Fields asked me.

I shrugged again, "She follows me around. Sometimes she speaks, most often though she follows me. I don't know who she is. I'm certain I didn't know her in life."

"Why are you certain of that?" she started walking again.

"Because she doesn't feel familiar to me," I answered her, my tone even.

"She is someone who had power to her," came the next response.

Double checking my walls, I played ignorant, "What do you mean?" I got the feeling she saw through the ignorance ploy. "Can you see her?"

Dr. Fields leveled a glare at me. "Surprisingly, no I can't. I can see where she is at, but I can't see her, which is odd to me, since I can see all the other spirits here flocking to you," she snarled like I was purposely hiding Winnie. Her admission kinda stumped me.

"Spirits are flocking to me?" I repeated.

"Yes, there are about fifteen of them behind you right now," she retorted smugly. She was getting on my nerves.

"Well ask them what they want then," I shot back at her.

"That's what I find so odd about this," she said, her eyes focused behind me, "they all say that they want you to give them admission."

Winnie was frantically shaking her head no. Now, if this was the test, I was sure I was failing. I had no damn clue what she was talking about. I wrinkled my eyebrows in confusion. "I don't get it. That makes no sense to me."

"Me neither, but that is telling in itself," she expressed. Dr. Fields suddenly went stiff as a board mid-step and started to fall forward. Directly in front of her was a headstone that she'd surely crack her head on. Without thinking, I dove in front of her and jammed my arms out in front of me as a brace to stop her fall.

The air whooshed out of my lungs as her weight fell on me. At least one of us had a soft landing. I lowered my arms until I could easily roll her to the ground without injury and gently put one of my legs under her head. She might be rude, but I didn't want her to get hurt. "Dr. Fields?" I said loudly. "Can you hear me?"

I shook her a little and got no response. Her eyes were sightless staring straight up, her body so rigid I'm surprised she didn't crack when she fell over. "Fascinating," Dr. Stone said looking at me. "She will be fine, she's having a vision."

I blinked slowly, staring at him, saying nothing. Blinking again, I looked back down at Dr. Sarah Fields and roamed my hands over her face, opening my senses just a little to make sure she was okay. Not seeing any signs of distress, I walled myself back up, and just sat there until she came back. Her body slowly losing the stiffness underneath my leg.

She sat up and looked around and then stood up, finally turning around and noticing me sitting on the ground sporting new grass stains on my brand new high fashioned discount store clothes. "You are glowing," she said in wonder.

Shit, not this again. I stood up and started dusting myself off and stretching out my now aching body. "You okay?" I questioned her.

"Did you catch me?" she looked at me in amazement. I nodded. "Thanks." She looked at Dr. Stone, "I think we are done here."

Stunned I stood there frozen in place as she started to walk away. What the fuck just happened? I looked over at Dr. Sone who seemed just as confused as I was, but he had started following her, so I trailed behind them. I looked around for Winnie and saw her looking slightly concerned, but she shook her head at me, then shrugged. Well, okay then.

Dr. Stone told me to go ahead and sit down when we got back in the lobby of the building, so I took a seat on the bench and leaned back against the window. Winnie settled in beside me, "I'm pretty sure she just had a vision about you. In any case, she was rude." I nodded slowly in agreement, knowing better than to say anything out loud.

Five minutes later Dr. Stone reappeared with Asher Vance. I briefly wondered why he called himself by his first and last name. Why not just Asher? Ego probably. Winnie blinked out and I remembered that he was the medium. Asher was wearing an entire proper suit, with vest, tie and everything. He looked like he belonged on the cover of a magazine.

He was good looking, but his self-entitled attitude detracted from it. His hair was a dirty blond, had a slight wave to it and he wore it a little longer than most people that would dress in that kind of suit. His face was chiseled, his eyes a vibrant green, but cold. As they approached, I saw Asher glance over my disheveled state, though he didn't comment. Wise on his part.

Dr. Stone was looking at his phone, studying something. He looked away from his phone and settled his unwavering gaze on me. "Your heart rate and stress level didn't fluctuate at all last time, impressive considering the physical exertion you used to catch Dr. Fields."

"What can I say, I'm active," I responded and saw Asher's eyebrows go up slightly at Dr. Stone's comment.

"At the moment you aren't exhibiting any signs of stress, or exhaustion either," he noted.

"I'm going to have to fall back on the previous comment, I'm active normally, and that didn't push me. I'm a little sore from the impact, but nothing that would slow me down," I admitted truthfully.

"Let's proceed then, Mr. Vance, lead the way," he held his arm out like he was a gracious host.

"Very well then," Asher said in his clipped British accent. "Let's head east."

I felt my sarcasm level notch up but refrained from mocking them both and just followed silently. Winnie wisely stayed wherever she had disappeared to. I opened myself up slightly to try and get a read on the emotions of these two and felt an atmospheric shift in energy that usually told me of an incoming storm.

Which brought my mind back to Winnie and her telling me of the storm that had hit at home after I left. She had said it was violent and I had hoped the neighbor had remembered to check on my cats, or if she even could. If the power had gone out, she wouldn't have been able to get in. I made a mental note to text her this evening to check. I glanced up at the sky and saw it was clear. Odd, usually when I felt that shift there were clouds present.

I put it out of my mind but noticed Dr. Stone watching me closely. Covering, I took a deep breath in and said, "I love fresh air, it reinvigorates the soul." Then I felt a wave of something hit me and remembered I had opened my senses a little. I focused on it and felt it came from Asher, and I went deeper and felt fear. He was scared of me?

"Let's turn here," Asher said, his tone flat. I walled

up again, feeling no cracks, I plastered a calm smile on my face and followed.

We were on a narrow street, a park across from us, businesses on the other side. I didn't notice anything remarkable, other than the park looked pretty. A nice break opportunity for the businesses there. Asher crossed the street, there was no car traffic, just people scattered about, and he stepped on to a paved path that meandered along through the park.

I followed more cautiously now, something felt off to me. There was an energy that was crackling in the air around me and while I didn't open my senses to it, I was on alert. Someone was close by with intentions that were less than honorable. I watched around me as Dr. Stone continued to study me and make notes.

At this point I felt he was inconsequential compared to what I was picking up on, but to look at me you wouldn't know something was off. "Pretty park," I commented inanely.

Asher had slowed down considerably and looked jittery. "My guide tells me there is evil here."

This was a test. "Your guide is correct," I responded.

"You can feel it?" Asher questioned. "Can you tell what form it takes?"

Dr. Stone had gone completely still and paled a bit. Even for someone with no empath skills he was picking up on something. I placed a hand on his arm to calm him, but he jerked like I had shocked him. "Are you okay Dr. Stone?"

"What? Of course, I am," he declared, insulted.

I couldn't help the rolling of my eyes then. Ignoring him, I walked away from them both just feeling out the air. Something was ahead of me and my senses tingled, wanting to open, but I didn't. It would leave me open to attack if this was something evil. I looked back at Asher and he was visibly shaken.

"My guide said we need to leave," his voice quivered.

"Why don't you pull out your phone, call the police," I suggested calmly.

"And tell them what, my spirit guide said something was evil?" he fired back at me.

"Well if your spirit guide is correct, then wouldn't you be better off trying to help? Maybe say you saw something, like a person being attacked, keep it vague," I said, irritation lining my voice.

"You want me to lie?" he said disgusted.

"It's not a lie," I replied. "It will attack."

"You have premonition?" Asher scoffed at me, disbelief heavy in his voice.

"No, but I can read intent in the emotions hitting me," I growled back at him. "Call the damn police you fool. Before someone gets hurt."

Dr. Stone shifted and pulled out his phone, making the call himself. "Asher's spirit guide is never wrong," he claimed. "I like being alive. I don't have a problem with a little white lie." Good to know.

I turned around and stilled myself, my ears straining at every sound, my instincts on high, though my senses were still walled up. There was a copse of trees off to my left, about fifty yards from the paved path and I felt the energy strongest from there. I wasn't sure what I was going to do, but I headed in that direction.

"What are you doing?" Asher hissed. Then he appeared as if he was listening. "My guide said you are glowing bright, what does that mean? Are you using your abilities right now?" he questioned me.

"No, I'm not using them right now, it would leave me open to attack since I can't tell what this is, I'm not a mind reader. Kindly shut up," I said, tension creeping into my voice, though I still appeared calm.

Dr. Stone was rapt with attention, his eyes glued on the trees like he had seen something. I focused my eyes there, but still didn't see anything. Out of nowhere, lightning cracked across the cloudless sky, and in that tiny moment of illumination a figure was revealed. A human one.

My hair was staticky from the bolt of lightning that had to have stuck somewhere close by and I felt it floating around my face, and then the boom of thunder rolled across the air, the sound reverberating through my chest making my bones shake. Maybe that had been the atmospheric change I had picked up on. They sky was still cloudless.

Asher and Dr. Stone forgotten, I inched my way closer to the figure, the feeling growing more intense the closer I got. The figure hadn't moved, though it felt like it was watching me intently. Unable to move forward anymore, I dropped to the ground and jabbed my fingers into the earth, seeking the energy that resided under me.

"He has a weapon Airiella," I heard Asher say somewhere behind me. I couldn't take my eyes off the figure though.

Slowly I became aware of another person behind him, the earth energy trickling into me giving it away. It was weak and small. Injured, I thought. We'd interrupted something. I said quietly to Asher behind me, "Did your guide know this was happening?"

"No, he just told me he felt we needed to go this way, he told me you would understand," Asher whispered back.

"If it, or he, whatever, comes towards me, run to get the child behind him and get out of here," I said urgently.

"What child?" Asher said, confused. "I don't see a child."

"It's behind him, I can feel it," I shot back. "Just trust me and do it."

"I'm not wearing the right shoes for this," he whined. Seriously? This is who they are testing me with?

I stood up again, wondering if I should take the risk and open my senses, when the figure moved. Most definitely a man, the guide was right about that. Not a large one though. Dirty and somewhat menacing, something dark flittering across his face. A possession? Nah, it didn't feel right. Damn it, I needed my senses, but my instincts were screaming at me not to use them.

I took another step forward and he bolted at me, the sunlight glinting off the knife in his hand. Calm flooded through me and I told Asher, "Go. Now." I saw Asher run around me to the now revealed kid as the crazy man came at me.

I easily dodged the blow and elbowed him in the back, some unnamed unknown fighting instinct in me taking over. I had no idea how I knew how to do this, but I went with it. The man fell forward and smacked his face on the ground. I heard his nose crunch and smelled the coppery tang of blood, some of it splattering on me. The second it touched my skin I got crazy dizzy and swayed, flinging my arms out for balance. What the hell was that about?

The guy rolled, swinging the arm with the knife out in a wide arc that got me on the back of my forearm, the skin splitting open and blood welling out of me and dripping on the crazy guy trying to kill me. That shit hurt. I heard the sirens getting closer and hoped they got here before he finished me off.

Asher was running back towards Dr. Stone with the kid in his arms and I felt a moment of relief before the guy beneath me started retching violently. I jumped back out of the way of his projectile vomit as the cops screamed up the street, doors slamming and people shouting as the guy flew off the ground and tackled me.

My body slammed into the ground for the second time today and my temper sparked. Without thinking I opened my senses and grabbed the violent emotion radiating from him and yanked with all my might, feeling something eerily similar to the darkness I pulled from Winnie. As the guy folded in on himself, I slammed my walls shut and tried to focus on calm.

Suddenly there were arms lifting me up and setting me upright. The world tilted and I would have toppled over if the medic hadn't been propping me up. He was wrapping my arm that was bleeding profusely and checking me over for other injuries. There was a rushing noise in my head and a blinding light that flared in front of my eyes as Winnie appeared repeating to me to just breathe. I focused on her and got myself under control to find the medic repeating, "Ma'am? Ma'am, where else are your hurt? Can you hear me?"

"I'm not old enough to be a ma'am," my voice came out all wobbly and weak sounding.

The medic bit back a smile, "Okay, now that you are back with us, can you tell me where else you are hurt?"

I shook my head at him, "I'm fine." I tried to stand up and had a sketchy moment where I thought my battered body would betray me, but it held.

"You need stitches miss," the medic gently said.

"Miss is way better than ma'am," I replied. "We have a medical team back at the office I work at, they will stitch me up," I thought quickly, trying to get out of a hospital trip.

The medic eyed me but walked with me over to Dr. Stone and a quaking Asher. He left me in their care and joined the rest of his crew looking at the kid and crazy man. The cops of course questioned me until I was ready to pass out, took my info and were then busy going over the scene.

"I told them there was medical at the office that could look at my arm. I can't handle a hospital right now, way too many emotions," I said, my strength slowly leaking out.

"We do indeed, I'll call ahead. Give me a moment please," Dr. Stone stepped away.

Asher looked at me, fear in his face. "I don't know what you are, or if I believe what my guide says," he started, "but are you mentally ill? What were you thinking?" he barked at me.

"I was thinking of an innocent child's life," I worked at tamping down my anger.

"What happened out there?" He asked, his curiosity winning out.

"I really don't know. I tried not to use my abilities, but at the end I had to, or he was going to kill me. I've got some nasty vile shit in me that needs to get released, and soon. And this arm fucking hurts," I bitched, cradling the one soaked through bandage to my chest.

"He'll have one of the healers look at it," he nodded

at Dr. Stone. Then he looked directly at Winnie hovering next to me. "There's also something odd about your friend there, I can't place it. You are either incredibly brave, or incredibly stupid. I can't decide," he muttered.

"Probably both," I replied, pain lacing my words. "Can we go now?"

He nodded stiffly and stood up, leading me surprisingly gently over to Dr. Stone. "One more thing before we have more ears, you have my vote. Your strength is amazing. My guide is in love with you, I think," he said smartly.

"Well, thanks, I think," I didn't know what to say to that. "Oh, can you suggest the priest be next please? I may need his help with this energy trying to take apart my insides."

He nodded. "My guide said it's not a demon, it's something manifested by emotions, if that helps." It didn't, but I'd take it.

They helped me back to the office and sat me down in the room with the elderly Native American, Taklishim, I think his name was. His face was alarmed as he looked me over and pulled out his medicine bag.

"She will need stitches after I am done. Please bring some water for her to drink," he said and started grinding up some herbs, dismissing Dr. Stone, who was again taking notes. He didn't leave though, so Taklishim kept working.

When water was brought in, he poured a little into the herbs and made a paste. "I need some towels, washcloth, water basin, bandages and the stuff for sutures please. Now." His tone brokered no argument from Dr. Stone or the unnamed assistant doing his bidding.

I felt another wave of nausea and dizziness hit me and gripped the table with my other hand. I felt Taklishim still and watch me. "Did it touch you?" He asked cautiously.

Struggling to remain focused enough to understand, "Did what touch me?" I questioned.

"The blood of the other," he said slowly, his eyes changing color as he looked at me. Whoa, that was weird.

"Yeah," I responded, "his blood splattered on me,

and I bled all over him. Why?"

"Your body is fighting his infection," he said angrily, turning to Dr. Stone. "You fool, this could set her back," he snarled, his voice dripping with venom.

"Whoa there buddy, back the train up. What infection, and how do you know?" Now I was worried, this nightmare just kept getting worse. Officially the worse interview I have ever had.

"My animal can smell it," he said caustically. "I bet your blood killed it in him though, he will unlikely remember anything."

I shook my head. I wasn't even going to try to understand this right now. I watched as he smeared the paste on my arm. It caused a soothing sensation, while cooling it and numbing at the same time. Relief was immediate, but the pain was still there. I looked at it and felt the feeling move up my arm, soaking into my blood.

He cleaned off my skin that had blood all over it and his eyes changed colors again as he scanned over me, then started grinding up a different set of herbs. These he mixed in a glass of water and told me to drink it. With a leap of faith, I took the cup and downed it. My stomach settled and my head cleared.

He started mixing another round of something and had me drink that as well, then he started stitching my arm up and wrapping it in gauze. When he was finished, he muttered something under his breath and an odd sensation washed over me, like a burst of energy, then he stood up and left.

My stomach rumbled in hunger and I reached for my bag to grab a banana and shoved it in my mouth as fast as I could. It was the most delicious banana I had ever eaten. Dr. stone had settled back in his chair and watched me, the psychoanalyzing still not done.

"Your heart rate and stress level elevated this time," he said. "Heart rate quite a bit more so than the stress, but still lower than most. Though to be fair, I'm pretty sure my heart rate skyrocketed, and I wasn't in the same position as you. It's very impressive I'll admit."

"So how many more today?" I dreaded the answer.

"Just one," He stood up. "I'll take you down to Father Roarke now."

Thank God. I think more holy water was in my immediate future and I wasn't looking forward to it. We went down many floors in the elevator, and I figured we were below ground somewhere. I saw Taklishim leaving a room as we stepped off the elevator. "Thank you," I told him gratefully as he walked past us. He nodded gently at me and kept going.

I'd never tell either of these men I now stood with, but I was at my limit for the day. Exhaustion was seeping into my bones and I knew that dark energy had something to do with it. As we stepped through the doors, I found myself in a church. Not quite the catholic ones I remembered from my childhood, but close enough.

The energy in me shifted and I grew nervous. I didn't want to talk about this in front of Dr. Stone. "I request privacy for this meeting, please."

Dr. Stone looked affronted, but Father Roarke nodded his head at me and turned to Dr. Stone, "It is her right." Clearly pissed off, he stormed out, slamming the door behind him.

Father Roarke waited a few minutes, then walked over and locked the door. "This room has no monitoring, and is soundproof, he can't see or hear you."

Relief swamped me and I sank to the pew behind me. "Have I got a story for you," I started. I spilled the story of my last meeting with a priest and told him about what I experienced today. Finishing up with what Asher had told me, and then what Taklishim had said.

Father Roarke looked astonished at my tale, but said, "Taklishim was just here and told me his theory. I'd have to agree with Asher, it's not a demon. And it may well be a manifestation of emotion, but I think there's more to it than that or you wouldn't have reacted to the holy water as you did."

I agreed with him, but that made this an unknown thing, and that sat heavy on my soul too. "So what does that mean for me?" I asked, resigned to whatever fate had in store for me.

"Sadly, it means since the holy water worked, we will do that again until we know more and can find a better way. In my years of dealing with the odd occult things, I've learned that salt water can be effective too. Seeing as how you need to get it out of you sooner rather than later, we won't experiment yet. Though I do want to try an additional step to maybe keep you safer," he said, thoughtful. I would have agreed to anything to keep hearing him talk.

I told him as much, and then was about as happy as I could be in the given circumstances to hear his rich laughter. He was maybe on the higher side of middle age, and not hard on the eyes. Ginger coloring, red hair, fair skin. Deep brown eyes with kindly wrinkles at the edges. I watched as he went to the pulpit and pressed a button on something, and the jolted ad the pew moved off to the side with me sitting on it.

The pews were on rotational circles that as they moved, they opened the center of the room and exposed what looked like to me a witch's circle. I must have had a befuddled expression on my face, and he told me that in some situations the priests were trained to use circles like this for protection. I wasn't about to question it. If it kept me safe, I was all for it.

There was more to this priest than met the eye, that was for sure. He excused himself to go prepare and I sat there, trying to remain calm. Winnie popped in and said, "I hope you know what you are doing. Last time was traumatic for both of us."

"I remember," my voice quiet. "This energy is vile Winnie. I'd rather drink toilet water than feel this creeping around inside me."

"I'll be here," she smiled softly at me, concern filling her eyes. "I do have to admit though; my testing was a lot less eventful than yours has been. I wouldn't have passed. You are beautiful Airy, everyone who looks at you sees you shining with it."

"Don't, not now Winnie. I can't process anymore

today." A look of sadness crossed her face and I didn't want to delve into if that look was because I didn't believe her, or because I refused to admit that I was what she claimed. I closed my eyes and waited.

It wasn't long before Father Roarke came back in, carrying a glass of holy water I assumed, a bag of something and a vial filled with a green liquid. He pulled some white candles out of the bag and placed them around the circle, lighting them and whispering a prayer in Latin. He then reached in the bag and pulled out what to me looked like a bag of weed, but I guessed was some herbs of some sort, then pulled out a bag of rock salt and sprinkled them around the circle as well.

This felt anything but holy to me, but I was out of my element here and I really wanted this crap in me gone. He then dipped his fingers in holy water by the pulpit and came over to me and said another prayer and made the sign of the cross on my forehead, which made the energy in me cramp in pain.

"In the circle," he said. I gingerly stood up and moved into the circle, then feeling unsteady, I laid on the floor. "I don't have magic lass, so I can't say that you'll be safe, but I think this will keep you safer than if we didn't use it." His voice was kind and soothing.

"I'm going to recite a couple of prayers while you drink this, I have a strong suspicion that someone up there is watching out for you," he pointed up. I didn't know if he meant in the building or heaven, and I wasn't going to ask. "Whatever this manifestation is, the circle and the prayers should keep it contained to this area within, that is why I put the herbs and salt down. The holy water should keep it from having it re-enter you," he explained gently to me.

He handed me the cup of water and I sat up to drink it as he started reciting prayers in both Latin and English. Once it was all gone, I laid back down and closed my eyes. I didn't feel anything at first, nothing like the last time, and I got scared it wasn't going to work. I opened my eyes to tell him when it hit me.

Pain roared through my body and I distantly heard

screaming again, realizing it was probably me. I went in and out of consciousness, the pain relentless in its need to take me apart. I'm sure I heard snippets of the prayers between bouts of consciousness, but I couldn't make any guarantees.

I had no idea how long the agony lasted, but I finally blacked out for good, sure I was bleeding from my eyes. I don't know how long I was out, but it wasn't long enough. Pain woke me to hear Father Roarke repeating, "Lass? Can you hear me?" And patting my cheeks.

I think I nodded, but maybe not since he kept asking. I cracked open one crusty eyelid and saw him with a bloody gash on his cheek and Winnie looking pale even for a ghost. Suddenly I was very awake as I saw how rumpled Father Roarke looked and I mistakenly tried to sit up too fast.

With a guttural cry my body gave in to the pain that tore through me and I couldn't move. "Did I do that to you?" I croaked through my hoarse voice. I motioned with my head at his face, misery flooding through me at the thought of hurting him.

"It happened because I failed to understand the level of pain you described to me from when you did this before, and I was too close. It's entirely my fault," his kind words didn't detract from me having hurt him. "Drink this, quickly now." He handed me the vial of green fluid. "Taklishim left if for you." As if that explained anything.

I downed it like a shot of tequila by a thirsty man, feeling a numbing sensation much like a shot of tequila would do, without the burn of the alcohol, spreading throughout my body. "Water," I pleaded.

"Not yet, let the medicine work first," were the gentle words I heard.

"Your arm, Airy," were the next words I heard as I lifted my arm to see blood soaking through the bandage again. This day needed to be over.

I moved around until I positioned myself in a seated position and peeled the bandage off and replaced it with the one Father Roarke silently handed me. I stood slowly and moved to a pew and plopped down ungracefully. "Was it as bad as I feel?" I asked, not caring who answered me.

I heard Winnie's quiet yes from next to me but was too tired to look at her. Father Roarke must be walking around as I heard movement and then a scraping sound in front of me. I opened my eyes again to see him sitting in a chair he had moved, and he was holding a wet washcloth to his face. I winced.

"I'm so sorry, Father." Words couldn't convey it properly.

"You my lass, have a great gift for understatement," he joked.

I blanched, "No, I truly am sorry," completely misunderstanding his statement.

He leaned forward and tipped my chin up, "I'm talking about what you described to me from last time. Not this," he pointed to his face. "If you must explain this again, please don't undervalue the pain that it puts you through. I've seen some awful things, but nothing quite like that."

His face got gravely serious. "You stopped breathing lass. I thought I had lost you. Then, you lit up with a glow that I can't even describe, but this entire room filled with love and I saw your chest fill with air again. You have been given a rare gift, or better yet, you ARE a rare gift that this world will exploit given a chance."

I shook my head in denial, but I could feel that every word he spoke was true. My walls had been shredded by this last go around and my senses were wide open. "I'm afraid I don't understand Father." My voice thick with tears I refused to let fall.

"I don't either lass, but I'm getting a better picture. You are exquisite and divine, I consider myself blessed to have been here for this. You are my hope for the future, and also my fear that it will get taken away. You must be very careful in your upcoming trials that I am sure will be coming. Never fear the darkness, lass, for you can shine brightly in any corner and expose it for what it is hiding. This will not be the last time we will speak, but rest assured I will be searching for answers in how to better help you than this. Your humble strength brings me to my knees," his eyes were shining with tears as he cupped my cheek in his hand and made the sign of the cross on my forehead again.

Winnie was sobbing noisily next to me, and I needed food and sleep. "Father, I can't find the words to tell you how much it pains me that my actions hurt you, but I am also reduced to a jumbled-up mess at the beautiful words you just gifted me. Thank you will not be enough. Though, I don't understand any of this, I will do my best to live up to your hopes. Right now, I find myself lacking much of the strength you say you see, but I will take my leave and hope for a brighter tomorrow."

I stood bracing myself against the pew for a moment. He stood with me, "Wee lass, think about this for me please. The fact that you can offer me hope, without understanding, stand after that ordeal, without assistance, and carry on this path you find yourself on, without knowing what awaits you, that my child, is strength."

I didn't care if it was proper or not, I hugged him. Then turned as quickly as I could and left the room for the elevator. Dr. Stone waiting in the hall, and I inwardly groaned. "What I find amazing is that your heart rate tracker stopped working for five minutes while you were in there, care to explain that?" he asked as I got in the elevator, his tone impervious.

"Nope, I don't care to explain it. All I care about now, is eating and sleeping," my voice harsh.

"The car is waiting to take you back," he said as the elevator opened at the ground floor. Dusk just setting. How was it only just now dusk? It felt like today had been three days. "The car will pick you up at 7:00 am tomorrow," he called after me. I gave him a thumbs up and kept walking, feeling shattered.

"Hotel please," I said to the driver and passed out.

Chapter Thirteen

Winnie watched in horror as Airy passed out in the car, unable to get the attention of the driver or to help her. She started to panic, worried about the energy exertion Airy had used, the battering her body had taken, the blood loss, lack of food, the list went on and on and added up to nothing good. And the testing was going to continue tomorrow. She shuddered thinking of what would happen next.

The car stopped and the driver noticed Airy slumped over. Concerned she watched him bolt out of the car and try to wake her. She was out. Winnie yelled in her ear, trying to help, but no response. The driver carefully lifted her out of the back and carried her inside the lobby, asking the front desk to please help him get her to her room.

Winnie almost laughed as the front desk clerk took in the bloody clothes and battered appearance and gave the driver a look of disbelief and lack of trust. She insisted on calling security to escort him to the room to ensure Airy was safely inside. Winnie was grateful for the extra care shown.

See Me

Once Airy was safely placed on the bed and the driver out of the room, security shut her in and left. She sat there keeping an eye on her, but the worry not diminishing at all. She cursed at her lack of ability to communicate clearly with anyone else. Making songs play on the guys phones would not convey this.

Suddenly she noticed Airy moving. She got up dazed, moved stiffly and stripped her clothes and got in the shower. Maybe all was okay, Winnie started to think. Then she heard deep wracking sobs coming from the shower. All was not okay. She popped out and into one of the guys rooms, she didn't know which one. She saw Aedan playing with an Ovilus and Mags curled up on a sofa reading.

The Ovilus would work, but Aedan wouldn't get it, she needed Smitty or Ronnie. An idea came to her and she played with the device on her side of the veil separating them and the device spoke, "Art."

Aedan started, dropping it in surprise and Mags looked up. "Did that just say Art?" she asked.

"Sure did," Aedan said, confusion coloring his face. It was a start, she had their attention.

Winnie played with it again, and got it to speak two words, "Need" then "Art".

Mags jumped, her book forgotten. "Holy shit Aedan!"

"Yep," he looked at her in amazement.

"I'm getting the guys," she yelled behind her as she ran out of the room.

Winnie was excited it was working and clapped as Ronnie and Jax ran into the room followed by Mags. She played with the device again and got it to say "Air" and "Bad" but that didn't get the message across. They were all confused.

Her mind racing, she tried again. "Angel, need, help" it spoke, and Ronnie jolted.

"It's Winnie," he stated. Mags and Aedan staring at him like he was crazy.

Smitty carefully said out loud, "Airiella needs help?"

Yes! Winnie knew he'd get it. She made the device

178

say yes.

"Is she in her room?" Ronnie trying to narrow it down, standing like he was ready to bolt to her rescue.

Winnie made it say yes again, knowing now that they would help her. Ronnie started to go but Smitty pulled him back. Mags and Aedan still staring, dumbstruck.

"Winnie, should we go, or should Mags go?" Smitty turned to Ronnie, "She might not need someone with a penis around her right now, dude. We don't know what she went through today."

She thought about it and understood what he was getting at. While Airy would enjoy their being there, she would not like them seeing her like that. She manipulated the machine until it said, "Magenta."

The guys all looked at Mags, who just nodded and asked Smitty what room, then left. Winnie felt a wave of relief. And went back to Airy.

That had been Mags first experience with what the guys called an intelligent spirit. It was exhilarating, but unnerving at the same time. Smitty and Ronnie had filled Aedan in on Airiella, sharing their impressions and wonder at their reactions to her. Mags was sure she would like her but had no idea what was wrong enough to send a ghost seeking help.

She knocked on the door and waited. Pressing her ear to the door she could hear movement and knocked gently again, then heard a shuffling sound. The door opened and Mags gasped in shock at the sight. This girl indeed needed help. Mags jumped forward as she started to drop, like she had no bones.

She helped her back to the and sat her down. "Hi there, my name is Mags, short for Magenta. My parents were horrible at names," she chattered, giving her time to check this poor girl out. "I'm Aedan's wife, you haven't met him yet. But he just got a stunning message on one of his devices that you needed help, so here I am."

"I'm not at my best," her voice was rough and weak. "I'm Airiella, please call me Airy," her voice nothing but a whisper by then. Mags heard her stomach growl.

"Are you hungry? Don't talk, just nod," she prodded. Airy nodded and Mags got up to grab the room service menu and bring it back. "Okay love, point to what sounds good," she instructed.

Airy pointed to a grilled cheese sandwich, french fries, a cup of soup, and chocolate cake. Mags chuckled, she chose all comfort foods. This girl needed some love. Mags ordered the food and had them add chamomile tea, some honey and lemon.

She went back to Airy and got her back in bed, tucked in and propped up. "Don't talk until after you eat and drink the tea I ordered. Your throat needs some rest," Mags ordered sweetly. Airy smiled at her, not a huge smile, but she saw what Ronnie and Smitty meant about a draw. She felt the overwhelming need to protect her. "I'd love to hear about your day, but right now, I am just going to provide some TLC, okay?"

Airy nodded and sagged again. Mags sat next to Airy and pulled her into her body to just hold her. Airy's body shook as silent sobs claimed her. Mags fought back her own tears as she realized just how deep whatever it was that shook her up was. Airy curled up into Mags and just cried.

Mags stroked her still damp hair, checked the bandage on her arm, cataloged the bruises she could see, and silently cursed the council that pushed her this far. There was a knock on the door and Mags eased out from under Airy and let the room service in. When he left, she helped her up and over to the table, set the food in front of her and prepped the tea while Airy started eating. It was slow going but she was keeping it down.

Mags brought the still steaming tea over to her and plopped an ice cube in it, so she didn't burn her mouth. She felt like one of those helicopter parents just hovering around, but Airy wasn't her kid. She just wanted to anticipate any of the needs she had. She felt so bad for her right now.

She was beautiful, even in her misery. She was pale

right now, washed out looking like she'd been running on empty too long. Dark circles rimmed her bloodshot eyes, and they were swollen from crying. Despite all that, she exuded strength and a sense of love that just made you feel like she was happy to be in your presence. It was a surreal feeling. Something not of this world.

Mags saw Airiella finish her tea and noticed that she had ate all her food. This was a good sign. She smiled softly at her, hoping she wouldn't push her out the door yet. Mags got up and sat down at the table next to her. "Feeling better?"

Airy moved her lips in a semblance of a smile and nodded. "Thank you. You kind of saved me there." Her voice still raw sounding, but better.

"Are you sick?" Mags gestured at her throat.

"No, it happens as a byproduct of trying to rid myself of a certain type of energy. So, Winnie huh? She communicated somehow?" Airy changed the subject.

"I have to say; my heart was racing when I realized someone from the other side was actually talking to us. It was my first time being a part of that. I was half excited, half scared out of my mind," Mags said, a tremor of excitement running through her voice. "Though I am really glad that I was there and could now be here to help. I thought Ronnie was going to bust straight through the door to get out here when he realized the message was about you."

Airy blushed. "I'm glad it was you, I would have been so embarrassed for Smitty or Ronnie to see me like this." She shook her head. "Actually, I am embarrassed for anyone to see me like this. It's what I call my aftershock period. I'm calm during intense situations, and then once I'm alone, the adrenaline, fear or whatever hits me. I think everything that happened over the past couple of weeks has just caught up to me. Maybe, I don't know."

Mags stayed silent, getting the feel she wasn't done, and started clearing the table off to put the dishes out in the hall for room service to pick back up. She also started making another cup of tea for Airy. "Well if you need to talk, I am at your disposal," Mags decided to lead with as she walked back to Airy with the cup of tea.

"I'm awful about opening up to others," she started, "it's something I've been working on, but there are so few that I trust, that working on it becomes hard. I have to be selective about what I open up to others with because I don't trust them with some areas. It's exhausting. My usual MO is just to deal with things in my own way. This," she pointed at Mags, "is something that wouldn't have happened at home. I probably wouldn't have even answered my door."

"I can understand that, and I know that words are cheap, but I can assure you that I am trustworthy. The only time I would ever betray a trust is if I thought your life was in danger, and even then, I would try to find a way to help without breaking that. As a female, I've had my trust broken by too many people and often find myself in the same boat as you. It wasn't until Aedan that I started letting people in. At first it was only him, now, slowly, the other guys I let in too," Mags admitted.

"I already figured out that you were trustworthy," Airy smiled, "or I don't think Winnie would have sent you. I'll give you a brief rundown of my day minus certain aspects of it that I haven't come to terms with myself."

Mags nodded, it sounded fair. And she sat there and listened to the astonishing tale that this girl had lived just in this day. But when she finished with her day, she told Mags about her life, what brought her here, how she met Winnie, her reactions to the guys. Mags was stunned silent. She cleared her throat and said the first thing that came to her mind, "Sex is a great stress reliever."

Airy burst out laughing and the sight of the joy on her face settled on Mags like a blanket of softness. She grinned, "Mags, did you just proposition me?"

Startled at the question, Mags blinked her eyes, "Well no, but now that you mention it my fantasy has always been to be with a woman and my husband at the same time." She thought about it and then added, "But I think the penetration would have to be with me only, I don't share well."

Airy's clear happy laugh filled the room again and Mags couldn't help but smile too. "I've never been with a woman myself, but if I were to try, I'd pick you, you're gorgeous," Airy said.

Now Mags blushed and tried to turn the argument around, "Have you seen you?"

Airy replied, "Every day I see me. But let me tell you what I see when I look at you. Confidence, strength, compassion, bravery and love. What you look like on the outside doesn't matter to me. What I can see shining from your eyes and your soul is what matters most. Your outsides happen to match what I see within you. You are tall, willowy with that runners frame. Your blonde hair is amazing with the magenta ends on it. Your eyes are a deep brown that see way more than you admit. Your ass, it's just perfect," Airy said with a smirk.

With that, Mags just fell head over heels in love with Airiella. Tears sprung up in her eyes and she tried to laugh them off and smartly replied, "Well your boobs are perfect, so we're even." They both doubled over in laughter howling until their stomachs hurt.

Airy dragged herself back over to the bed. "I'm wrecked. I'm sorry, I need to sleep," she apologized.

"No need to apologize, after the day you had, I'd be comatose on the floor," Mags told her. "Need anything else or should I just go?"

Airy blushed again, "Would you mind staying? I just don't want to be alone right now," she said shyly.

"Oh sweets, of course I'll stay. I'll text Aedan and tell him I'll be here for the night," Mags pulled out her phone and started typing a text.

"I'm going to stay the night here with her tonight," Mags wrote.

"Everything okay?" Aedan responded. "Ronnie is driving me crazy."

"She said she didn't want to be alone, she's had quite the day. By the way, my fantasy? She might be the one."

"I don't know what to say to that."

"You'll get it when you meet her," Mags replied mysteriously.

"Is that what you are staying for tonight? Because I just got excited."

"No. She genuinely just needs someone to be here."

"If you need anything shoot me a text. We all can help."

"I know. I love you."

"Love you Babe," Aedan sent.

"All set," she told Airy. "I'll lay down on the couch here. Just let me know if you need anything."

"Please, no. Up here with me. Though I do need to warn you, since my energy dump earlier, my skin is really irritated for some reason and I need to pull my nightshirt off. If that makes you uncomfortable, I'll deal with it," she said looking down at her hands. "I promise, I'm not coming on to you."

Mags laughed. "I'm fine with nudity. Are you sure you want me that close?"

Airy nodded, "I'm just feeling raw. My walls are down, my skin feels weird, I have zero energy, I can't process any of these thoughts. Sleeping between Ronnie and Smitty last night was the best night of sleep I have had in years. I could really use that. If any of this makes you uncomfortable you can send them in."

"I'm honored that you asked me Airy, just relax," Mags said, pulling off her jeans and climbing in the bed. Airy smiled weakly at her and pulled off her night shirt and rolled onto her side. "I'm going to touch you, just a forewarning. When I feel like that, I find human touch soothes me."

Airy nodded her head, then looked back over her shoulder, "I haven't forgotten about your fantasy, and I'm intrigued enough to want to help you. But just not tonight, I'd like to have enough energy to enjoy it."

Mags sucked a breath in, "Deal. Let me give you a goodnight kiss." Mags leaned over and brushed her lips lightly over Airy's and groaned at the spark that happened from the contact.

"Same thing happened with skin to skin contact with Smitty and Ronnie," she told Mags. "Not sure what it means. Winnie said it's a bond. Guess we are bonded now too," her voice getting sleepier. "Goodnight."

Just like that she was out. Mags looked at the bruises all over her back and gently stroked her skin, feeling the tingle that ripped through her body at the contact. She kept up the stroking until Airy's breathing got deep and even, and then she wrapped her arm around her and spooned her. A feeling of contentment washing over her and carrying her off to sleep too.

Since earlier in the day Ronnie had been feeling out of place, jittery and had a variety of emotions roll through him. He didn't make the connection until Smitty said something similar was happening to him and he remembered the feeling they had when they touched. He was feeling her emotions to a degree, where he felt something was off, but he didn't know how bad it was.

After Mags left, he tried tapping in to it, but it almost felt like the connection wasn't complete yet. He didn't know a whole lot about this stuff, but his mind was racing trying to think of everything that could have gone wrong. He'd been itching for Mags to come back so he could grill her and then go see her.

When Aedan said Mags was staying the night, he got more worried. He kept looking at Smitty to see if he was on the same train of thought. Smitty finally said, "Stop staring at me. Yes, I'm worried, but if Mags needed help, she would ask. Or Aedan would have freaked out."

Ronnie nodded, knowing it was true, but it didn't stop him from worrying. It wasn't until he had gotten a text from Dave, one of the producers that he freaked out a little bit. "That girl is the real deal," it said. "It made the news. She got through three tests today. Offsite tomorrow."

Ronnie showed the text to Smitty and they turned the TV on looking for a local news show and watched as the breaking news talked about a child abduction gone wrong and the tourist who saved the day. The shots only showed Airiella being interviewed by the police, but she was covered in dirt and blood with a medic tending to her arm.

"What the fuck?" hissed Smitty.

"No shit, she's covered in blood. What kind of testing did they do? Who is that with her, Asher?" Ronnie growled reaching for his phone.

"Yep, but you know he won't reveal anything," Smitty argued pulling the phone out of his hand. "Save it for a face to face so you can get a feel for something."

Ronnie acknowledged that with a flick of his hand and went to stare out the window at the night. He was trying to work out if he'd be able to go on the tests tomorrow, however he knew it would be pointless to ask. The offsite ones Dr. Stone wasn't even allowed to go on. The tribes were secretive. Maybe instead he would spend the day grilling the others. He'd think of something.

"Let's grab the other guys and go eat something," Ronnie said, needing to move.

Chapter Fourteen

I woke up with a hand on my boob and was confused until I looked over my shoulder and saw Mags. My aftershock came rushing back to me and I winced knowing I had told a stranger all my secrets. Well, almost all of them. The angel thing I kept under wraps. Noting that the sensation wasn't unpleasant I left her hand there and just enjoyed the comfort for a moment.

I knew today was going to suck just as much as yesterday, and I wanted to get more food in me. I didn't feel like my energy was fully restored yet. I gently pulled away trying not to wake Mags and touched my lips as I remember she kissed me. Hmm, was I brave enough to experiment with a female? I had to figure I was considering it, as I had asked her to stay.

I shrugged and got dressed and checked the wound on my arm as I got ready for the day. Whatever poultice Taklishim had used was a miracle, it had scabbed up already, but it still hurt bad. I scrawled out a quick note for Mags thanking her for her help and staying last night and left it next to her jeans, so she'd see it. I grabbed my purse and snuck out.

SEE ME

As I was pulling my door closed, I head a throat clear behind me and I jumped. Ronnie and Smitty were standing there leaning against the wall waiting for me apparently. Smitty gently took my chin in his hand and looked at my face, noting a few bruises, while Ronnie took my arm and checked it over. Thank God my clothes were covering the rest of the bruises or this would take all day.

"I'm fine," I told them, "but I'm starving." Smitty pulled me into a hug, tight, but not painful and it felt so good that I forgot about food. I melted into his body.

"We saw you on the news," he said into my hair, then pulled back and looked right into my eyes where I promptly drowned. Then he kissed me, his lips soft against mine and that connection flared to life and burned through me fast. I groaned and opened to give his tongue permission and I swear my bones melted. He tasted like cinnamon. Too soon he pulled away, his breathing ragged and his eyes dark with need. I wanted to drag him to the floor and continue.

He had stepped back and suddenly my vision was filled with Ronnie. "Angel," he moaned and crushed his mouth to mine. Where Smitty had been soft, Ronnie was hard, and the connection burned even hotter and I tried to mold myself to him to absorb more. He ground himself against me and I suddenly hated clothes. Ronnie's tongue sweeping my mouth insistently. He tasted like raspberry.

These two were going to undo me right here in the hallway, and then he was gone, and I felt dazed. That was definitely a good way to start the morning. I touched my swollen lips and ran my tongue over them, tasting both cinnamon and raspberry. Jeez, it was hot in the hallway.

Knowing I couldn't pull it off, but I did it anyway, I smiled wickedly at the both and sashayed past them to hit the elevator button. In my lust filled eyes, I completely missed and stabbed the wall instead. That was how well I pulled off that move. I heard Smitty laugh behind me.

"Baby girl, we will join you in a moment, as soon as our pants un-tent," he joked.

There was no way I could keep my eyes forward

after that. I turned around, and sure enough, both stood there, unashamed with their pants sporting a good size tent. I flushed but couldn't stop that smile that came on my face. Totally worth it. Whoever I was around these men and Mags was someone I wasn't familiar with.

I hopped in the elevator before I could do something stupid and managed to stab the buttons to take me to the lobby so I could get food in the hope that I survived today better than I had yesterday. I walked into the dining room and immediately lost my grin and man candy high.

Jax felt her walk in. He didn't even have to turn around to know it was whoever they had called to interview. He felt it. Every cell in his body was drawn to her. She called to him in a way he had never felt before and the darkness in him revolted. He was going to look like an idiot if he didn't move. He continued down the line, pretending he didn't notice her presence. Every step he took that brought him farther away from her felt like he was killing all that was good in life while at the same time the farther he got the more the darkness eased. His body was at war with itself. His limbs started shaking as anger in him shifted.

Unable to fight off the urge anymore he turned to face her. Instantly, the darkness swallowed him whole, the plate dropping to the ground, food flying, glass shattering, and her. She was fucking glowing. This bright light that the darkness hated. It despised her. Jax fought hard for control, he couldn't cause a scene here, there were too many people, and he didn't want to hurt her. Himself as a person that is, the darkness in him wanted to rip her to pieces and then burn them to a crisp.

Inch by excruciating inch he fought his way back and stalked over to her, the darkness boiling under the surface of his skin, driving him mad. "You will never beat it, best me, or tempt me with your seductive body," he growled at her. "Prepare for war."

She looked at him with wide eyes and looked insulted. Then reached out to his face and he instinctively recoiled, fear gripping him tight, an odd sensation flicking over his skin. She moved with him though, her fingers tracing a path down his cheek. At her touch something flared to life within him and the darkness receded enough for him to regain full control. He stared at her in amazement as he took in her shocked expression, he knew she felt it too.

"What the fuck just happened?" he whispered dramatically.

She dragged her finger down his cheek more and slipped it under his chin, stood on her toes and said breathlessly in his ear, "If I was trying to seduce you honey, you'd know. I walk my talk." And she walked away, turning after a couple of feet, "Oh, and tell that shit in you, it was nice meeting it."

He saw her trembling, so he knew it was partially an act, but still. The combo of her and that darkness in him was dangerous, and how she overcame it with a touch was beyond his comprehension. He was terrified as he walked fast out of that room, flying past Smitty and Ronnie without even seeing them. Shit just got real.

I was shaking. I picked up the large pieces of broken plate off the floor as someone from the kitchen crew came running out to clean up the mess. That was one hell of an introduction. I grabbed a plate and mindlessly loaded food on it, not even paying attention to what I grabbed and sat down.

I jumped at the sound of a voice behind me and saw it was Smitty, concern etched on his face. "Um, everything okay?" I saw Ronnie standing in the doorway looking between Jax's retreating figure and us.

"Well I just met your illustrious leader, kind of," I muttered and stuck food in my mouth. I don't even know what it was, it was all tasteless now.

"The food on the floor and broken plate was him?" Smitty tried to piece it together. I nodded. "He knew who you were?"

"Well when I walked in, he froze, didn't even look at

me. When he did turn around the plate dropped and he accused me of trying to seduce him and that I couldn't beat him or best him," a little shame washed over me at my own reaction.

Smitty had a stunned look on his face. "He doesn't even know your name, but he knew it was you. I get how you knew who he was, you've seen him on TV," he worked it out in his head. "Did you feel anything?"

"We had a pretty damn strong connection between us. I may have pushed him a little, but I could see the darkness trying to take over, his face kept changing and I could feel it in him trying to break free. No doubt that it doesn't like me."

"He must have felt you come in the room, you have a certain presence about you," Smitty talked through it. "You pushed him? Physically?"

I laughed at that thought. "No, verbally. I got pissed after the seduction comment and ran my fingers over his face, that's when I felt the connection. But I also may have said something along the lines of he'd know if I was seducing him because I walk my talk." Blushing, I shoved more food in my mouth as Smitty roared in laughter.

Ronnie came over at that and Smitty filled him in, making Ronnie laugh too. "You can certainly hold your own with him," Ronnie declared and left to go get food. Smitty followed behind, still laughing. I kept shoveling food in my mouth

They came back and ate like normal people while I rushed, realizing my time was shorter than it had been the day before. Smitty put a few granola bars in front of me to take with me and asked me for my cell phone. I handed it over without a thought as I put the bars in my purse and pushed my now empty plate away. He handed my phone back and I dropped that in my purse too.

"I programmed our cell numbers in there. When you get back today, let one of us know. Also, let us know if you need help," Smitty chastised, his blue eyes sparkling pools I wanted to drown in. I nodded mindlessly, not sure where my head was. I saw Ronnie nod behind me and glanced back to see the driver standing there.

"Off to another fun filled day of hellish crap," I mumbled. Smitty gave my hand a squeeze before I walked off. To my surprise we went to the same building as I was at yesterday and I was led back upstairs to the same room.

Dr. Stone was there, looking furious, which I admit, made me slightly happy. "Good morning Airiella, I trust you slept well?" He didn't pause to let me answer. "I will not be going with today, but each of the members will be debriefing me when they return. We will meet tomorrow morning again for a recap to see where things stand. You will be taking a helicopter with the remaining members to a mountain cabin today where the tests will be concluded. Do you have any questions?"

A helicopter? I was excited now. I shook my head no and stayed silent though. Father Roarke walked in right then and ignored Dr. Stone to head over to me. He handed me a card in a subtle move as he shook my hand and asked if I was alright. I nodded that I was, and he left. A befuddled Dr. Stone looking at him as he left, and I palmed the card and slid it in my pocket out of sight.

Dr. Stone gave me a questioning look to which I ignored and smiled. Pompous jerk. Taklishim got up and walked over to me, gesturing at me to follow him. As I got up so did the remaining council members and we all went out onto the roof where a big helicopter sat.

The pilot got us all loaded up, buckled in and ear safety on and started the rotors up. Exhilaration shot through me, I'd always wanted to go on a helicopter ride. As we lifted off and flew over the city, my head was glued to the window, watching everything pass underneath us. I wasn't a fan of heights, but I loved this.

I watched the city fade into rocky terrain and mountainous landscape, and I felt something shift inside me at the thought that I would be in nature, a more comfortable element for me, less emotions of random people to pick up on. I smiled at the beauty that reminded me of home. Rivers glinted off the morning sunlight, small hidden lakes sparkled in bright blue tones. I loved it.

I suddenly remembered the card in my pocket and without Dr. Stone here to see, I pulled it out and looked at it. It was a business card for Father Roarke with his cell number on it. I glanced at the back of it and saw he had written a message on it for me. "Lass, I have more information for you, call me at your earliest convenience. I'm actively searching for more in the meantime." He signed it Roarke.

The good of the day, so far, outweighed the bad with Jax in the dining room. I put all my attention into the happy feelings and just lost myself in the landscape below me, ignoring everyone else on the helicopter. Until we landed, it was just me, the landscape and my happiness.

Kalisha came up to me once we were all out of the helicopter and it was safely out of the way. "You will be with me first," she said, her accent captivating and her beauty oddly alluring. I nodded at her and reinforced my walls before following her to a large wooden log house. Hardly a cabin, closer to a lodge. There was smoke coming from a couple of chimney stacks on the roof already which meant it was warm, compared to the bitter chill of the mountain air. Oh, but that fresh crisp air lifted my soul.

Taklishim brought me over a heavy fleece lined jacket that I was thankful for and immediately put on. He then handed me some lined boots that were too big but were much warmer than my tennis shoes. I gave him my heartfelt thanks and buried my icy hands in the pocket of the jacket and followed Kalisha.

Chapter Fifteen

K alisha led me off to the side of the house into a dense forest area, but she kept walking in an almost straight line until we came to a quiet clearing. There was a rug on the ground and a small fire pit in an area that was free of grass, weeds or plants, it was just dirt. There was a distinct feel of energy here that I could feel without my senses being opened and it hummed through me.

"Airiella, sit please," she told me, pointing to the rug, her voice was light and musical. I was thankful the coat was long because that rug and my thin leggings weren't going to keep me from freezing to the cold ground. I sat down and watched her light a fire in the pit. I was really looking forward to my time with Kalisha. I didn't know very much about hoodoo, only what popular myth said.

Kalisha settled down in front of me, both of us an equal distance to the fire, the warmth already seeping into me. She gazed at me in silence like she was expecting something from me. Since I didn't know what, I just sat there and took in her beauty. She wore bright colors in what I had always assumed was traditional African clothing, but instead of sarongs, she had on a type of pants and long-sleeved shirt on under a coat.

Her hair was long, black and dreadlocked. At the meeting yesterday, she had the dreads pulled back in a band, today they were loose around her face and I noticed some beads in some of them. Her face was narrow, skin ebony dark that glowed with life. There was a pink tint to her cheeks, and her plump lips. She had a straight nose, a small piercing on the left nostril. She wore no makeup that I could see but had thick eyelashes that curled perfectly and framed deep charcoal colored eyes that glimmered with a sparkle when the sunlight hit them. Her cheekbones were high and defined, but not sharp. Her neck was long and graceful, her ears plain with no piercings or adornments.

She had on a necklace that had some charms hanging off it, as well as some on her wrists as well. Her hands were long with slender fingers. She was taller than me, gracefully slender and moved like a gazelle. She also had that nice round butt giving her a very sensual look, coupled with high rounded breasts. She smelled of cocoa butter and an earthy scent I couldn't place.

"My name, Kalisha," she started, "it means sorceress. I come from Ghana, a city called Sunyani. It's clean there, and I live on the edges near the Ashanti Uplands. It's a beautiful forest area filled with life and energy. Mystery and spirits." Her voice and accent had me riveted. "In hoodoo, the guardians of the forest taught us about the plants around us, to help us heal. Those guardians we call Azzizas. From them we learned how to heal our tribes and conjure the spirits to help us fight what you here call evil."

"You don't believe in evil?"

She ignored me. "Today I am going to teach you some of our ways. You learning is my test. I can already see in you what I need to see. You are rare, a gift to us. I want to help you learn how to protect your tribe."

"Thank you Kalisha, I am eager to learn," I bowed my head to her.

"In hoodoo, there is no evil. There is good, and there is bad. It is determined by what you wish to accomplish with the conjuring or poultice you make. If your intent is not set and a mix you made caused someone harm, then it is bad. If your intent is to harm and it comes to fruition, that is bad. If what you conjure has intent to harm, it is bad. Now if you conjure something bad to help you do something good, that is different. But it always has a cost. As above, so below," she said.

As above, so below. I had heard that before. "So, if it happens here, on this plane, it happens on the other side too?" She nodded at me.

"A priestess of hoodoo can be anyone that practices it, but only a few of us have powers. Some things I cannot tell you about. Legba is a spirit that is a messenger for the gods. He delivers messages to me that allow me to help in ways that others can't. But if I conjure him to ask for help, I must pay him. The most common form of payment is rum, they all want blood as well. Therefore so many people over here think hoodoo is dark magic. They don't understand we don't bring the dark, it's already here."

I nodded my agreement, it was one of the problems I had with organized religion. There were too many double standards that allowed ignorance and hate to breed.

"In hoodoo," she continued, "we use the earth and it's gifts to us, minerals, plants, animals, water to make medicine, or Gbo," she pointed to her charms on her necklace and bracelet. She reached into the pack she had carried with her and handed me a small pouch, maybe the size of two fists. "Please open it," she instructed me.

I opened it and pulled out a book of Psalms, and various containers of herbs, and an amulet and stone. I held them in my hands and looked at her with a question in my eyes.

"We use the book when we feel something is wrong and we read a psalm. Your Moses, to us he was a Mountain Man. He performed much magic, and he freed the slaves. When you need the psalm, it will help you. Read them. The amulet I made for you to wear as protection from the bad. You have too much power in you for the amulet to stop it, but it will help. The stone we are going to use today and make a talisman, what we call Gbo. This Gbo will be for you to use to help absorb some of that energy you take, and it will be purified in this stone. It is not an easy task to make this. Also, because your own power is so strong, what this will hold will seem like very little in comparison. It is just meant to help in a fast moment of need. What I teach you today, you will be able to recharge it for use again but you will have to do a cleansing ritual as well."

Kalisha pulled out some candles and herbs from her bag, a knife, some water and a bowl. Then she pulled out some more stones and set it all in front of her. "The priest, he showed you a circle, yes?"

I nodded, "Are we doing one here too? Will you teach me how to do that?"

"Aminda will teach you the circle, but I am going to put one up since I need to conjure a spirit to help me." She stood up and began placing candles in particular positions and quietly chanting, and then she spread some salt and herbs around them. "Salt injures the bad energy, it can't cross the salt lines. Some energy the salt can kill. If you are near a sea and need help, simply sitting in the water, or dunking yourself can cleanse you, restore you. It carries great power."

"But won't the bad energy infect the water and harm the life it contains?" I asked.

"Not salt water. The salt cleanses the bad leaving only good. Fresh water, yes, it can leave the bad intact sometimes. It depends on the energy," she explained. "Water can be very powerful, it magnifies things. Makes it stronger, or makes it weaker, it can heal, it can kill."

I told her about my experience with the river and how the wildlife got infected and how I needed to go back and pull the energy back in, and then what happened with the holy water. She listened carefully and had a somewhat astonished look on her face.

"You can do this? Pull the energy from water, from animals?" I nodded. "You are indeed rare. It tells me a little bit about this energy that you will be dealing with. I understand it has affected one of the tribe that you will be joining." I nodded again. "It's strong and sentient then. The flowing water didn't dilute it like it should have. It stayed together. But the holy water destroyed it." She paced looking thoughtful.

"Does that mean that salt water will not work?" hoping like crazy it would.

"That would still work, though it does lead me to believe that it might still be painful for you to some degree. Water itself holds a certain energy, it's filled with life. Salt water holds even more. Holy water is water conjured with a holy spirit, the spirit is essentially in the water. I believe that means that the spirit in the water is what cleansed the energy in you. Salt water may take a little longer to work since that will be outside your body, while holy water you take inside you where the energy resides," she gestured to her middle, thinking out loud.

She was knowledgeable and I was soaking it up. As far as I was concerned any information and brainstorming was welcome since I didn't know the first thing about what I was dealing with other than how it felt inside me, and when it left me.

"We are going to make two stones," she decided, pulling what looked to me like a gemstone of some sort from her bag. "This stone has grounding properties as well as protection properties. We will conjure Damballah and Ezrulie. I will need a sweet dessert and a piece of silver," she said to herself rooting through her bag again and pulling out a silver chain and a wrapped cupcake. "This second stone we will be asking Ezrulie to bless with an abundance of love, which you embody, and to allow that love to flow through the stone to the holder of it. Damballah we will ask to bless the stone with his love of the earth and all that reside on it and allow the pure energy to flow through to the holder. Both will take us some time."

"So how do I use them then?" I wondered.

"You will hold them, feel for the energy in them and allow it to release. Like what you describe doing when you let go of the energy you need to cleanse out of you. To recharge them, you will need to feed your energy into them under the moon and burn sage to clean it," she told me.

"How can I help you?" I desperately wanted to be a part of this.

"First you need to open yourself to the area, allow the energy to flow through you, and you to flow through the energy. Ground yourself to the earth and let love flow," she spoke, her tone light. I dropped my walls and opened myself, feeling the ground below me and allowing the energy to fill me and seep back in. "You glow," wonderment filled her musical words. "Legba has touched you already."

She handed me the bowl and a rock. "Use this rock and crush these herbs into a fine powder," she told me and handed me a bag filled with different little baggies of herbs in it. "As you crush the herbs, feel the energy they release, and seek out what they contain. Feel their power in your blood as you breathe in the scent."

That was a bit more mystical than what I was used to, and I divided my attention. Part of me maintaining control of the energy flowing between me and the earth, and the other now focused on the herbs I was crushing. I was starting to pick up on the energy they contained and felt a buzz in my veins as I crushed them.

"Chale," Kalisha spoke, "I can feel Ezrulie." She looked at me and gasped.

Confused, "Chale? What is that?" I didn't know what was happening.

"You have Ezrulie's blessing," she said. "It's in your glow."

"Um, okay, but what is chale?"

Distracted, she replied, "It means friend."

I had the herbs crushed into a fine powder now and handed them back to her. She went about mixing something else into them and chanting. I felt the air around me change and sat absolutely still, my eyes glued to the chanting priestess in front of me.

It looked like the very air around her was vibrating, which didn't make sense to me because you couldn't see air, and then I saw out of the corner of my eye, all the candles around us light up. I was most definitely in the presence of something I didn't understand as I felt energy being drawn from me.

Kalisha got up and placed the silver and cupcake on the other side of the fire pit. "They are here chale, show respect," she told me reverently.

Kalisha spoke rapidly in a language I couldn't identify as she bent in supplication facing away from me. Suddenly I saw them, two figures in front of her, a man and a woman. The woman was pale, ethereal and stunning. Wearing a pink and white dress and adorned with gold jewels. She smiled at me and I felt love fill my body. "You have the power of Balianne," she said to me.

I bowed graciously now knowing what else to do. "Thank you."

The man shone as all white, I couldn't depict any specific features, but he moved like a snake. I did my best not to recoil and watched as they both picked up the stones that Kalisha had laid before them. They flared bright and then they put them down again. I heard a hissing sound and watched in rapt attention as Kalisha pulled out her knife and slashed open her hand, bleeding over the rocks and down into the earth.

She motioned me forward and I figured I wasn't going to like this much as she took my hand and did the same thing. Our blood combined in the soil beneath the stones, a new energy pulsing in the air. The blood on the stones vanished as if it had never been, and in a flash the cupcake and silver were both gone, along with the figures.

Kalisha pressed herbs into my palm and the gash healed before my eyes. She did the same to hers, and then all the candles went out. "Our offerings were accepted, and blessings bestowed. The gods favor you."

She stood up and motioned for me to pick up the stones. I picked them up and held them in my palms, one in each hand. They felt alive. "Those are very powerful, treasure them, keep them safe from those that would wish to use them for bad."

I walked back over to the rug and went to put them in the pouch and Kalisha stopped me. "Not in there, they must be kept separate." She pulled another silver chain and some wire and started weaving the wire around one of the stones and attached it to the chain, which she then fastened to my wrist. She used more wire and twisted it around the other stone and connected it to the chain that the amulet was on and handed it back to me. I put it around my neck and tucked it in under my shirt. She nodded in approval.

"Remember, to use them, direct your energy to the stone, feel it and release it." She reached into her bag and pulled out a bottle of rum. "I'm going to leave extra, maybe Legba is thirsty." She placed the rum in the same spots our blood had spilled and then started packing up everything.

I unrooted myself from where I stood and scrambled to help her. I had no idea how long we had been here, or that I was even sure what had just taken place was real. The energy in the stones was unmistakable though. We got everything packed up and I looked around to made sure we left nothing there.

She looked at me, "Your path is difficult, but you have the spirit of a warrior who fights for love. The power of that is unbeatable. You need to remember that. Use the psalms. Carry that bag with you always," she pointed to the pouch she gave me. "Remember what we did here today. You will know when you need to use it. You have my support," she tapped on the amulet and stone on the necklace. "My blood is powerful, yours even more so."

We started walking back and she turned to me again. "I notice you often are between two worlds, don't let them make you choose." She tapped my head, "Protect yourself." I put my walls back up and she nodded.

I was trying to piece together what she said about the two worlds as we got back to the house, but I couldn't make the puzzle fit together. I felt fuzzy and realized that my energy was low, so I fumbled around in my purse until I found a granola bar and ate it. She handed me an apple too as we walked in and I munched on that happily starting to feel better.

Before Kalisha could walk away I stopped her. "One more question if I may, Kalisha?" She nodded at me. "My, er, friend, told me the first time I took on the energy that I needed to get rid of it, that my glow was turning darker. Any idea what that means?"

"That even as strong as you are, you are not immune to it. Given a long enough time period, you'd become one of the dark ones. Fallen." She gestured at the stones, "Those will help, but given that information you'd better not hold on to it for too long."

"It also felt like I took a piece of her when I pulled it from her, is that possible?"

"Yes. It all depends on how this energy attaches itself to the soul. Maybe like tentacles, or needles instead of wrapping around. I'm sorry, I do not know because I haven't felt it."

This world I had been thrust into would take some getting used to, and aspects of it were a bit frightening, but I wasn't scared. Aminda came up to me and smiled kindly. "For us we will use a room in the house and stay warm."

Chapter Sixteen

Aminda led us to a room that must have been in the very back corner of the house. It had a small table with what looked like a shrine on it, draped in swatches of fabric in royal blue, satiny white, and red. I'm guessing they meant something other than our flag colors.

Aminda sat on the floor and motioned me to do the same. She was a petite woman and had an ageless quality about her. If I had to guess I would say late forties or early fifties was her age, but for all I knew she could have been younger than me. She was wearing all white in a kind of shapeless outfit but had beaded necklaces in that were in a rainbow-like color scheme.

Her skin was the mocha color that so many had from the Caribbean area, but her accent suggested to me that she was Latina of some sort. Her eyes were the softest gray color that I had ever seen, they reminded me of a soft cashmere sweater. Framed with dark lashes and eyebrows and short curly chestnut colored hair.

"We won't have to spend long together Airiella. I'm from Cuba, just outside Havana. My family has always practiced Santeria. Do you know much about it?" she started.

SEE ME

I shook my head no. "Not really. I have heard of it, most people assume it's a form of voodoo, but I don't believe that is correct. Isn't it more similar to Catholicism?"

"In a way. To become a priestess like me is a very difficult process, and one that takes quite a bit of time. Santeria is a term that was forced upon people that practiced this religion because they drew conclusions that we worship saints that most closely identify as those the Catholic religion recognizes. Vodoun pray to Loa, similar to hoodoo, which is a similarity that all three have. We just all call them by different names. Vodoun and Santeria are both religions, where hoodoo is a magical practice."

"Okay, that's a bit of a clearer distinction between them," I drawled.

"You don't need to know a whole lot, but a general overview of the religions can sometimes help you identify what you are dealing with. The name we use in Cuba is Regla de Ocha, and we worship nature and the saints that it deifies. I would call the saints themselves a cross between the Loa and catholic saints. Many crossovers and are found in a variety of religious beliefs. In Cuba, they are called orishas. Like others, Santeria uses blood sacrifice as well."

I blanched at that, not because I was afraid of blood, but I didn't like the thought of killing things. I understood it to be a necessity in some cases, it just seemed like a waste of life to me.

"I can see that bothers you, but I can assure you that it is not dark in practice," she pointed out.

"Oh, I wasn't thinking that," I corrected her. "I just don't like killing things."

She nodded at me. "In Santeria, it is not a waste. The sacrifice itself is an offering to god and the orishas. The blood is for them and the sacrifice. We then use the animal to feed everyone in the ritual and ceremony. We use drums and dances to in our rituals to communicate our intent. We do have prayers and chants as well. It's a very holistic approach to healing, to life in general. Heart, mind and body are our focus. Is this making sense to you?"

"Yes, please continue," I replied.

"We worship at an altar," she pointed to the shrine, "that is made in the image of the orisha we are praying to. We use these colors to honor the kings, queens and deified warriors. Like Catholics, we have one God, Olodumare, though there are many orisha that carry out work in his name. We also believe our ancestors should be venerated as they become our spirit guides when the die, influencing our lives through their wisdom, they are still with us."

There were so many similarities to other beliefs that it was getting hard to keep them all straight. I was following what she was saying, but if I had to take a test on paper and relay all that had been told to me, I wasn't sure I'd be able to pass it.

"I think that in relation to you, I can feel touches of some of the orishas in you. I am aware of what others think and believe you are, and it may very well be true. The blessings that have been bestowed upon you are many, and you have great power in your blood. Even with not having done a ritual, I can see the glow surrounding you. But I would like to do a small ritual with you to ask the orishas to guide you on your journey."

I nodded wanly. It appeared whether I believed it or not, these people clearly saw something in me that I didn't see. I was tired of arguing about it and I decided to let it go. There was a part of me that agreed with the fact that if this many people are seeing the same thing, then it was probably true. But there was also a part of me that believed people were susceptible to influence and would see what someone else pointed out to them.

"I'm going to use a circle because it's been asked by Father Roarke and Kalisha that we show you these, and how to make one. Instead of teaching you right now, I wrote the directions down for you. I know that a lot of information will be given to you today, and it will be hard to remember everything. I'd rather have you do it right, than miss a step and have something bad happen." Now I smiled at her in thanks. "However, you still need to pay attention and watch what I do. Oh, do you practice a religion?"

"I was baptized Roman Catholic, but it's not

something I practice. I have more of an open spirituality belief," I summarized.

She went about making a circle in much of the same way that Kalisha had. While she added salt around it, she didn't add any herbs, though she did use white candles. "This shrine is for Yemaya. Father Roarke told me that he is thinking water from the sea might be able to help you. Yemaya is the Spirit of Motherhood, the Ocean and the Moon. Today we will be asking her for her favor for you. That she grants you the cleansing properties of her waters, purified in the moons light. Yemaya is often related to Mother Mary."

Aminda grabbed a small MP3 player and drum music filled the room, the beating cadence both exhilarating and soothing at the same time. She sat back on her heels and looked at me. "I'm going to do a dance, it's not difficult, but you may also try to follow my steps along with me, within the circle after I light the candles and say a prayer to Yemaya." She reached out and took my hand in hers and ran her finger along my palm. "I can feel Eleggua strong in you, he is a messenger."

She ran her fingertips over my wrist, resting on my pulse. "Yes, he is very strong in you. So is Oya, and Oshun. Oya is the Spirit of storms, a warrior, she runs in your blood. Oshun I can feel in your soul, she is the Spirit of love, beauty, sexuality and fresh water." She took my other hand and touched the back of my hand this time, her fingers resting and still. "Obtala has gifted you as well. He is the father of peace and harmony, humanity. You are very blessed indeed."

She abruptly let go of my hand and it dropped back into my lap. So Legba and Eleggua might be the same spirit called by different names, I tried matching the spirits to make more sense. Oshun might be Ezrulie, and Damballah might be Obtala? Or was she feeling those spirits due to the stones and amulet I was wearing.

"Are you feeling those spirits because of these stones I have on?" I decided to ask her. She shook her no. Clear as mud then.

"Those spirits will come when you call them to the stone, these spirits are already in you." She had started lighting the candles now and was saying a prayer in her native language. I stood up to join her and bowed to the shrine when she did. When she started dancing, I did my best to follow her moves, but I felt clumsy and awkward. She had a grace that flowed easily with the drum beat, her feet in perfect timing. I tried giving myself over to the music which made it a little easier, though I still didn't quite know what I was doing.

She stopped dancing and dropped to her knees in front of the shrine, "Repeat after me," she said, and spoke in a different language, slowly so I could repeat it. "We asked Yemaya to bless you with the powers of her waters, to heal that within you that needs healing. We asked her to allow the moon to purify your heart and bathe you in her love. She will take care of you." She made a mark on my arm with her thumb. "Go in peace Airiella."

She bowed to me, and I bowed back. My head a jumble, although I felt oddly rejuvenated. Aminda handed me the directions she had written out, as well as a few herbal remedies that might possibly help me. I'd have a lot of research to do to learn which plants these were to make sure I didn't use something wrong. I folded the papers into smaller squares and put them in the pouch that Kalisha had given me.

"Thank you for your time and patience Aminda, it was a pleasure spending time with you," I told her honestly as I headed to the door.

"Blessings on your journey Airiella," she returned with a smile.

I walked back out to the grand room where the others were sitting, waiting to see which one would be next. If I remembered right, it was Degataga that was heading towards me now, he was the Cherokee Medicine Man.

Chapter Seventeen

H ello Airiella, let's head outside," Degataga smiled a small smile and led the way. I took him to be around the generation of my parents, though he showed his age very well and could possibly be a lot younger than I suspected. He had dark hair that was long and straight, falling below his shoulders. He had it tied with a leather strap in a loose sort of fashion. His clothes were just regular clothes, no traditional clothing from his tribe that I could see.

His face had the lined look of someone who had spent years outdoors. It was broad, his nose somewhat large and flat, thin lips to a wide mouth. His eyes were widely spaced, and very dark, lined with black eyebrows. He was clean shaven. I'd call him handsome, and he had a somewhat gentle nature to him.

His gait was long, and he walked fast, my shorter legs having to work harder to keep up. He led us into the forest, no marked path that I could see, though he seemed to know where he was going. His steps sure and solid on the uneven terrain. Mine were clumsier as I had on boots that were too big and I was moving faster than I would have normally trying to keep his pace.

We hiked for about ten minutes and we were a good distance away from the house, surrounded by dense forest. Moss hung heavy on some of the larger trees and underfoot, dampening the sound as we walked. After about another five minutes we came to a little creek that had a few very large boulders on the edge of it.

Degataga easily scaled one and leaned over to give me a hand up and we settled down on top of it. This was exactly the kind of spot I would search out when I went into the woods on my own. Secluded and quiet, filled with life though. The energy alive and palpable in everything around us. Degataga leaned back against a tree that butted up to the rock we were on.

"Airiella, I am less formal than the others, yet also more secretive. Many of my tribes' ways are not to be shared with outsiders. My name, Degataga means "standing together" which is also a way I think and live. While some things I can't share, some I think you should know. You are a different being than what I expected," he told me, his voice strong, but kind.

"You are Cherokee, correct?" I asked, letting him take the lead.

"Yes," he nodded his head.

"I admit that all I know about your tribe is what I learned in school which is not much. What stands out to me is the Trail of Tears, though I am sure there are many tales just as heartbreaking as that one in your history."

"This is true. Cherokee is one of the few tribes that had a written language, but in our way of life, many more things were relayed verbally. The stories the elder tell are usually for a reason, and there are many myths that circulate through humanity. While not all of them are true, many times within that myth is a bit of truth, which is where the legends come from. I myself have the gifts of being able to see spirits, good and bad, and I can take the energy from something and manipulate it. I understand that you have something similar."

"Well kind of. I'm an empath, well at least I thought

I was, now everyone is telling me I'm something else. Regardless, all my life I have been able to feel the emotions of others, which if you break it down into science, is a form of energy. I can't change it into something else, but I can weaken or strengthen something that already exists," I tried explaining.

"Airiella, you might be more than an empath, but you are still one, don't forget that. What I am not supposed to tell people is that I am a Medicine Man. In my tribe we don't share that information, it is information for my tribe only, and even then, not all of them know who I am. Cherokee are very strong in medicine uses and plant knowledge. Our language helped preserve some of that, but it is also written in a way that not everyone would understand. To make things even more difficult, some parts of remedies were left out and only passed down verbally. It's one of the ways we preserve our way of life."

I nodded, understanding that he was telling me he couldn't share that part of his life with me. I was okay with that. "I truly find it fascinating," I told him.

"I know Taklishim said you were a raven, and I will admit that I see what he means, however, my strengths lie in the energy around us, and that is what I am going to be working on with you. I will be testing you in my own ways, though I will also teach as we go along. I want to get a feel for you and understand more, that's the Medicine Man part in me," he winked. "I am curious though, I don't feel the energy that some of the others have said pours out of you."

Startled, I didn't know what to say at first. He was the first one who hadn't said I had a ton of power. Then it hit me, I had my walls up and sealed tight. "Oh, I have what I call walls up. It blocks that energy from escaping and from letting anything in," I said, the light bulb over my head clicking on. "Otherwise it leaves me open for an attack of sorts by those that know how to. Plus, it gets overwhelming and exhausting being bombarded with emotions all the time. It drains me fast, as I start to take on those emotions of those around me. It can get hard to separate what is mine and what belongs to others."

213

SEE ME

"I see. You created a type of mental block?" he questioned me.

"That's exactly what I did. When I tap into that power, or energy inside me I would picture in my head, a sealed-up area, surrounded by thick heavy bricks that were impenetrable. After a bit of time it got easier for me and then became something I could do instantly and focus parts of it to allow things in or out, search for leaks, and revise on the fly. Sometimes when an emotion is very strong, either by me or someone else, what happens is what I call a leak. It can take a bit of work to fix it, but usually I just let it be unless it's really bad."

"What do you mean by really bad?" he said, curious.

"Bad emotions. Hate, violence, negative energy that is harmful. Sadness carries a weight to it that can shift quickly depending on the stability of a person or situation as well."

"Do your walls come down any other way than you taking them down?" he asked good questions.

I sighed. It bothered me to have so much of my life an open book with these strangers, but I saw the reason for it. "Since this path started for me, there have been two instances where the walls just shattered. Both times were when I was trying to rid myself of the bad energy I took on that was really invasive. From what I understand of myself, is that the pain that came with the releasing of that energy is what caused it. The pain was just too severe for me to hold on to the stability those walls provide. Also, both times afterwards, I was so depleted of energy that I couldn't rebuild them, I just had to feel so to speak. It was excruciating."

"Are you willing to drop them now?" his voice gentle. "I mean you no harm."

I nodded. "Just to warn you though, I can tell when people try to feel me out or get in my head."

"So noted. I do not intend to manipulate you, I just want to see the way it flows through you and around you. If it makes patterns when you use it."

I dropped my walls and felt his curiosity instantly.

214

"Right now, without doing anything, I can feel how curious you are."

"Very good," he said. Looking away from me, he studied around us. "In the Cherokee tribes, the numbers four and seven are very important. Four, for the directions on the compass, the seasons, the elements. Seven for the number of clans in our tribe, also with the three extra directions, up, down and center. Meaning, the world above us, the world below us, and the world we are in right now. Seven is also the highest attainable level you can achieve in purity and sacredness. This tree behind me is a seven," he ran his hands along the bark. "It is also a sacred tree."

"Is that cedar?"

"Very good," he smiled, "it is. Now if you will look around us, this spot is rich in those numbers. It spoke to me as we crested that hill, telling me this was a sacred place, one that was pure and safe. Look around and tell me if you notice anything, feel with your energy," he told me, leaning his head back against the tree and closing his eyes.

I looked around and reached out with my energy to actively seek through the area. I immediately noticed that right here we had seven large cedar trees around us, the only ones I could see in this area. The number of the large boulders like what we were sitting on was four. "There are seven cedar trees and four boulders," I said quietly. He didn't respond and I momentarily wondered if he had fallen asleep.

My emotions tingled with the feeling of curiosity from in the woods. "I feel animals out there curious about us," I continued. The energy from the creek hummed with the energy spots I used back home to release emotions. "The creek has an energy vortex in it," I noted aloud, "as well as it drops in level four times."

Degataga opened his eyes then and watched me. "There's something I can feel, almost void like, out beyond that small cluster of pines off to my right," I pushed more, trying to zero in on it. "I can't tell what it is, it's appearing to me like a black spot, not good, but not bad. Just there." His eyes narrowed on me in scrutiny.

"I can feel residual energy from the rock we are on, and if I focus hard enough it's almost like I can see it how it used to be before erosion brought it to this point." My mind was buzzing. "The woods here, don't mind our presence, but there is warning there as well."

Mother nature decided to use this point in time to scare the hell out of me with the clear blue sky above me lighting up in a flash of light, immediately followed by the roar of thunder as it tore through the atmosphere. We both jumped in alarm, me because I hadn't felt the shift in the atmosphere until it happened. Degataga looked at me in wonder.

"You can't see spirits?" he asked.

"No, just the one, and I don't think she is here with us," I replied, wondering where he was going.

"Can you feel them?" he continued.

"Sometimes I think I can, though because I can't see or hear them, I'm never entirely sure if it's a spirits emotion I am picking up, residual energy, or animals, depending on where I am," I responded, paying closer attention to emotions now.

The curiosity was still strong and coming from multiple directions, the black spot was still there, and I felt a tiny trickle of fear, but the direction wasn't clear to me. Degataga looked as though he was concentrating, and his fingers were moving slightly. "We aren't alone," he said, but he didn't sound concerned.

Suddenly in front of me the creek started rushing faster and I stood, thinking it was a flash flood even though it wasn't raining where we were. The boulder we were on was high enough that it wasn't a danger, but the water wasn't rising, it was just now rushing instead of gently flowing.

I felt around the water for its energy signature and felt a strand of energy going back to Degataga. My eyes widened when I realized it was him, and then my curiosity took over. I gently tapped into his strand of energy and fed my own into it in a rush, and the creek roared to life like a raging river. Fascinated I fed more into and watched it rise.

Realizing it would pose a risk to any life around us I backed off fast and let it go.

I had a giant grin on my face now, that was the first time I had ever really influenced my natural environment intentionally and it felt a little crazy. I looked back at Degataga to find him open mouthed staring at me. Oops, I wondered if I had crossed a line. I sat back down, arranging the jacket underneath me and waited for him to say something.

Instead of talking to me I felt something close to me and looked around until I saw a deer, watching us with caution. I glanced at Degataga to see if he was manipulating it at all, but I couldn't really tell. I felt out around him and felt his strand of energy that was leading out from him to the deer. There wasn't any emotion to it at all, so I pushed some of my calm into it and saw the deer relax, like we weren't even there.

The energy flow suddenly cut off around me. "Incredible," he said, studying me. "You could be extremely dangerous under the influence of the wrong energy. Yet, I don't feel anything malevolent in you at all. Pure intentions. Very rare in an adult."

"Dangerous? The water you mean? I wouldn't have let it flood. There's too much life around here that could have been adversely affected by that," I answered apologetically. "I'm sorry if that crossed a line."

"Oh no, you didn't. That was a test to see if you could feel what I was doing, apparently you did."

"I did, but it took the visual of the water moving faster for me to narrow my focus down to that. Once I saw it was you, I just decided to experiment."

"The lightning, was that you?" he asked me.

"No, I can't influence the weather," I denied. "No one can that I know of. I can usually feel an atmospheric shift that signifies a change, but I didn't feel anything that time until the moment it happened. That's the second time lightning has struck like that with a clear blue sky above."

"Even curiouser. Can you show me what you can do with emotions?" he pointedly asked.

"I did to an extent. I calmed the deer down so it wouldn't be afraid of us."

"To me, though. Can you do something to me?" he pushed.

I read him, picking through his emotions looking for something that would stand out and pulled out a very thin thread of fear. I didn't want anger or something to make him react in a bad way, and he was mostly calm and curious, but there was a sliver of fear. So I pulled on it, adding to it, amplifying it slowly. I watched his face pale, and his eyes shift as he started to frantically look around, his body tensing.

"Is that you?" his voice shook a little. I nodded at him. "Okay, can you fix it please? This is unnerving me."

I giggled, "That was kind of the point." I released the fear and fed the energy back into his normal calm.

"Incredible," he repeated, the color returning to his face. "I had no idea what I was afraid of, or that I even was."

"I can only feed what already exists, I can't give you a false emotion," I stated.

"You are finely in tune with what's around you when you are paying attention. What do you do when you are distracted?"

"I can usually sense strong emotions even when I'm not trying to and depending on what it is will determine how I respond. In dangerous situations like yesterday there are always several clues that have nothing to do with the empath abilities. Especially when in a nature surrounding. In the park, people were actively avoiding the area where the man was, animal life was not there or making noise, there was an unnatural feel to the area, things like that. In normal everyday life, even though I am not using my abilities, I pay attention to my surroundings and go off cues like that."

"Yet you still don't see spirits, very interesting. There are several around us that appeared when you dropped your walls, they are drawn to you, but you aren't picking up on them. I will admit though, you are extremely powerful. The rush of energy I got when you fed the creek was the craziest high I have ever experienced, and it was pure joy. Can I make an observation?" he tilted his head looking at me.

I nodded, "Of course."

"I feel you may not be receptive to this, but there may be something to what the others say," he started.

"Are you talking about the angel thing?" I interrupted, my tone a little harder than I intended.

"Yes, but hear me out. I don't know if it's true or not, because I have never encountered an angel, at least not in the flesh that I am aware of. Being Cherokee, we see things like that differently than others. Spirits are not paranormal, they just are. They are a part of normal life like this rock and tree. By all accounts you should see them as they are pure energy. In some circles, it is rumored that angels can't see that which is between worlds, here in what we call center. Maybe when you add all these things together, there is something to it."

"I don't know," I started to argue and stopped when he held up his hand.

"Just keep your mind open," he stood. "Being a healer, and a damn good one at that," he literally patted himself on the back, and I laughed, "I can feel something in you that is damaged, and it may be that part of you that is keeping you from the full potential I can feel in you, and it's enormous. I am going to make something for you back at the house." He jumped easily down off the rock.

I sat down and tried to maneuver myself to slide down it without falling on my ass. As I turned, I felt him grab my hips and help me down. "Thank you," I said gratefully. We headed back the way we came.

"What I will make is something you will add to water and drink. It will make you dream, and you will see things clearer. You will see what we see, but you will also see what you see. What you see will be the damaged parts that are keeping you from where you could be. It won't be pleasant, it will feel like a nightmare, but that is only because those damaged parts are what scare you. To reach our full potential we need to heal mind, body and spirit."

"Honestly that doesn't sound very fun," I said bluntly.

"It's not, but it's necessary." He reached into his pocket and handed me a carving of a raven. "I made this last night out of cedar, it will help guide you."

It was exquisite and I went to put it in my pouch. He shook his head no, "You'll need to keep it in a white cloth when not holding it and using it. Cedar is sacred." He reached in his other pocket and pulled out a white handkerchief. "Wrap it in this." I wrapped it and placed it carefully in with the other items.

We walked back to the house in a comfortable silence, and as we returned, he stopped me before going on. "Remember Airiella, ravens fly. You need to heal your wings." He chucked me under the chin and walked in.

Chapter Eighteen

The twins met me outside and told me to follow them. I wasn't sure which was which, but by now my mind was a mess of thoughts so tangled up I didn't even try to work them out. I just followed them silently, in yet a completely different direction than I had gone with the others.

I was hungry again, so I pulled out another granola bar and munched on it while we were walking. We were in the woods, but it wasn't dense like where I had just come from, and I could hear water this time, perhaps the same stream I was just at, just farther downstream. Without looking at a map I had no way of knowing.

We soon came upon the stream I heard and entered a little bit of a sheltered area. Still not dense woods, but it was closed in enough that it felt like it. The twins sat on a fallen tree and faced the stream. I wasn't sure what to do so I sat next to one of them.

The one closest to me spoke. "Raven," she called me. "I am Tama, we come from what people call one of the Chinook tribes. I understand we travel the same areas." If she meant the whole state in a broad term, then I guess she was right. "My name means thunder, and I am what some would call a powerful shaman. It's not something we really talk about with outsiders."

I nodded silently, understanding more after my time spent with Degataga. Tama fell silent for a few moments and I studied her. She was identical in appearance to her sister. Long black hair fell to mid back. She didn't have it restrained it all, it flowed freely with her movements. Her face was long, narrow, and while her nose wasn't large, the nostrils flared out a bit. Her lips were full and ripe looking, and her skin had a tan tone, but she wasn't dark. Her eyes were a deep chocolate color that had a spark of mischief in them. Her eyebrows dark and thin. It was hard to tell her age as she looked somewhat timeless. She was taller than me, and athletic. She moved with an easy grace and effortlessly quiet. Neither wore any makeup, but they both wore beaded necklaces.

"Do I meet with your approval?" she asked with a good nature.

Taken aback, I stuttered out an apology, "I-I'm sorry. I didn't mean to stare."

Tama laughed, "It's all good. I'm sure you have a lot of questions and I don't want to take up any more time than we need to. Taklishim will need to spend the most time with you is my guess. He is my mate," she said fondly. "We broke with traditions and didn't marry within our tribes. I'm a bit of a rule breaker."

Her sister spoke up, "She's not kidding. My name is Onida, it means the one searched for. I too am a powerful shaman, and while I help many within the tribes, I help just as many outside of them. I received a medical degree from the university and became a doctor. Neither of us really follow the laws of the tribe. Though I am unmarried."

"Our Father was a clan leader, but the government doesn't recognize the Chinook as a nation. While his clan followed him, we moved north of where many of my people were, to a smaller area, near other tribes. He didn't agree with some of the Chinook ways and he met a lot of resistance from other leaders when he broke traditions. So maybe rule breaking is in our blood," Tama explained.

"We both have what people call paranormal gifts, but to us, it's just a way of life and part of who a shaman is. We both have visions, can see spirits and the veil between our worlds. We both have animal guides. I am what some would call a spiritual warrior. Onida is much like her name definition, people seek her out, to carry messages to the spirit world, to heal them, to gift them sight."

Onida piped in, "We have the ability to take the shape of our animals to help us in tasks we need to accomplish. They also speak to us, though only we can hear them." She leaned forward and looked at me, a mirror image of her sister. "If we were to shift, and hide in the woods, would you be able to sense us?"

"I believe so. I can often pick up other animals, though their emotions are much less chaotic than peoples are."

"You carry the divine light with you," Tama said thoughtfully. "Do you know what a Raven is?"

"A bird," was my automatic response, which made both sisters laugh cheerily.

"I like you Raven. You are a protector of secrets, a messenger between the heavens and this world. When you appear in people's lives it means you are there to help them change, be reborn, in a way. Your courage and magic are very strong, you are highly sexual and gifted at healing, a Raven is rare."

Blushing at the sexual comment, "If I am a Raven why does everyone keep saying I'm an angel?"

"Different symbolism for different beliefs. The root of what you are is the same, just called by a different name," Onida explained simply.

"So, a Raven is an Angel?" I asked, confused.

"Both have the divine light guiding you. You have the power of the heavens on your side, whatever you decide to call yourself. Your purpose is the same, to heal and bring about the changes that need to be made to set the world back to what it needs to be," Tama said bluntly.

"I'm sorry, it's just not clear to me how that is

possible. Angels are supposed to be pure and holy and all that crap," I argued.

"Airiella," Onida said, "why do you think you are not this?"

"Because my life is a train wreck most of the time!" I exploded. "The things I've been through left an ugly stain on me, marking me forever." Tears welled in my eyes and I stood, walking to the edge of the creek, fighting the damn things back.

"Raven," Tama placed an arm around my shoulder and hugged me to her. "Your experiences do not define your soul like you think. The bad spirits of the world attack you, because of who you are. They don't want you to survive, because if you do, they don't. You will always have struggles, it is the way the world has become unbalanced. Your very presence here on earth is a warning that transformation is coming. The very fact that you survived all that has befallen you is a beacon of the strength you have within. The glow around you is so bright and engulfing that is strikes terror in those that have bad intentions."

"I went through cancer because a bad spirit wanted to end me?" I said choking on my tears.

"Essentially, yes," Onida spoke softly from the other side of me now. Sandwiching me between them. "In our beliefs, a sickness is the result of a bad spirit. Other beliefs have different answers. In a generally broad answer from my animal guide, he is a hawk. They have the ability to see a larger picture," she told me. "You are a gift to the world, one granted by the highest power."

Onida grabbed my wrist that had my cancer ribbon tattoo on it and ran her thumb over it. "It is said that your kind, being a gift to the world, you aren't allowed to have children. They can be taken, corrupted and turned to the other side. But your blood has the power to heal anything, it is how you share your gift. Not through birth do you give life, you give it in other ways."

"I don't understand any of this," I sobbed, my heart torn open and bleeding at the loss of the dreams I once had.

"You do," Tama said, lifting my chin to make me look at her. "You just have to let go of your own shadow."

"What the hell does that mean?" I spat out.

"The pain you hold inside is a shadow. Darkness cannot exist without light, nor can light exist without darkness. It is not a stain on your soul as you think it is, it is a testament of your soul that you still exist and are stronger than what tried to take you down. It doesn't make it hurt any less, and it is okay to feel sad. You need to know it is okay to heal yourself, not just others. Life itself is a balance, good and bad will always exist. If you didn't suffer, how would you know when something is wonderful?" Tama pointed out.

The sisters looked at each other and nodded. I wasn't sure what to do when they both started stripping down out of their clothes in the freezing cold Colorado air. Suddenly both began to shift, their limbs changing shapes right before my eyes.

My self-pity and tears forgotten as I witnessed something I hadn't known was possible. Before me sat a cougar and a hawk. I was halfway terrified and rooted to the ground when the cougar advanced towards me. I thought for sure I was about to become dinner for this magnificent creature, but she just butted my hand with her head, and I stroked her fur with my fingers, amazed.

I dropped my walls and felt for the women in both animals and found their energy and happiness easily enough. I was in awe. Tama's feline grace made sense to me now. I looked over at Onida and reached out tentatively to brush a finger over her feathers. She stretched her wings out to make it easier, her wing span impressive.

Several things happened simultaneously then. With my senses opened I felt an atmospheric shift again. I also felt that same blank energy I felt with Degataga very near me. Onida let out a chilling screech as she launched into the air, the feathers of her wings brushing my face. Tama roared ferociously sending ice through my veins and leaped behind me knocking me flat to the ground as tree bark exploded behind where my head had been. I never even heard the crack of the rifle. The first time or the second time.

But I heard the wounded cry of a cat, the sound gutting me as I rolled to my feet to see her step falter, a chunk torn out of one of her hind legs. Time stood still for me then. Every aspect of everything around me in sharp focus, something inside me woke up and called out, a scream tearing out of my lips. I raised my arms to the sky like I could physically grab the electricity I could feel building. I pulled that energy as hard as I could, furious that something injured Tama, and I threw it all at the space I felt the void.

Lightning struck, the force throwing me off my feet and sending me flying backwards into a tree, the area illuminating in a flash charged with my anger crackling the air, the scent of burned ozone permeating my nose. Ten seconds later the biggest eagle I had ever seen flew in screaming a deadly call that had me scrambling to get away followed by deafening thunder that left me shaking.

The scorched earth where lightning hit was left with a very burned body and melted rifle. Suddenly a naked Taklishim, Onida and Tama were in front of me. Tama bleeding as Degataga ran into our no longer peaceful spot and started applying a poultice on Tama's leg.

My ears were ringing, I couldn't hear anything, my body shaking so bad I couldn't stand, so I just dropped. My eyes were going in and out of focus, my back felt like it was bleeding. I passed out.

My eyes opened to see Onida standing over me. "What happened?"

"In a word, you."

"Me?" I wasn't following.

"It isn't the world that shapes your thoughts, it's your thoughts that shape the world."

"Philosophy?" I shouted at her. "You are going to spout philosophy right now?"

"Ariella," Onida said calmly, "when everything happened, what was your intention?"

"To keep you both safe," I replied numbly,

"obviously that didn't work."

"To the contrary. We are both alive, and whatever was after us is not. I'd call that successful."

"Are you saying I killed it?" I was stunned. "It was hit by lightning."

"Lightning that you called," she told me gently.

"I don't understand," my voice weak and shaky.

"What I saw in the spirit world was for lack of a better word, a black hole. Bad energy was pooling on the other side to fill that spot. If you hadn't done what you did, we would still be fighting," Onida explained.

"You saw it from the other side? For me, I just felt a void, like a blank spot," I puzzled.

"Your intention was to save us, the divine light that fills you, you manifested it and used it to create your intention. It was actually pretty incredible," Onida breathed.

"I agree," said Tama, limping over. Blood soaking through her pants.

"Oh my God! Are you okay? I saw you get shot and flipped out," I admitted in a rush.

"It hurts," Tama told me softly, "but I am alive because of you."

"I have so many more questions," I muttered.

"I bet. But for now, I think Taklishim is going to take over and finish the day. I need to go sit down for a bit," Tama said and Degataga walked over and helped her up and head back to the house.

"We will answer any remaining questions before the process is through, I promise you," Onida said, touching my forehead with two of her fingers. She followed and took up the other side of Tama.

Well, time to face the music I guess, I thought to myself. Taklishim was the only one left. Coincidently he was also the one that intimidated me the most. I'm just ready for this to be over with. I needed to process all this, and I didn't know where to start.

Chapter Nineteen

I walked over to Taklishim who was squatting over in front of the scorched earth. I suppressed a violent shudder that ran through me and told myself to suck it up and go over there. His hand was stretched out over a spot as I approached, and he pulled it back to look at me.

"This is an impressive display you managed," he said calmly.

"I wasn't even aware that it was me that did it, or how it happened," the words rushed out of my mouth.

"He wasn't human," Taklishim said carefully, using his finger to poke at a pile of ash. "No bones here." He then pointed to the warped and twisted pile of metal and plastic that used to be a gun. "Not sure how he got that, but only your kind of light can do this," he pointed back to the ash.

"But how?" I whispered, condemning myself for having killed something.

"My guess is extreme emotional response from you called it."

"What does that even mean?" I cried, dropping down from my squatting position to sit on the ground I burnt.

"I don't know Raven," he admitted, sitting back next to me. "When this happened, what were you doing?"

"It's all a jumble, everything happened so fast," I closed my eyes trying to remember the sequence of events. "I think we all realized something was here at the same time. Tama knocked me down, I'm guessing to keep me out of harm's way, and she ended up shot. I didn't hear either shot, or maybe I did and didn't recognize what it was. But I remember seeing she was hit and knowing it was a shot and I got really angry that someone would shoot such a beautiful animal. I wanted to save them. Onida had flown up and was circling. I know I screamed because my throat hurts again. I think I tried to pull the energy from what I assumed was a man, but I couldn't find any to pull and I grabbed whatever energy I could and focused it on this," I gestured before me.

"You couldn't find the energy to pull because there wasn't any, it was gathering on the other side. If you had waited, there would have been a large amount, but it is also my understanding that pulling it comes at a great cost to you. What you pulled was your light."

"I killed something," I choked, my eyes once again filling with tears.

"No Raven, you can't kill something that isn't really alive. You instead protected life with a heart of pure intention. You carried the message that whatever that energy is, it has no place here. It's what you are made to do. You protect with love. Tama is my mate, I would have lost everything if she had died. Do you understand?" he asked me, his eyes sharp.

I nodded warily, taking him in. He wasn't as old as I thought, but the color of his hair threw me off. "I take it that the gigantic eagle that came swooping in was you?"

He nodded at me. "I heard Onida's cry and felt the pain Tama felt. I also had been feeling something growing on the other side for a couple of days now. None of us know what it is, just that it is intelligent in its actions, and has bad intentions. It's not something we have ever seen before."

"Because Tama is your mate you can feel her?" I asked curious.

"Yes. You have bonds, correct?"

"I don't know, but I am starting to suspect I do," I replied.

"Do you feel something pulling at you?" he asked.

"Yes, so far with five different people. Is that even possible?"

"It is rare, but then again, so are you. Their seed will cement the bond, making it unbreakable in life. Death will break it, but you lose a part of yourself. The bond will also make you stronger," he explained.

"By seed, do you mean..." I trailed off, embarrassed.

"Sex, Raven."

"Well shit," I mumbled. "I have to sleep with five different people?"

"You don't have to, but in order to feed that bond and keep that strength you need contact. Sex will cement it in, make it a viable living thing that can heal you, or him, ease pain, bring comfort. Without sex, it's still there, but it doesn't help as much. It takes constant work and energy to keep it viable."

"I was baptized Catholic, and while I don't follow or practice the religion, it's ingrained in us since children that sex before marriage is a sin. I'm not saying that I didn't do it anyway, but it doesn't make sense to me how I could be an angel given that. It means I am not pure. I can't wrap my head around this."

"Being pure doesn't mean you haven't taken part in pleasure of the flesh," he coughed. "It more means that you are pure of heart, your intentions are pure, not selfish, not harmful. You act out of love, not hate. Every belief system has a different opinion of sex. It's a part of nature, it's natural. Have you taken someone by force?"

"What?" I asked, stunned by the question.

"I am unused to having these conversations, I apologize. Have you raped someone?" he reworded the question.

"Of course not!" I replied hotly. Then more quietly,

"But it's been done to me."

"I'm going to give you my perspective on this, and remember, this is just a perspective Raven. If your creator wanted you to be here as a divine light, someone to win through love and fight the imbalance the bad has created, he might make you go through things that are bad so that you can understand it when you see it others. If you go through it, you can help them through it, you'd be walking on ground you've already navigated. I don't like to call it a test you go through, because it leaves marks in here," he tapped his chest, "but the premise is the same."

Damn these tears. "I understand what you are saying on a logical level, but emotionally it's harder for me to accept that a benevolent god willingly puts someone through these things."

Taklishim nodded at me and stood up, reaching his hand down to me and helped me to my feet. "My name, Taklishim, means gray one. When I was born, my parents said I was gray, that I straddled the line between this world and the spirit world. I was taught from birth that I am a spirit warrior. The Medicine Man taught me his ways, the greatest warrior of our tribe taught me his ways. I was told I was destined to be both. It's hard to understand as a child that you are meant to heal, be magical, spiritual and good, while at the same time being taught to kill and hurt."

I listened closely, picking up the caustic tone in his words. "My father was chief in my village, I was being groomed to be the next chief when he died. No one ever asked me if that was what I wanted, if they had, I would have said no. I've always had to straddle that line between life and death. I can look in the spirit world and see what is happening around me, and I can fight in the spirit world. I'm the highest skilled warrior alive right now. But I didn't ask for that."

"I can heal almost anything, save children and appreciate every breath the living takes. And while I may value that skill more than the other, I am wise enough to know that it has given me a balance. When I was a teenager, my younger sister was taken. We had been close, she followed me everywhere and copied all the things I was learning to do. In her own right, she was a good fighter, but she couldn't save herself. I couldn't save her either. When she died, my hair turned this gray color, to match my spirit."

I held my breath as tears fell unchecked down my cheeks. "The spirit world denied me access that day, and I had to fight my way in, and I searched for her. I searched until I was almost permanently a part of that world as well. I too felt the way you did, that a benevolent god wouldn't take such an innocent and pure life. That was a turning point for me. I continued my lessons, learned both trades as a warrior, and a Medicine Man and when the time came for me to take my place in the tribe, I left."

"You left?"

He nodded, "I couldn't stay there, the loss of my sister, of one so close to my soul had damaged me too much. I wandered from tribe to tribe, visiting and helping where needed and eventually made my way to where Tama was. My soul had pulled me in that direction, I followed not knowing why, but did so anyway because it took me farther and farther away from where my sister had died."

"Did it work?" I quietly asked.

"No, running never works. The pain of losing her is with me every day. Distance allows me to not see the grief in my parent's faces, but it doesn't go away. However, in this case, leaving all that was known to me allowed me to see the ways of life of others, both good and bad. It allowed me to see with eyes that have experienced my own grief. And it brought me to Tama."

"So you found your silver lining," I said.

"Not just in Tama but in all that I learned from leaving my comfort zone. I was in my eagle form when I first saw her. Her animal is dangerous, but beautiful in a way I'd never experienced. I felt her every move while I soared above her. Her sister was flying too and thought I was after her prey and kept trying to keep me away. I finally had to settle on a low branch and just watch. I didn't think my heart had the capacity for that kind of love anymore, but my animal recognized it for what it was. Hers did too."

"Love at first sight?" I asked, skeptical.

"In a way yes. Animals know their bonds, their mates instinctively. My eagle was following his instincts leading me to her. There's a tug that comes from your soul when you are around them. You are pulled to them, and the closer you get, the stronger it is. When you touch skin to skin, there is a spark of current that tells you it's right. The heart bond grows stronger over time, but the mate bond is there. Those of us who spend a lot of time in our animal form understand it for what it is."

"You are telling me that my soul knows I am supposed to be around these five people?"

"Kind of, yes. It doesn't mean that you must have a mating relationship with all of them, but if you make the connection with them permanent at least once, they will always be your family. You don't even have to have sex, just remaining in close contact with them will work, it will just be harder. I say this because I think those five are the chosen ones to help you with your mission here on this world. They each play a part. I can't say what that is, but if you feel that way with them, it's for a reason. That is what my own pain has taught me. I've learned to listen, even when I don't understand."

"I hear you," I said thoughtfully. "You don't know what my purpose here is?"

"If I had to guess, it's to restore balance and teach the world to love again," Taklishim said honestly.

"You make it sound so easy," I snorted in laughter.

"Make no mistake Raven, your task is anything but easy. There is growing unease and tension in the spirit world. Hate is breeding faster than anything here on this world. People are uneducated in ways of keeping their own balance between heart, body and mind. Religion is bringing a divisiveness that is unparalleled. Violence is making its way to be the leading answer to disagreements. The light that surrounds you, it encompasses those that are around you, filling them with hope bright enough to fight back the despair. Your capacity to love is a powerful weapon."

"What about these powers of mine everyone keeps referring to?" I asked.

"They are tools for you to use to restore balance," was his blunt answer.

"But if I don't know what they are, how do I use them?" I replied in frustration.

"You need to heal in here," he tapped my chest. "You carry the same pain I carried. Plus, you don't fully believe yet." He walked some more, "Degataga said he was making you a tea to help you heal," he looked at me, "I suggest you use it."

"He said it wouldn't be easy," I hedged.

"No, healing never is, but it's always worth it in the end. You are a raven. You have abilities beyond your wildest imagination, as your very being is magic. There is not one person here who is stronger than you are. Even combined, we could not defeat you."

"I don't see how that would be possible," I started.

"Because you don't believe yet. When you believe, you will have no limit. At the very least, right now you make our abilities stronger, without you, they are just as they always are. With you, new levels are seen. It is your very nature to lift and help people soar on the winds that carry you. It starts with you. You've heard the saying, you can't expect anyone else to love you if you don't love yourself?"

I nodded, suddenly feeling inadequate. "Yes, I know. I have issues."

"Everyone has issues. No one is immune to them. It's how you deal with them and move on that matters. For you to see what we see in you, you must heal. No one on earth escapes suffering in some way or another. It's just part of life," he said, his tone matter of fact.

"Once I begin healing, I'll be able to use my powers better?"

"I think that the way to use them will become clearer when there is no self-doubt in the way. You manifested lightning today in your desire to keep others safe from harm. It may have taken an extreme emotion to

SEE ME

get you there, but you got there," he gently said.

"This is just a lot to take in," I said haltingly.

"It is," Taklishim agreed. "If anyone can do it though, it will be you. I have no doubt about that. I will even give you my number so you can contact me with questions you may have, or for Tama or Onida for that matter. It's against our rules as a council, but I think in this case it might be warranted to break with tradition. No one knows what your presence here means in the larger picture, but I fear it doesn't mean anything good for us as a planet."

"Ha! No pressure or anything, right?"

"I'm sorry Raven. I'll do what I can to help along the way."

"I am extremely grateful already. I know more than I did when I came here, and I know what I have to do to get to where I need to be. I won't run from it, but nor am I running into it. I'm scared, I won't lie about that, but if there is one thing you should know about it, is that fear doesn't stop me."

"You have my support," he put his hand on my arm, "in however I can provide it. No journey is without pain, and some have more of it than any of us can anticipate. Here on this world, everything is temporary, even pain."

I took a deep breath in and exhaled slowly. "What happens now?"

"We go back, meet with the shrink, and then tomorrow, all of us meet again with you to go over recommendations for the job you applied for. The extra part is, our recommendations will also have advice for how to continue to navigate this path that we all understand you are on. The shrink does not, he isn't a part of this world we share. So while some things may not make sense to you for the job you will be working, it will for the larger picture."

I nodded. "All this info you all shared was for me for the larger picture? Not for the job I applied for?"

"Exactly. We all knew within minutes you'd be able to handle that job without issues, even with no training. It's the rest we all were gearing for with these talks and, well, let's call them adventures." He chuckled then got serious as

236

he looked at me again, "I am going to recommend physical training in a fighting manner. You will need to learn skills to fight."

"Um, okay, if you think I need to," I stammered, pushing back the fear that fighting triggered.

"I'll recommend Ronnie train you," he suggested kindly.

I silently nodded as we walked back up to the house where all the others were waiting. The helicopter ride back was solemn for me as I went through everything in my head, feeling overwhelmed. This was so much more than I bargained for, and I wondered not for the first time where Winnie was for all this.

Chapter Twenty

Smitty happened to be in the building when the helicopter came back, so he knew Airiella was back now. Jax and Ronnie were off trying to work things out so they could all be in the same room together and not be choked by tension.

Aedan and Mags were off by themselves having alone time. Odd man out, he came to the work building to look over equipment they had, and new stuff that came in. Plus, he was feeling nosy and wanted to make sure that everything went well.

He had talked with Asher to see what had happened with that situation, and then he talked with Father Roarke, but hadn't gotten anywhere with the priest. So Smitty didn't have a lot to work with on trying to figure out where to direct their attentions to regarding what they were dealing with. Which led him to the conclusion that no one really knew.

He started putting things away and making his list of things to take with him for their next investigation. He'd have the guys here ship it to the next location. As he was finishing that up his phone chirped in his pocket and he pulled it out to see a text from Airiella.

"I don't really want to be alone right now, is anyone not busy that could hang with me?"

Smitty glanced at his watch, noting that it was dinner time already and wrote back, "Jax and Ronnie are out trying to work out their issues, Aedan and Mags are on a date. I'm available if you aren't uncomfortable with that?"

"Of course I'm not. I'm waiting for the driver to bring me back to the hotel, where should I meet you?"

"No need for the driver, give me three minutes and I'll be down, I'm in the same place you are."

Smitty grabbed his notebooks, his coat and flew out the door, taking the steps instead of the elevator and couldn't help grinning. Ronnie was going to be so jealous. It made him laugh, but he was also glad that he would have some time with her alone to try and see what it was she knew.

He flew out the door and immediately saw Dr. Stone cornering Airiella and Smitty slowed, staying out of his sight line, but still eavesdropping.

"How are you feeling Ms. Raven?" Dr. Stone was asking her.

"I'm fine, just tired and hungry and needing a shower," Airiella told him tightly. Smitty could see she was holding something back.

"I see. Well we will meet a little bit later tomorrow, I will have the driver call for you at 10:00 AM to bring you here for the final part of the interview," he told her coldly.

Smitty cringed at his tone. Something had set the Dr.'s teeth on edge and he was taking it out on Airiella. Smitty fought his instinct to go to her and just continued to watch.

"Thank you, Dr. Stone, I will be ready," she responded with a small smile. "If that's all, I'd like to get going." He gave her a curt nod and spun around and stomped off.

Smitty slid around the corner and rushed over to her, sliding an arm behind her back as he walked her out the door. "Sorry about him, he's always been kind of an ass." He felt her relax under his arm and he couldn't fight the grin that popped on to his face.

"I'm used to people like him, it's just been a long day," she told him easily.

"You look a little tense, and a little dirty," he mused, looking her over.

"I was outside for a good portion of the day," she smiled, "only a few mishaps. It was a beautiful location though."

"Somewhere out in the mountains?" he guessed.

She nodded. "I'd hoped to get to spend time getting to explore there before I went home, so mission accomplished I guess."

"You have mountains where you live, right?" he prodded.

"Yes, a lot of them. And the ocean, and desert. I have all the terrains. I love it," she gushed.

Smitty helped her out of the car as they got back to the hotel, "Want to eat?"

"Can I shower first? Actually, can we hit that store across the street first, then can I shower?" she asked hopefully.

"Sure," he held out his arm to her and they walked across the street to the little boutique store. He watched as she picked out a few items of clothing and not bothering to try them on paid for them and they headed back to the hotel.

"I really need to shower, I feel like I stink," she said shyly.

"You don't, but I'll go change too. Give me your key card so I can get back in," he held out his hand at her door.

She handed it over without an argument and went straight to the bathroom. Smitty dashed to his room, changed his clothes and checked his appearance over. Presentable enough. He hoped she would be open to going out of the hotel to eat somewhere. He didn't want to run into the guys.

He went back to her room and waited for her to finish up. He paced for a few minutes trying to burn off some extra energy, then finally sat down and waited. She came out about fifteen minutes later; her skin had a freshly scrubbed glow to it, and she smelled fantastic. Her hair was still wet, and she was trying to shake some of the moisture out of it.

"Here, let me help," Smitty said, getting up and leading her back into the bathroom. He grabbed the dryer off the wall and put it on the cool setting and dried her hair. It was still cold outside, and he didn't want her to catch a chill, especially in that dress she picked out from the store. Which he wasn't going to complain about since she looked amazing.

"This is completely decadent," she purred, feeling like putty in his hands. When her hair was mostly dried, he fluffed the wild curls and buried his nose in her hair. He stepped back and noted the bruises showing, an erratic feeling surging in his blood.

"How do you feel about Mexican food?" he asked her, trying to get himself under control.

"I love it," she said smiling.

"Grab a coat then, let's go out," he told her, dropping a kiss on the top of her head.

"No arguments from me!" she grabbed her coat, which was a thin little jacket and he decided they wouldn't walk, they'd take the car, or she'd freeze.

He'd asked the driver to be on stand by and was suddenly happy about that as they headed down and to the restaurant. He felt the connection to her he'd felt since the first time, and he was getting used to it, becoming comfortable with the pull he felt to her as if it was natural.

She chatted about nothing of importance, places back where she lived that she liked to hang out, asked him questions about the show, the conversation light. He itched to ask her about the day but got the feeling she wasn't ready to talk about it.

They ate dinner, talked, laughed and the more they touched, the more Smitty felt like he was right where he was supposed to be. Bellies full, they walked back to the hotel Smitty putting his own jacket on her and held her hand. He could feel a shift in her as they walked, like she was looking for a way to bring something up.

He didn't say anything, it was up to her if she wanted to talk to him or not, all he could do was make sure she felt comfortable, so he lifted her hand up and kissed the back of her hand and smiling at her. "Do you feel a connection between us?" she finally asked him, her voice sensual and hesitant.

"Sure do. Buzzes right along my skin," Smitty told her.

She looked up at him, her eyes unreadable but her voice giving away the nervousness she was feeling. "Will you stay with me tonight please?"

Smitty swallowed and asked, "Are you sure you want me to and not someone else?"

"Right now? Yes, I'm sure," she said but her voice still held a bit of fear.

"Airiella, are you scared of me?" Smitty stopped and turned her to look at him.

Startled, she said with pure honesty, "No, not at all. Should I be?" She searched his face.

"No. I just hear fear in your voice," he said, pulling her closer.

"It's not fear of you," she said softly, her voice taking on a husky breathless tone that undid him.

"Are you going to tell me what the fear is for then?" Smitty asked, a growl in his voice responding to her tone.

She nodded slowly, "I think I might."

"Good enough for me, let's get inside where it's warm," he started walking again, a purpose to his step now. She scrambled to keep up with him, tugging on his hand to slow him down a bit.

"My legs aren't as long as yours," she reminded him.

"I'm sorry, baby girl," Smitty's voice was rough, but he slowed. "I was just anxious to get back in the room."

She giggled and blushed and didn't say anything. Honestly Smitty hadn't been thinking of sex until that moment. Her blush put him directly on that track though. He had just wanted to be alone with her and hear what she had to say, to get closer to her. But now, that connection they shared had a different buzz to it that went straight to his crotch.

He briefly thought of Jillian, and the relationship they had. It was an open one, she slept with others and he was okay with it as long as he knew, and she was safe. He hadn't slept with anyone else even though they both defined theirs as an open relationship, he hadn't felt the urge to go that route, until now.

They got up to Airiella's room and Smitty slapped the Do Not Disturb sign on the door and took out his phone to shoot a text to Ronnie telling him he was out for the night, that Airiella asked him to stay with her. He was going to be honest and not lie.

Ronnie responded immediately, "Lucky fucker." Smiling, he set it to silent and put it on the table. Airiella had taken his jacket off and pulled off her shoes and stuffed her feet under the blanket that was on the little sofa she sat on. She watched him closely and he wondered if she was reading him.

He sat down next to her and pulled her feet into his lap and started rubbing them. She moaned and dropped her head back. "That feels amazing," she told him.

"I need to be honest with you and I hope you are the same with me," Smitty started. "I'm in a relationship, her name is Jillian. Though it is very important for you to know that what her and I have is an open relationship. She is a very free person, and she follows many of her urges which are typically sexual in nature. We are both free to sleep with whomever we want. While I have not done that since I have been with her, it's mainly because I haven't felt the need." Smitty cleared his throat. "Until now."

Airiella stared at him, her eyes roving over his face and so deep he felt lost. "I understand," she said slowly.

"This connection between us, I know you feel it with the others too, and that doesn't bother me. I mean, really, how could it if my girlfriend sleeps with others, right?" He chuckled a little. "What I feel with you is very different than what I feel for her. I don't understand it, and I'm not talking with my dick here, but I feel like I am where I am

244

supposed to be right now."

"Does your dick often talk for you?" she asked deadpan.

Smitty let out a howl of laughter, "Baby girl, you fill me with some amazing feelings. No, my dick doesn't talk for me."

She reached out to stop his hands that were still rubbing her feet. "I get it Smitty. I feel the same way and the fear you heard was because I am afraid of all this, of following where this wants me to go. I'm not afraid of any of you, just of what facing this all means to me, how it will change my beliefs and where to go. This is as unknown to me as it is to all of you."

"Is that all the fear was?" he asked carefully, feeling like he was on a slippery slope with that question.

"No." He watched her take a deep breath and saw the fear in her eyes. "When I was a teenager, I was raped by someone I knew and trusted. My next relationship after that was an abusive one, where sex was a weapon. After that I was married to someone who is an alcoholic and has trust issues. Ultimately, I paid the price for that in my own self confidence that never recovered from the two before that. My last relationship I thought was The One. He was the one person I let all the way in, I held nothing back. He used it against me, he broke me. My fear is a culmination of those relationships, the belief I hold within myself that I don't deserve to feel the good things I feel with you or Ronnie, or even Mags. It's emotional baggage that I need to clean up. The *situation* I find myself in scares me, not you. The things I learned today terrify me and challenge me in ways that make my brain just stop. This connection we share," she pointed to a spot between them, like she saw a tether, "this I can't explain, and I don't want to try. I just want to enjoy it. You are like the cool breeze that allows me to breathe when I feel suffocated."

Smitty had visible reaction to her story. "Baby girl," his voice was thick with emotion, "I will never abuse you in any way. Rage boils in my blood to know you dealt with any of that. Happiness flows that you still aren't living that life, sadness fills me that you still suffer from those scars. Beyond those emotions, a deep respect for you covers it all. I'm not an emotional or trusting person by nature, but around you that doesn't seem to be true."

"I don't want pity," she said, her voice hard. "I enjoy sex, have a dirty mind, even filthier mouth and am curious about new things and experiences."

"I don't have any pity," his words ringing true. "I do feel love though."

She sighed. "If I'm honest with myself I do too, but I'm not there yet. Ronnie's declaration of love scared me a bit. Let me tell you about the past couple of weeks of my life." She told him everything, trusting the instinct she had inside. She talked for about an hour straight without interruption. Everything about the testing and what she learned coming out. She told him about the bonds and expressed her concerns and fears about it, and social stigma that made her pause.

For the first time in his life, Smitty felt completely floored and unsure of what to say. Airiella had certainly been thrust into this life at a dizzying speed that he was sure would have stopped others in their tracks, including him. He resumed rubbing her feet, then suddenly stopped. He pushed her feet from his lap, ignoring the look of surprise on her face and he pulled her arms, pulling her forward until she was in his lap. He wrapped his arms around her and just held on to her like she was going to disappear.

Her body relaxed into him once she realized he wasn't rejecting her and molded herself to him. Jillian filled a spot in his heart, Airiella filled a gaping hole in his soul he didn't even know he'd had until he met her. He was overcome with emotions and shocked silent when he felt tears slipping down his cheeks.

"I'm feeling everything you are," she told him softly. "I opened myself up for you. Thank you for not holding back," she whispered against his lips as she kissed him gently.

"You're a real live angel. Here on earth. On my lap,

kissing me," he said between kisses.

"Will you be my experimental guinea pig?" she asked him, her eyes wide and shining with a love that he couldn't explain if he tried.

Smitty groaned, "I don't know what you are asking of me baby girl, but I will happily be your guinea pig for anything if it means you are touching me." He shifted under her so she could feel the affect she was having on him.

"It's not going to be weird between us after?" she clarified.

"Not for me no. It might be different with the others, at least until they know the reasons behind it," he thought out loud.

"When I first met you," she said, dragging her lips down across his jaw making his breath catch, "I saw flashes of the future. You are a part of it, but you aren't mine, you belong to someone else, maybe it's Jillian, I don't know. I feel greedy wanting this," she went on, switching to the other side, "but I want that permanent connection with you that Taklishim told me about. I don't believe in love at first sight, but at the same time, I know I love you in a way that comes from somewhere deep inside."

"If it furthers the cause and helps, I don't see that as greedy," Smitty groaned as she slid her hands under his shirt. He tore the damn thing off making her smile a sexy smile, and as she ran her tongue along her lips, Smitty had to fight to control the urge to throw her back on the couch and devour her.

"Are you sure you are okay with this?" she asked, her voice pure sex, her nails skimming down over his chest and his blood feeling like it was on fire as it raced through his veins. He swore he was going to come from her voice alone.

"Baby girl, if you don't touch me more and keep going, I think I will literally go insane," he growled, capturing her lips in a deep kiss, his tongue stroking hers in the way he wanted to taste the rest of her. He loved how she was just taking what she wanted as he gave willingly.

247

She ground herself down on his lap as she kissed him.

He stood abruptly, cupping her ass in his hands and walked them backwards to the bed where he dropped them both. "I don't have a whole lot of experience," she said, straddling him. "But I'm willing to learn." Her eyes held a light that captivated him, they almost looked amber.

"Fuck," he ground out, "you are doin' just fine baby girl." He pushed up against her again. She slid down him a little bit and groaned at the contact. She reached forward and unbuttoned his jeans and Smitty stopped breathing. The buzzing along his skin intensified to a point just shy of painful. He lifted his hips and she pushed his jeans off him.

Climbing off his lap, she pulled them free of his feet and he was naked before her. Smitty saw his cock standing up begging for attention and it nearly undid him to see her standing there before him, staring at him in awe. "Don't leave me hanging baby girl, get your sexy ass over here," Smitty rasped.

She suddenly looked at him shyly, "I-I don't have a very nice body," she whispered, her own fears taking over.

"Look at me Airiella, does my body's reaction look like I'm disgusted by you?" Smitty pointed gently. "I want you so badly that I'm afraid it will be over way too soon," his voice ragged.

Her chest was heaving with heavy breath's she was dragging in and out of her lungs. She put her hand out in front of her and Smitty felt his blood go electric. "Can you see it?"

"See what baby girl? You're killing me here," he gritted out.

"Can you see me?" she asked, captivated by something. Smitty felt every move she made with her hand even though she wasn't touching him.

"Yes, I see you, you are damned beautiful," he growled.

She pulled her dress off and stepped out of her boy shorts. She touched the tattoo he had on his thigh and his cock bounced with need. His body was strung so tight he vibrated. She leaned over and licked the tattoo and hips bucked as she ran her tongue up and over his balls. He knew she wanted to set the pace, but he was pretty sure his heart was about to beat right out of his chest.

"Airiella," he warned and then lost all rational thought as she sucked his cock down her throat. She moaned and he came in wild jerks, the connection they shared now visible to him as she touched it and swallowed him down.

His control snapped, and even though he came he was far from done with this angel. He yanked her up and had her on her back with her legs over his shoulders spread beneath his hands in two seconds flat. He lapped at her, letting her taste fill his mouth and he groaned as it was her turn for her hips to be bucking under his mouth as she shuddered into an orgasm.

He kept licking, loving the sweet torture he was giving her. She clawed at his arms trying to pull him up. Kissing his way back up to her lips, he slid into her, his cock still hard as a rock. Smitty forced his body to slow down, she was so tight around him he felt like he was going to hurt her, but she rocked against him increasing the pace.

Every point of contact their skin touched was sparking with energy, Smitty could swear they were glowing. Nothing in his entire existence had ever felt this good or this right and nothing he could do would make it last longer, it pulled him down and he felt her tighten around him even more as she came with a cry, he fell right into it with her, the connection between them slamming in to place as she bit his shoulder shuddering beneath him.

He didn't have any words, he just pulled her tight to him and rolled to his side, their bodies both trembling. He ran his fingers over her skin and tentatively touched the connection he could now see and watched in amazement as they both glowed. He rolled onto his back, pulling her on top of him and held her tight to him.

She laid her cheek on his chest and as their breathing slowed, he realized he was still buried in her body. He started to get hard again and felt it when she smiled into his chest and gyrated her hips a bit. "Let's finish this in the shower baby girl or we will both be sleeping in wet spots," he said with a laugh in her ear.

She slid off him and his body felt empty without her, but she took his hand and pulled him into the bathroom. Thankful it was a large shower he cleaned her off, then made her all sticky and dirty again. Finally, clean and spent they crawled back into bed again. Smitty smiled as he drifted off to sleep holding her, knowing every word she told him was true and having no clue how to explain it.

Chapter Twenty-One

Ronnie woke up early in the morning fighting back waves of jealousy. Jax and him were the only two not in relationships. Granted he knew about how open Smitty's was, but he was still jealous. If he had been the one in the building when she got back it would have been him in that room with her.

Ronnie was happy though that he and Jax had a few moments to work out some of the tension they had. It didn't feel good to be fighting with him like that, and while he knew it wasn't fixed, he could be in the same room without wanting to hurt him now.

Jax was pretty harsh when he talked about Airiella, but Ronnie didn't think that was really Jax talking. It was either that darkness inside him, or his fears. Maybe a bit of both. He rolled over and looked at his phone and decided to hell with it, he was texting the lucky bastard.

"Smitty, you awake?"

"Yep," was Smitty's reply. Followed by another text, "About to be busy. Talk to you later."

Ronnie growled and punched his pillow. Totally not fair. Well, at least it wasn't Jax in there with her right now.

SEE ME

He was pretty sure that would have sent him over the edge. Especially after the talks they've had about Winnie. He wasn't ready to share Airiella with him yet.

Knowing he wasn't going to be able to go back to sleep, he got up and decided to hit the gym in the hotel to release some of this energy. They were all going to be there for the final meeting today back in that damn room. Who knew how long that was going to last.

He spent an hour in the gym and headed back to shower when he ran into Airiella and Smitty coming out of her room looking all shiny and happy. Ronnie couldn't help the grin that lit his face as he saw them. Airiella blushed, but he just gave her a lip tingling kiss, smacked her ass and kept going.

She had quite an effect on him. He showered as fast as possible so he could join them in the dining room before the others were up. Getting dressed he chose a little more care with his outfit than just jeans and a t-shirt, but not really thinking it mattered what he wore. He ignored the interested glances from other women he passed, there was only one that captured his attention now.

He found them sitting at a table with a chair open for him. He grabbed some food and sat down, grinning. "Have a good night?" he joked.

Airiella blushed and Smitty smirked. "Good morning Ronnie," she said, ignoring his question.

"Hi angel. I'm just messing with you because I'm jealous," he said with a smile.

She blushed even more, and Ronnie laughed warmly. "Back off bro," Smitty said in a tone that told him to not argue.

Curious now, Ronnie looked him over, "Everything okay?"

"She had a rough interview process," he said slowly. "Let's just keep things light for now. We can talk more after the meeting today."

Ronnie looked Airiella over carefully, noting a few more bruises and tamping down his need to demand to know how they got there. "I'm okay Ronnie. I promise, I'll tell you everything that I told Smitty. We'll have our chance." She smiled at him, her face softly glowing, her curly hair wild around her head. He melted. He felt cheesy, but that's just how it was with her.

He nodded at her; a promise held in his eyes that she didn't even try to hide from. Smitty noticed and started laughing. "You've met your match dude," Smitty told him.

Ronnie widened his eyes again at Airiella, "Oh angel, challenge accepted," he purred, his voice low and husky. She blushed, bit her lip, which made him hard, and held his gaze with heat in her own. He was a dead man.

I felt so invigorated after last night, that I was openly challenging Ronnie to a wild ride in the middle of the dining room to Smitty's delight. Secretly I was pleased that it wasn't an awkward morning after scenario. Incredibly enough, it was anything but that. It was perfectly comfortable. I had no idea who I was anymore.

The connection experience was amazing. If I had the balls, I would tell Taklishim that, but it wasn't his business. I felt the jealousy on Ronnie, but he wasn't angry, and I started to think that just maybe all this was really real. Maybe I could have actual connections with all these people I felt something with. Even if they didn't turn into a sexual relationship it was something I could see happening at least once to make the connection solid.

After the sex with Smitty I noticed that I could feel more from him without having to use my senses. Almost like I could anticipate his moves as if he were an extension of me. I wondered if it was the same for him. In my usual style of speaking what comes into my head, I asked, "Smitty can you feel me now?"

Ronnie looked flabbergasted, while Smitty got thoughtful. "Well I can feel the connection you talked about, and I can even see it without touching you. I can feel your mood, but not really read your thoughts. I guess that's a yes. I'm assuming the reverse is true, which is why you asked me?"

I nodded, biting my lip again. I felt the jealousy

coming off Ronnie again and put my hand on his. The connection between us was stronger than it had been with Smitty so I can only begin to imagine how strong it would be after sex. He calmed under my touch and stroked my palm with his thumb.

That gave me little tingles inside that I didn't want to think about just now, so I carefully pulled my hand away and continued to eat. "So, today they will either tell me to take a hike or offer me the job?" I asked diverting my attention.

"They'll offer the job after Stone gets his rocks off by throwing his professional opinion around about your mental state. Be prepared to get pissed off at him," Ronnie said, sounding sure.

Smitty nodded his head in agreement as he ate his waffle. "You think they will offer the job?"

"I'm sure of it," Ronnie said.

"After last night, I am too," Smitty added. Ronnie narrowed his eyes again.

I patted him on the leg. "So, then I go home and do what? I am assuming I'll have to move?"

"They'll go over all that. I'm not sure what their plans are. I know they want you on the next shooting location," Smitty replied.

"Because big, old, bad me can't be trusted to do my job," came an angry voice from behind me. I jumped, surprised I hadn't felt him come up behind me.

Smitty stood, "Jax," his tone hard in warning.

"Relax, I'm just here for food before we get to this circus act," he fired back over his shoulder as he walked off. His body tense with anger, his tone dripping in derision.

I clicked my tongue. "I have a feeling this is going to be a very hard job," I said quietly. Neither Smitty or Ronnie answered, but their stiff postures told me they thought so too. "I'm not going to let him win, nor do I need you guys fighting my battles for me," I told them sternly. "I can handle him."

"Never doubted you, baby girl," Smitty said, finished with his breakfast. Ronnie had pushed his plate away and sat there with his arms crossed over his chest saying nothing. Damn testosterone.

"Okay then," I stood up. "I'm going to go pack my bags up and bring them with, so I can just go straight home. I miss my cats."

Smitty's eyes followed me. "We'll ride their together," he said.

I shook my head no. "I think it's better if we arrive separately." His eyes narrowed at me, but Ronnie was nodding his head in agreement. I smiled at them both and went back to my room.

I got all my stuff packed into my backpack, throwing away both the shirts I had picked up at the discount store as they now had holes in them, and I called the driver telling him I was ready whenever he was. I still had an hour left before he was supposed to even be there to pick me up, so I told him I would wait, I had a book to read.

I spent the time alone reading and allowing it to relax me, then grabbed my bag and headed down to the lobby. Mentally preparing myself on the way, to get belittled by a pompous psychiatrist. I focused my emotions on how it felt connecting with Smitty instead. Immediately my confidence was boosted. I found he was a rational, calming influence on me.

When I arrived at the building, I noticed right away that something felt off to me. I pushed it off as nerves, but the closer I got to the conference room, the stronger it got. As the receptionist led me in to the conference room, I felt the energy easily. The vibe in the room was hostile, and it put me on edge. I opened my senses half way to read the energy and quickly found my connection with Smitty and felt the others. That explained the energy to me then. Jax was back there.

I sat at the table and waited. Degataga was the first one to come in and he gave me a small smile and flapped his arms like wings. He slid across the table a container. "What we talked about. Drink it in hot water before you go to sleep." He winked and sat down.

I put it in my purse and made polite small talk as

Dr. Fields, Aminda, and Kalisha walked in. Both Aminda and Kalisha said hello to me, and Dr. Fields gave a brief nod. Not unfriendly, but it wasn't warm either. Asher came in next with Father Roarke. Asher gave me a weak smile, while Father Roarke came around the table to give me a hug before he sat down.

Then in walked the twins and Taklishim. Tama had a noticeable limp but seemed to be doing okay and was walking unaided, and I was thankful for that. The only person missing was Dr. Stone. Taklishim was trying to get my attention so I looked over at him. He tapped his head and had a question in his eyes, but I wasn't picking up on it.

Two minutes later Dr. Stone walked in. The tension in the air ratcheted up a notch and I did some yoga breathing to calm myself. I think Taklishim wanted me to open my senses, so I did a little bit and noticed immediately again, that bad energy. I felt bad for Jax having to carry that around all the time.

"Let's get started then," Dr. Stone said brusquely. "I have the reports from everyone, and I have to say that they are all complimentary. Given your abrupt nature with me, I don't agree with these reports that you will be sufficient to do this job. Unfortunately, the decision is not mine, it is theirs, he gestured to the table."

At that moment, Numbers One through Three walked in to the room and I felt a moment of shame for not remembering their names. "Dr. Stone," Number One said, "we went over this already and have spoken to each of the members here. You are the only one who seems to have anything negative to say." The three sat down and Dr. Stone stood.

"It is unwise to dismiss my concerns gentlemen," he fumed. His face was turning an interesting shade of red. Taklishim tapped his head again, something was definitely going on.

"Airiella, we do apologize for the unprofessionalism being shown at the moment, but it was an almost unanimous vote that you will be able to handle the stresses that taking this job would provide, and that your unique skill set would benefit the team greatly. Dave, Tom and I would like to offer you the job, we will provide details after the council gives its recommendations on things that can aid you in the duties," Number two said.

"Thank you, Stephen," said Number one. "Dr. Stone please take a seat."

Okay, Stephen was number two. Got it. I was pretty sure number three was Dave, that left number one being Tom. Process of elimination for the win. I smiled and saw my connection with Smitty glowing and moved my arm a bit so I could touch it, loving the soothing feeling that rushed into me.

"Kalisha, do you have any recommendations for Airiella in regard to this job?" Stephen asked.

She smiled warmly at me, "Carry your stones everywhere and the book of Psalms." That was easy enough to manage. I nodded at her.

"Aminda, you're next," Stephen said, taking notes.

"Just words of advice. Remember to set your intentions," she spoke to me. I nodded at her.

"Thank you Aminda. Father Roarke, your turn," Stephen continued.

"My recommendations are that Airiella check in with me weekly," Father Roarke said.

"Airiella, is this something that you can manage?" Stephen asked me, making more notes.

"Of course," I replied. I wonder if that meant he had more information on how to cleanse the energy.

"Asher, please give your recommendations," Stephen droned on.

"I have none at this time," Asher responded in a monotone.

"Very well. Dr. Fields," Stephen gestured at her.

"I would recommend weekly spiritual cleansing," Dr. Fields said.

Startled I gave her a surprised look.

"It's for your own protection," she told me quietly. I nodded at her.

Stephen made another note. "Degataga, you're up."

see me

"I have made an herbal tea for her to drink to help with the healing she needs, and one for pain that is caused by spirits. My recommendations are for her to use those," he said carefully.

Stephen looked at me, "Is this something you are comfortable doing?"

"Yes, not a problem," I said, giving Degataga the acknowledgment he wanted that I would drink the nightmare tea.

"Tama, Onida, is there anything you would like to add?" Stephen said, looking them over.

"Believe," Onida said, tapping her chest.

"You can make it happen," Tama said.

"Thank you for those words of advice ladies. Taklishim, the floor is yours," Stephen said.

"First I would like to recommend that Ronnie teach her basic fighting skills and self-defense," Stephen started writing. "Second, more meditation and self-reflection when things are more intense, she will find the answers there. Third, that she utilizes all bonds she has to complete the circle."

Taklishim gave me a strong look, "You will do this." I nodded at him, grateful for the hidden messages of support woven in there. If anything, this panel showed me that I just may have made a few new friends that I would need for this.

I took a deep breath in, "Thank you all for your time, patience and energy in talking to me, teaching me and working with me. It has been an honor to meet all of you."

"The honor is ours," Onida said gently.

"I'm sorry this is complete and utter bullshit," Dr. Stone burst in standing up again.

"Sit down," Taklishim thundered. Oh, now I see the warrior in him, and he's terrifying.

Dr. Stone sat, but if the vile look on his face was any confirmation, he was far from done.

"Airiella, during filming season, we rent a house in a location close to the studio where we can do the editing and the computer work for each aired show. We keep the equipment at the studio where the team can go over it, check to make sure all is working properly and prep for the next location. It is at this house we can set up appointments to have the recommendations that the council has made completed after each location. Are these agreeable conditions for you?" Dave asked.

"To clarify, I would share a house with the rest of the team during the filming season? And then after I would get to go home? I don't need to permanently move?" I asked. What was I going to do with the cats?

"Correct. Living expenses are paid for while in the house," Tom said.

Dave slid an envelope across the table to me, "This contains an offer of employment and the salary details and benefits offered. We will draw up a contract with the recommendations of the council as conditions of your employment. This is to keep you safe."

I nodded my understanding. "When would this position start? I have a few things to wrap up at home before I can jump in."

"Ultimately, we would like you to start now, but we understand you have a current position that you need to wrap up, and personal matters to attend to. Please take the night to look over the information provided in the envelope and if you can, let us know tomorrow if things need to be changed, or if you accept," Tom said.

"If you accept, I would like to send Aedan with you back to your home, he doesn't need to stay in your home," Dave amended, "but he would be able to fill you in on what it's like on location, the things that we would be looking for you to do, and train you a bit on the equipment while you take care of what you need to take care of there."

I was feeling cornered, but I already knew I was taking the job. Aedan coming home with me wouldn't be a big deal, neither would letting him use my extra room. I think the energy in the room was getting to me. "That's fine with me, and I do have an extra room in my house that he can use. It would cut down on expenses and travel time. I would like to ask that his wife come with as well."

SEE ME

I don't think they expected that as all three of them looked startled, but they nodded their agreement. As they were nodding, a crash sounded from behind the glass where I knew the guys were sitting. Everyone at the table jumped and looked over.

Suddenly the speakers roared to life with a voice shouting, "Fuck you!" I sighed. Jax. The energy was reacting to something.

The producers cleared their throats looking extremely uncomfortable. "Um," they all stammered, and then Dr. Stone stood up. But it wasn't Dr. Stone. My senses picked up the energy rolling off him and the room smelled of danger.

Dr. Stone pointed a finger at me, "Do you really think you are better than me?" he snarled. "I will show the world your lies and defeat you in a way that will leave no doubt about who is in control here."

"Dr. Stone!" Dave shouted; fear spreading across his eyes.

Dr. Stone shifted and then shoved Dave across the room. Well damn. This got out of hand fast. I glanced around the table seeing a variety of expressions, but just fear on the producers faces. I stood up and stepped around the table to stand between Dr. Stone and the producers.

"Get out of my way bitch or I'll kill you now!" Dr. Stone spit at me.

I looked at the three men standing there stupefied. "Please go stand in the corner or leave the room. Out of the line of fire," I told them quietly.

"No one leaves here unless I say they do!" Dr. Stone yelled in my face; way too close for my comfort.

There was commotion in the room with the guys as well, that was being picked up by the activated microphone. "Aedan, Ronnie, Mags, please restrain Jax, I think he is going to react to what will happen."

"Got it angel," Ronnie's voice came through tight.

"Smitty, I'm going to need you in a matter of moments," I looked over at Father Roarke. "Can you help me again after I do this?" Father Roarke nodded his head.

260

"Smitty, if it's ok, you'll need to help Father Roarke."

"Whatever you need, baby girl," I head Smitty agree. Then the door opened and Smitty came out, showing Ronnie behind Jax holding him in a head lock.

"What the fuck makes you think you are in charge here?!" Dr. Stone roared, still not advancing towards me. I ignored him. I knew he wouldn't touch me; he was afraid of me. It was rolling off him.

I looked over at Aminda, Kalisha, Dr. Fields and Asher. "Can you go with the producers?" As one they all nodded and joined the producers in the corner.

"Degataga, use your sight to see if you can see what's happening. Hawkeye, Cat Woman and Gandalf," they all broke out in laughter at that, "can you do what you do and see if you can spot any way that we can make this easier? I'm going to do my thing, looks like you'll get a front row seat."

I waited for their signals that they were ready, and motioned Smitty over to Father Roarke. "Thank you."

"If you so much as dare touch me, it will be the end of you," Dr. Stone shouted, spittle hitting me in the face.

"Why are you so hostile Dr. Stone?" I asked slowly. I took a step towards him and opened all my senses fully. The negative energy slammed into me hard from Jax, it was violent and hot. Writhing in him. I focused on Dr. Stone, the energy in him was the same, but on a smaller scale. "Are you afraid of me?" I taunted.

"Why would I be afraid you, whore?" He sneered. I heard Ronnie cuss in the background. "You are nothing but a stupid whore."

"Maybe. Maybe I'm more than that. It's not for me to say. I'm pretty sure I'm not talking to Dr. Stone though, so why don't you tell me who you are?" I stepped closer again and latched on to the bad energy, seeking out other threads I could use to help. He was full of insecurities, fear and anger. There had to be something else in there to counteract those. I kept digging as he hurled insults at me.

Found it, he had love, though it was by far the smallest amount out of all the negative in him. I pushed energy into the love and watched his expression change. At the same time Jax roared so loud it almost broke my concentration. I yanked hard on the bad energy, not caring if it hurt Dr. Stone or not, I didn't have time to wait and go slow with how Jax was reacting.

I heard gasps from behind me and Winnie shouting, "Airy, no!" Wonder where she'd been. The bad energy leaped into my body and Dr. Stone screamed, collapsing in a heap on the floor. I swayed where I stood and latched on to part of the energy in Jax.

At least in him, I could feel hope, love and kindness. I grabbed those and shoved my own energy into those hoping it would ease the effect on him, but that energy fought, and I heard him screaming for help. A little piece of my heart broke. Tears began filling my eyes as the pain of what I was doing settled on my nerves. I pulled some of the energy from Jax.

"He fainted," I heard Ronnie yell. I gave a small prayer of thanks and stopped pulling and dropped to the floor. Sickness engulfed me, my stomach was heaving, my eyes blind. My skin felt like it was being stung by thousands of bees.

I felt Smitty, the connection we had easing some of the pain as his skin touched me. He lifted me and was carrying me. I heard the footsteps of others following, but I kept blacking out. The energy in me was so filled with rage that it was trying to consume me. It was too much; I took too much. The only way I knew we were in the church was by the way the energy in me reacted.

My own energy that was filled with hope and love was fighting being taken over by this darkness that filled me with despair, pounding against my soul so violently that I couldn't get a hold of anything to use against it. It was savagely ripping at me. My nerves raw now, pain was all I knew.

"Raven, I need you to drink this," I heard Taklishim say and something touched my lips. I opened my mouth and swallowed, the earthy mix hitting my stomach and immediately I threw it all up. "There's no time," he said.

I was put on the ground and cried out at the pain of my skin on the floor, the loss of the connection severed. I must have been in the circle. "I'm so sorry, Airiella," Father Roarke said, and I was drenched in water. Holy water, was my thought as my nerves exploded in fire, screams ripping through my throat my body rigid.

"Not enough," I choked out.

"Oh my God, baby girl, stay with me," Smitty's rough cry penetrated my head.

"I need to drink it," I rasped between screams. I felt the cup pressed into my hand and guided to my lips. I tasted blood, and my stomach heaved again. It felt like the scene in that alien movie where an alien comes out of her stomach. It was awful. I had little doubt that my life was about to end, and I only could hope that what I pulled from Jax was enough to help him.

"Stand back," I heard Father Roarke say and he started reciting prayers. I also heard Taklishim chanting, but my ears started ringing with a buzzing noise that drowned everything else out. Someone raised my arm to my mouth again for me to drink and I fought to get it down. It felt as if every bone in my body was breaking. Following that it felt like every one of my limbs was torn from my body, and then there was blackness.

Smitty's brain couldn't process the horror of what he was seeing play out in front of his eyes. Her body literally broke, he heard the bones snap. There was blood coming out of her mouth and the screams were deafening, echoing off the walls and ringing in his ears. Then in a split second it stopped, and the room was silent. Like someone had dampened all the sound in the room.

He glanced away from Airiella for a moment and looked around. Shock written on all the faces of those present. Destruction all around them, and as he looked back at Airiella, his heart stopped. She wasn't moving, she wasn't breathing. Covered in her own blood and drenched from the holy water, her beautiful face frozen in a grimace of pain. He stepped forward, but Father Roarke was suddenly in his way.

"It's not over, son," he told Smitty in a shaky voice.

"She's not breathing," Smitty sobbed unabashedly.

"Wait," the priest told him. Before his eyes, Airiella lit up in a blue glow, her body six inches off the ground, her hair floating around her face as her body snapped back into place. The sounds of the bones sliding in to place making Smitty cringe in pain. The light around her flared so bright he couldn't even look at her anymore, he shielded his eyes and looked over at the three that followed him, Taklishim, Tama and Onida.

All three were on their knees, their heads on the ground in supplication. As he snapped his gaze back towards Airiella, he saw Winnie, and his jaw dropped. "Winnie," he whispered. "What's happening?"

"She's gone," Winnie said brokenly. "She took way too much," she looked horrified. "There's so much damage inside her."

"What are you talking about?" Smitty saw her still floating there glowing.

"It made her bleed inside," she whispered.

Taklishim was by his side in an instant, "Can you tell me what that was?"

Smitty looked at him wildly, "How the fuck should I know?"

"The ghost, not you," Taklishim said patiently.

"Neither of us know, but she calls it bad energy, but it's sentient, it changes every time," Winnie told him.

"Every time?" Smitty was dumbstruck. "She's done this before?"

"Two days ago, when Mags stayed with her," Winnie said sadly. "Before that, it was the same stuff she pulled from me."

Taklishim had pulled out his medicine bag and was mixing ingredients and chanting, the priest praying fervently. Onida had walked over to them but looked directly at Winnie. "She's not gone, she's with her Creator," Onida said.

"In my world, that means dead," Smitty shot at her.

"She's in there, her soul isn't gone," Onida argued. "I can see it, so can you. That's what is glowing."

Smitty gasped. "That's her soul?"

Taklishim spoke up, "You sealed the connection, right?" Smitty nodded, at a loss for words. "Then feel for her. Reach for that connection you share with her. She needs your touch to make it back here."

"How?" Smitty asked, willing to do anything to see her breathe again.

"Close your eyes, remember the feel of the connection, how it felt in you. You saw it too, picture it. Picture yourself touching it, feeding it energy. It's alive, I can see it between you two, but it's weak right now. When she does this, whoever has those connections with her, you need to be there. You are her tether to this world."

Smitty was unable to provide any logical backup to the words, but he did as Taklishim told him. "Will doing this kill her?"

"Not in the way you think, but it does hurt her. It's a part of who and what she is, you will need to accept it. Skin on skin contact is best to help her, but you must wait until it is safe to do so, or the energy that was ripped from her will attach to you. It is why Father Roarke said it wasn't finished. That energy was not dead yet. Now, it is safe, you can touch her," Taklishim said.

"Do you know what that was?" Smitty whispered.

"No, it's never been seen before. But the ghost was right, it's sentient. It's evolving to try and learn how to survive. Your friend is lucky she pulled some out of him, it's almost too late for him," Taklishim said, stirring water into the herbs he crushed. "Take this paste, rub some into her mouth, on her tongue. It will absorb and ease some of the pain. Keep doing it until it's gone, or she wakes up." He handed Smitty the bowl.

"She's truly incredible," Onida whispered to him. "If you combined the entire council, we wouldn't have had enough power to do what she did. All we can do is find ways to help her get through this part of it. Take care of her," she pressed a card into his hand. It had their contact info on it and Smitty slid it into his pocket.

He took the paste over to Airiella. "Baby girl, I'm here." He scooped some of the paste onto his finger and slid it into her mouth, scraping his finger along her teeth to get it off. He put his other hand gently on the arm floating in the air next to him and felt the connection tingle to life and her body shuddered.

"Keep touching her son," Father Roarke said gently.

Smitty had tears falling down his cheeks, "I had no idea. She told me, but I had no idea."

"Neither did I, son. Not until two days ago when she came to me asking for help. It was so much worse this time. Believe me, I'm searching for ways to ease this process, I haven't slept since last time she was here. I see it in my nightmares," he told Smitty.

"She chooses to do this," Smitty said in wonder.

"Help her see herself," Father Roarke said. "She doesn't believe how amazing and beautiful she is."

Smitty looked at the priest sharply, "She doesn't?"

"She thinks she is unworthy to be called an angel because of her past."

Taklishim joined Smitty, sitting on his knees. "Add more paste. And the priest is right. Her true powers won't come into play until she heals those wounds. Encourage her to drink the tea that Degataga gave her, but don't leave her alone that night. She will need as many connections as she can around her to hold on to the love that she radiates."

"I can't claim to understand any of this. My brain is geared for science," Smitty said.

"Yes, but now you have seen that which others can't. You can see the truth of it in front of you," Taklishim pushed.

Smitty nodded numbly, his life forever changed. "She's here for Jax?"

Taklishim shrugged, "He's part of it, but not the whole reason. Give her more paste, she's starting to settle," he nodded at her body that had lowered closer to the ground. "This is very hard on her. I watched from the spirit realm as did they," he motioned to the women. "It's creating an imbalance, above and below."

"Do you know how to stop it?" Smitty asked as he put more paste in her mouth.

"She's what is stopping it," Taklishim admitted. "Imagine if the power that she had, to give love so freely was flipped, to someone doling out that negative energy everywhere they went, infecting every person they came in contact with. Imagine what that world would look like."

Smitty shivered involuntarily at the thought and winced as he realized that was what was in Jax. Airiella had to pull all that out of Jax. "How much more of this is in Jax?"

"I don't know, but he's very close to losing himself to it."

Airiella suddenly gasped for air, her body crashing down on to the ground, her chest heaving, tears clearing a path through the blood streaked on her face, but her eyes weren't open. Smitty clung to her hand, his own tears falling on her fingers.

"Her," Taklishim pointed at Airiella. "She is what will save us all once she believes in herself. You saw a piece of that today. Dr. Stone is alive because of her. Jax, is alive because of her."

"That's a lot of pressure for one person," Smitty said sadly.

Taklishim tapped Smitty's chest. "You need to believe, too. I am going to go make some more of this for her to take with, as well as a few other things. I'll label the containers and put directions on there, so she knows what they are for. She had you witness this so you understood, so you know, so you can help the others believe what is unbelievable. You are her voice of reason."

Smitty swallowed a lump in his throat as he looked down at Airiella, still seemingly stuck in the nightmare she voluntarily threw herself in to help others. He wasn't ashamed to say he didn't understand any of this, but he also wasn't afraid to admit that he had just been given a huge gift in her. He laid down on the floor next to her. "What does that mean? I'm her voice of reason?"

See Me

The priest brought over a blanket, and Smitty rolled so he could lay it on the floor, then he stripped his shirt off and pulled Airiella on top of him as gently as he could. Her blood and tear stained face resting on his bare chest as her body quieted at the contact of his skin on hers. His world had just been thrown completely off it's axis and was spinning wildly out of control.

"Each of you that shares a connection with her brings something to the table so to speak. From what I can see, you bring her reason. The voice that shows her the path she should be on when she strays," Tama answered him.

The priest came back with a pillow and Smitty raised his head as he wrapped his arms around Airiella, holding her tight. "Her walls are down, aren't they?" Smitty asked the room knowing someone in there would have an answer for him.

"Yes," Tama said quietly. "We will leave here so she doesn't get overwhelmed. Just make sure that what you are feeling is good. She needs to feel the good."

Smitty nodded in acknowledgement and focused all his thoughts on how many ways this one person had showed him things he would have never known about. He thought about her easy playful banter, her strength, the passion she carried within that she hid until she wanted you to see it. He thought about the connection they shared and the love she freely poured into it with no expectations of her own.

She moaned into his chest, her body tightening against him as she fought back the pain and Smitty started whispering into her hear, "I've got you baby girl, I'm not going anywhere. I've got you." He whispered it repeatedly until she settled, her eyes never once opening.

Airy, I know you can hear me, you better damn well respond to me!" Winnie shouted at her. Airy was with her on the spirit plane. Her eyes closed, looking pretty rough.

"I'm not joking around here Airy! Open your eyes

and look at me!"

Winnie paced back and forth in the same scene as the one on earth, just mirrored in the spirit plane. She got down on the ground to look in Airy's face that was pressed against Smitty. All that showed of him on this plane was his soul color as he was still very much alive.

Winnie noticed the rolling colors as Smitty tried to focus his thoughts on love and she smiled as she saw the color finally settle. "Damn it, Airiella Raven, you are not supposed to be here! Wake your ass up and get back in your body!"

Winnie was freaking out. That darkness had the power to break her body this time. Human bodies weren't built to withstand that much pain all at once. Winnie stroked Airy's hair and saw her sigh. "Airy," Winnie tried once more. "I need you to go back, you aren't finished yet."

Airiella blinked her eyes at Winnie. "Winnie?"

"Airy, go back to your body," Winnie pleaded.

"It hurts too much, and I'm too tired," Airy said weakly.

"Don't make me do this the hard way," Winnie said, tears pooling in her eyes.

"What?"

Winnie took a deep breath in and then shoved Airiella hard, her soul slamming back into her body violently. Winnie let the tears fall as she watched Airiella open her eyes and scream at the pain tearing through her.

The story continues in...

SEE ME
REVEALED

...coming February 2020

Made in the USA
Middletown, DE
20 December 2019